LUCKY FOOLS

LUCKY FOOLS

COERT VOORHEES

HYPERION
NEW YORK

First Edition

1 3 5 7 9 10 8 6 4 2

G75-5664-5-1212

Printed in the United States of America

Library of Congress Cataloging-in-Publication Data
Voorhees, Coert.
Lucky fools / Coert Voorhees.—1st Hyperion Books hardcover ed.
p. cm.
Summary: Eighteen-year-old David Ellison, a senior at Oak Fields
Preparatory School which is only a few miles away from the Stanford
University campus, tries to reconcile his desire to attend Juilliard instead
of an Ivy League university as is expected of him, while also wondering
why he seems dissatisfied with his long-term girlfriend after being cast
opposite an interesting new student in the school play.
ISBN 978-1-4231-2398-9
[1. Theater—Fiction. 2. Dating (Social customs)—Fiction. 3. Preparatory
schools—Fiction. 4. Schools—Fiction. 5. College choice—Fiction.
6. Palo Alto (Calif.)—Fiction.] I. Title.
PZ7.V943Lu 2012
[Fic]—dc23   2011026252

Text is set in 11.5-point Sabon

Reinforced binding

Visit www.hyperionteens.com

For Molly—
My rudder and sail

1

Vanessa Stern eased back against the small table and pulled me in with her left hand. I gave myself up, letting momentum carry me against her body. Her hair glistened against the black of her T-shirt like gold jewelry, and a few strands of it tumbled across her face. My fingertips brushed against her cheek as I tucked the hair behind her ear. We stared into each other's eyes.

"Are you sure we should be doing this?" I said.

Her voice was smooth, almost a whisper. "Absolutely."

We were alone. On the other side of the door were chaos and stress, finger pointing and suspicion, but in here there were only the two of us. I tried to push the distant and muffled screeching of metal against brick from my mind; I had more important things to think about.

She held me behind the neck and—slowly, slowly—pulled me closer. We'd done this a dozen times before, and yet I still felt my throat constrict, my pulse quicken, my lungs threaten to give out. My one thought was the same: I can't believe this is really happening!

"And then . . . kiss," I said, stepping back. "A three count."

Vanessa glanced down at the script in her right hand. "And then I push you away, right? After the kiss?"

"Yeah, but give me time to gather my balance. That way when you push me back, I'm stumbling, but under control."

Vanessa lifted herself up from the table. "Want to run it again?"

The stage was empty except for a black table and two black cubes that served as chairs. We'd blocked the scene at rehearsal the night before, and Vanessa wanted to perfect it before anybody saw it again, so we'd met an hour before school started. I'd unlocked the side entrance with the key to the theater Mr. Prokov gave me last year, thrilled to finally find someone as dedicated as I was, especially since that someone was Vanessa Stern. Vanessa Stern!

The screeching outside returned, this time carrying murmured conversation along with it. More people were arriving.

"David?" she said.

I turned to her. "Are you ready for the meeting?"

"You're going?"

"I promised my parents," I said with a shrug. "Besides, it's nice to have a safety school, right?"

"Safety school." Vanessa laughed. "Right."

"We still have ten minutes. Let's take it one more time from the top."

I knew she was there because she cared about her performance and not because she was into me. Drama was the only remaining hole in her résumé, and this play, a stage adaptation of *The Great Gatsby*, was just the experience to fill it.

Nevertheless, every time Vanessa brushed up against

me, I had to remind myself not to think about what I was thinking about. I had to keep it professional; otherwise I'd just be a jerk fantasizing about someone who wasn't his girlfriend.

"Actually, let me show you something," I said, moving upstage, where a small black metal ladder hugged the wall up to the catwalk above.

She checked her watch. "I don't want to be late."

"It'll only take a minute."

I climbed the twenty feet to a narrow walkway and stepped out onto the catwalk, a large suspended platform the same size and shape of the stage below. A wire mesh was laid over a grid of support beams three feet apart, and the stage lights were affixed to the metal poles connecting the catwalk to the ceiling. I was on the other side of the lights now, the ceiling just inches from my head, with a half-light illuminating me from below.

Walking across the mesh was like stepping on an inflatable mattress—a slight bounce, just enough instability to keep you from getting too comfortable. I moved to a spot almost directly over Vanessa, and she arched her back to look up at me, shielding her eyes. I was struck by how the light accentuated the sharpness of her jaw.

"Come on," I said.

"Are you even allowed up there?"

"Just check it out. Two minutes."

She looked at the exit, then back up at me. Finally she shrugged, tossing her script onto a front row seat. "If I'm late because of you—"

"It's not even going to start on time. Relax."

"Keep saying that," she said. "The more people relax, the better chance I have of getting in." She reached the top of the ladder and stepped out, her feet tentatively probing the mesh. "Wow."

"Sometimes I hang out up here during the day. Nobody bothers you. Nobody looks up, and even if they did, you're behind the lights anyway, so they'd never see you."

I detected a hint of disgust hiding out in the upturned corners of her mouth.

"I'm no peeper, if that's what that look is supposed to mean."

"Some kind of serial killer, maybe? Luring defenseless young ladies up to your suspended lair?"

"Nothing wrong with taking a break from time to time. The machine still grinds." I sat down and crossed my legs, leaning back against one of the poles.

"That it does," she said. "What kind of sausage is it turning you into?"

I laughed. "My parents always tell me I can accomplish anything I set my mind to, but even they have to know what a load of crap that is, right? I'm never going to play the piano or pro baseball. I won't be a financial planner or a brain surgeon or a quantum physicist—"

"Not many people are—"

"But that's okay with me. I don't need to hear that I can be anything I want to be—I already know what I want to be."

I realized, as my voice echoed in the empty theater, that

4

I'd been a little too emphatic. I may have even pounded an open palm on the wire mesh next to me.

Vanessa nodded and said, "Well, then I envy you."

My snort-laugh was out before I could stop it. As far as I was concerned, I was in no position to be envied by anybody, much less Vanessa Stern. She was smart, beautiful, and already her extracurriculars were legendary: Amnesty International, French Club, Art Club, Calculus Club, Humane Society, just to name a few.

"I'm serious." She sat across from me, all ladylike, leaning on one side with her knees together, somehow managing to look comfortable even on the mesh. "It's smart to have a plan."

"I don't know how much of a plan—"

"Stop with the modesty," she said. "Everyone knows about Juilliard."

Yes, I was a good actor; I knew that. Good enough to star in a regional ad campaign for Sparkles Iced Tea when I was in junior high: "Sparkles Tea! Mmmboy, delicious!" Fingers crossed, I was even good enough to get into Juilliard.

My audition was only nineteen days away, and no matter how much I tried to visualize success, I couldn't rid my mind of something Mr. Prokov said at the beginning of the year. It was a criticism I'd sworn to keep private, but Vanessa seemed to have cast some sort of mysterious hot-girl magic spell on me, and I said, "Big Pro told me I still have doe eyes."

"What does that even mean?"

"Actors can't reach their full potential unless they can find a way to get at the darkest part of their psyches, according to him. He thinks people who've never had their hearts broken look like doe-eyed little children."

The backstage door creaked open. I put my finger to my lips and motioned for Vanessa to watch. Mr. Prokov stepped onstage below us, the lights reflecting off his bald dome, a thick folder of wrinkled papers clutched against his ample belly. His shoes squeaked against the stage floor and then were quiet as he ascended the carpeted stairs of the center aisle. He rattled his keys in the lock at the double doors leading to the foyer and then disappeared through them.

Vanessa said, "How, exactly, are we not stalking?"

"I'd rather call it observing. You can learn a lot about people. You'd be surprised." I affected an outrageous British accent. "I'm a student of the human condition."

"Quite so." She laughed along with me—success!

"You always hear about how creative people have to experience misery in order to produce art with any lasting meaning, but my parents are still married, my uncle never sexually assaulted me at family reunions, and my little sister didn't die of leukemia when I was young—she didn't even have leukemia, and neither did I."

"Wait," she said. "You *want* to suffer?"

"No. But maybe it would be nice to *have* suffered."

"Important distinction." I couldn't tell if her nod was genuine or sarcastic. "But until then, you have to rely on your superhuman powers of observation."

"Something like that."

"Fine." She opened her arms wide and pointed to herself. "Come on, Mr. Student of the Human Condition, tell me what you observe."

The thing about being in school with the same people since the sixth grade is that by the time we were seniors, we were all pretty much sick of one another. When Vanessa and her brother showed up the first day of senior year, my class was desperate for new blood. She should have been instantly popular, but there was an odd distance to her.

Twenty minutes earlier, if anyone had told me that Vanessa Stern would be pointing to herself, asking me to tell her what I observed, I wouldn't even have bothered laughing in his face. Vanessa was Vanessa, and I was me.

Not that I'm such an ugly guy. About six feet, green eyes, shaggy black hair. I'm not jacked or anything, but I keep myself in good shape—you never know when some role is going to require a shirtless scene. In *The American Plan* the year before, I had to run onstage as though I'd just come from a swimming pool. I did push-ups in the wings to get the blood flowing while a cute freshman costume girl sprayed me with a water bottle.

And yet, there we were. I cleared my throat. "The light's not so good up here—"

"Excuses, excuses."

"All right. Here goes." I paused, trying to gauge her eyes for some sort of indication as to how I should continue. Was she joking? Did she want honesty? I had no idea. "You care what people think of you."

"Wow, David, that's amazing. A high school senior cares what people think of her. That's some serious Sherlock Holmes stuff."

I wasn't talking about the normal high school I-care-because-I-want-to-be-popular. I meant something else, but it was hard to put my finger on. Yes, she was gorgeous, but sometimes it was like she resented it, like she wore long skirts to hide her legs, to prove to everybody that she was more than just a fantastic body. But if that was the case, why wear such a tight shirt?

"Okay," I said. "Okay, here's what I—"

A latch clicked loudly, echoing through the deserted theater. One of the double doors swung open. "David?" a voice called out. Ellen. She poked her head in. "David? Are you in here?"

Vanessa looked down to where Ellen stood at the door. Then Vanessa turned back to me, her eyebrows raised in a sort of amused anticipation. She opened her mouth, but she must have seen the alarm on my face, because she stopped and bit a smile into her bottom lip.

We waited, the two of us—or three if you count Ellen—for what seemed like a full minute. Vanessa staring at me the whole time, me glancing back and forth from Vanessa to Ellen, who'd positioned her head slightly to the side, listening. I knew that Ellen couldn't see us through the lights, and knew I should have said something, but really there was nothing for me to say. Keeping quiet was much easier than trying to explain what I was doing up in the dimly lit catwalk with Vanessa Stern.

Ellen produced a sigh of disappointment—I felt bad for her, yet I still said nothing—before she shook her head and disappeared back into the foyer. Only then did I exhale.

"You guys have been together for almost two years, right?" Vanessa said.

"Don't look at me like that. I just don't feel like dealing with folding chairs."

Vanessa's grin was flat-out mischievous. "Want me to tell you what I observed?"

"We should probably get going, huh?" I said, but neither of us moved.

Did that make me a dick? That I was up there with Vanessa instead of outside helping my girlfriend set up the meeting like I'd promised? It's not that I thought there was any chance of Vanessa and me going out, but she was the hottest girl I'd ever talked to for longer than ten minutes, so what else was I supposed to do?

More importantly, being with Ellen meant being back in the real world and everything that came with it: pressure, expectations, college counselors. On the catwalk with Vanessa, I was literally and figuratively suspended, set apart from all of that.

Vanessa checked her watch. She leaned back against one of the posts and ran her fingertips along the wire mesh. "I can see what you like about this. It's peaceful."

"It must have sucked, moving to a new school before your senior year." I winced. Here I was with Vanessa one-on-one, and this is what I chose to talk about? A new school?

Her phone vibrated, a low buzz that echoed off the stage below. She reached into the small pocket of her skirt. "Hello? . . . In the theater." She put the phone to her neck and mouthed, "My brother." Then, into the phone: "Yeah, come in."

She winked at me and said, "Oh, and Colter, come in the side door, okay?" She snapped the phone closed and replaced it.

"Thanks," I said.

"Ellen's nice," she said. "We don't really talk much, but she's nice."

"Yes." I nodded again, like an idiot. "She is. Nice."

The outside door opened, letting in a shaft of bright northern California sunshine. It was a perfect day, just like the day before and the day before that.

"Use the ladder," Vanessa called down.

Her brother made his way to the back. Dull notes sang out as his feet struck each rung. He poked his head through the opening and looked around. "You guys making out?"

"David already has a girlfriend," Vanessa said. She sounded disappointed, but another quick wink let me know otherwise.

Colter hunched his way over. "This is weird up here."

He wore old flip-flops and faded cargo shorts with elaborate doodles in different colors of ink. His hair was dark brown and uncombed, and he could hardly summon the effort necessary to raise his eyelids above half-mast. It was as though he and Vanessa had formed the yin/yang symbol in the womb they'd shared.

"It's like cattle at a feed lot out there." Colter settled onto the mesh with his legs crossed and shook his head in disbelief. "Moooo."

Vanessa reached over and brushed something—a piece of dried leaf?—from Colter's shoulder.

"So, if you're not making out, what are you doing?" Colter said.

"We were just talking about being at a new school," she said.

There was a slight pause. Grooves appeared in Colter's brow. "Did you tell him why we moved?" he said to Vanessa.

"You called before I said anything."

Colter looked at me, then at his sister. She shook her head. A chuckle caught in my throat.

He waited for a moment and then finally spoke, his rasp just barely above a whisper. "You don't want to know."

Vanessa backhanded her brother across the chest, and Colter laughed through his nose, breathy and high-pitched.

"Our dad transferred," she said.

"We could have finished high school in Boston," Colter said. "But V figured, why waste our time so far away when Stanford's right down the street?"

Stanford. Vanessa and I checked our watches.

Colter hardly moved. "What's wrong?"

"The feed lot," I said, pushing myself to my feet. "Ellen helped organize it, and I promised to be one of the cattle."

We gathered around the ladder, and I motioned for Vanessa to go down.

"Dude," Colter said. "You totally blew it. If you'd gone down first, you could have pretended not to look up her skirt."

"He's not a peeper," Vanessa said from below. "He already told me."

By the time I pushed open the double doors and stepped into the foyer, the sound of scraping chairs had been overtaken by the low rumble of a hundred uncertain futures.

2

The foyer of the Cronyn Family Performing Arts Center featured an expansive vaulted ceiling lit by two crystal-and-silver chandeliers. Side walls of hand-chiseled marble tapered toward an end wall of tinted glass windows and doors that opened onto a landscaped quadrangle. Kids clustered amid the folding chairs that had been set up like church pews facing the opposite wall, where a single microphone played the role of the pulpit.

Vanessa, Colter, and I stood at the top of a small staircase overlooking the foyer. I noticed Ellen by the doors across the room, pulling on the fingers of her right hand, twirling the small silver ring I gave her for our six-month anniversary. She waved anxiously when she saw me.

I waved back and headed down the stairs, jostling through the center of the crowd. Halfway there, I glanced over my shoulder, but Vanessa and her brother had already disappeared.

"You said you'd meet me fifteen minutes ago," Ellen said. She was at least six inches shorter than me, but her energy, her aura, sometimes made me feel we were the same height. My mom always called her my little spark plug, and in direct contrast to me, she was actually someone who *could* do anything she set her mind to, as evidenced by, among other things, her four-year-old state record for pogo stick jumping: over thirteen hours. "I had to set up all the chairs by myself."

"Sorry," I said, and I meant it. "I was running lines."

"In the theater? I went in there, but I couldn't find you."

I looked around. "Do you still need help?"

The whine of reverberating feedback pierced the room, followed by Mr. Edwards, the head college counselor, saying dramatically: "One minute, ladies and gentlemen. We'll be starting in one minute."

"Come on," she said, "I saved you a seat."

We elbowed to the front row, where Ellen perched on the edge of her chair, leaving me the empty spot next to the wall. She reached under her seat for a spiral notebook—from her parents' life coaching business, with inspirational messages at the bottom of each page—and opened it to a fresh sheet. She then retrieved a yellow mechanical pencil from behind her ear and clicked it four or five times, saw that too much 0.5mm lead had sprouted forth, and pushed the lead back until only a smidge was available. She looked up at me.

"What?" she said. "I hate it when the lead snaps off."

I turned to her, reaching around the back of her chair. "It's not actually possible for you to get in today. You know that, right?"

She pursed her lips and smiled me a flat one. Then she looked down at her notebook and in the top right corner wrote, *Asshole.*

I laughed. "You still want to go to Keegan's party tonight after tutoring?"

"Don't call it tutoring. It's just me helping out."

"And it's me appreciating it. We should go."

She rubbed her eraser over the word, restoring the page to its pristine and profanity-free condition. She brushed the eraser shavings to the floor and crossed her legs.

Mr. Edwards returned to the microphone. A hush fell over the crowd and people scrambled to their seats. I looked around; every chair was filled, and the standers squeezed against one another behind the back row.

At Oak Fields it was generally cool to *not* want things, as if admitting desire showed a weakness. Everyone knew full well who was getting what award, who was interviewing for what summer internship, who was volunteering at what orphanage. But we pretended not to care about the things we wanted so people didn't see us disappointed when someone else got them. I guess that meant I'd already screwed up because, as Vanessa pointed out, everyone knew I wanted to go to Juilliard. And I was okay with that, as long as I got in.

But today, in a drastic break with the norm, the foyer was electric with desire. No amount of coolness could mask it.

"Ladies and gentlemen," Mr. Edwards said, tapping the mic with his index finger. "Can you hear me? Test, test."

Absolute silence.

"Good." Instead of raising the microphone stand, the

counselor hunched as he spoke, looking out at us over the frame of his tortoiseshell glasses. "I don't want to take up too much time, given that you're not here to see me. Two quick points, however. Number one: this Artist character."

A chuckle rippled throughout the room. The day before, a collage of photographs had been posted on the bulletin board outside the college counseling office depicting Sophie Meyers in various stages of debauchery—bong included, shirt not always. The caption read: How WELL DO YOU KNOW YOUR CITIZENS? and it was signed THE ARTIST.

"This is no laughing matter, I promise you! If anyone should find him or herself in possession of pertinent information, I'd strongly encourage that person to come forward."

"Bryan's got some pertinent information," said a voice, to stifled laughter.

I glanced back at Bryan Wilson, who as Sophie's most recent ex-boyfriend had made a shirtless cameo or two in The Artist's collage. Bryan's face flushed, and he looked down. A few of Sophie's friends glared at him from the other side of the room.

"You think Bryan did it?" I whispered to Ellen.

"I don't know," Ellen said. "Could be Zoë Franklin. She's finished second to Sophie in Model UN every year since ninth grade."

"Yeah, but why would she do it? Are they even applying to the same schools?"

"Number *two*," Mr. Edwards's voice boomed. "I wish

to remind you that the College Counseling Office requires a second draft of everybody's standard essay template by the end of the month."

There were a few assorted groans, some nods, quite a bit of pencil-scratching on notebook paper. Second draft. I actually laughed out loud, an obnoxious "Ha!"

"Did I say something humorous?" Mr. Edwards said, instantly narrowing his eyes at me. Thanks so much, Ellen, for putting us in the front row.

"No, sir," I said. "Definitely not."

"It is my duty to let you know," he said, settling his gaze on me for effect before looking out over the rest of the audience, "that your college essay is one of the most important documents you will ever write. And lest you think me guilty of hyperbole, remember that the strength of your essay determines where you spend the next four years of your life. In turn, statistics tell us that those four years will likely determine who your friends are and whom you marry, which will also play a role in where you choose to go after college and what you do for a living. In short, the entire path of your future may in fact depend on those seven hundred and fifty words, I'm sorry to tell you."

Ellen rifled a glance at me and whispered, "Have you even given them a first draft?"

"There's no essay for Juilliard," I reminded her, "just an audition. You should check out my monologues tonight. I made some changes."

Mr. Edwards spoke slowly, as though his words were

so heavy with meaning that he had a hard time getting them out. "It's my job to make sure you give yourself a chance at a future."

"And for that, we thank you, sir." Geoff Cronyn flourished a thumbs-up and raised it high, and a couple people around him laughed into their shoulders. I'd seen him more this semester than ever before because his mom had made him audition for a play just once, before he graduated, and in a stunning example of typecasting, he'd gotten a role as one of the wealthy freeloaders at Gatsby's parties.

According to the school's vibrant rumor mill, Geoff's parents had been so unhappy with the B-plus their son had received in eleventh grade British Literature that they'd demanded a meeting with Headmaster Lunardi and Mrs. Moore. Nobody knows what was said, but when the meeting was over, Mrs. Moore supposedly "found" a revised version of Geoff's final essay in the pile on her desk. Hello, A-minus!

Mr. Edwards glared at him, but said nothing. Geoff's parents, after all, were Platinum Level donors, and—according to the inscription on the bronze plaque near the entrance—the very foyer we sat in would not have been possible without their generous financial assistance.

"What about the applications for your other schools?" Ellen whispered, circling the inspirational quote at the bottom of her notebook page. "Need I remind you, 'The path to success is paved with the stones of preparation.'"

"You need not," I said.

Mr. Edwards suddenly transformed into a game show host. "And now, without further ado, I'd like to introduce our very own Michael Parson, Oak Fields Preparatory class of '92, and the current Assistant Associate Director of Admissions at Stanford University!"

Those last two words, finally spoken, sent a jolt of excitement throughout the room. The audience applauded fervently but politely, as if searching for the right mix of ass-kissing and West Coast Ivy–style decorum.

Stanford's Hoover Tower was visible from pretty much anywhere within a five-mile radius. Beige stone with a maroon-capped bell tower, it served as a constant reminder of where we were, of who was in charge.

Michael Parson bounced to the front of the room and snatched the wireless microphone out of the stand. Parson was a specimen of humanity. At least six-three, with a full head of jet-black hair and positive brown eyes. He wore a lime green tie in perfect contrast to the subtle blue pinstripes of his gray suit.

"Hello, hello, hello!" he said, and his voice filled the space. He waved his free hand in an attempt to fire up the crowd. "Who wants to be a Cardinal?"

I looked over my shoulder at the rest of my classmates. Children of venture capitalists and consultants and thousand-dollar-an-hour attorneys, heirs to the options of Google and Facebook and The Next Big Thing. Our lives up to this point were but prologue to the next step, and we had gathered to learn how best to make that next step happen. Michael Parson was the man to tell us.

Even with my heart set on Juilliard, I couldn't help but get caught up in the emotion and excitement. He spoke for twenty minutes about Stanford, what it had offered him, what it could offer us, and he peppered his speech with phrases like "fire within" and "touch points" and "stick-to-it-iveness." Parson talked about walking off that campus with his degree in hand and knowing that he'd been properly prepared for anything life could throw at him.

I rode Parson's speech like a wave, feeling more and more exhilarated as it propelled me forward. If only, if only! Maybe it *was* the place for me. Maybe I could even thrive there. I envisioned myself in front of the television at three a.m., a bag of greasy potato chips on my lap, watching Michael Parson convince me to mail four easy payments of $19.95 for his revolutionary three-book Redefining Success Tool Kit.

When he finished, he stepped backward and took a sip from a plastic cup of water. He smoothed his tie and quickly inspected the tip as if checking for lint. "Now, for the reason I came here today."

His mood changed. He replaced the microphone in the stand and put his hands in his pockets so that his shoulders couldn't help but shrug. He looked at us.

"There have been some changes in our admission policy, changes that we only finalized two days ago. They'll become public this afternoon, but given my love for and dedication to Oak Fields Prep, I wanted you to hear it from me."

"What's going on?" I whispered to Ellen.

She shook her head, her mouth slightly open, but said nothing. A restlessness grew around us.

"It's best I cut to the chase," he said. "This year, only one of you will get into Stanford University."

Silence. Followed by the exact opposite. Surprise turned to disbelief that was quickly replaced by anger. How was a limit like that even possible? There had never been one before. Ellen cleared her throat and blinked a bunch of times.

Parson held his hands up, motioning for quiet until it finally came. "Please let me explain, and then I'll answer questions for as long as you like. This wasn't an easy decision for the admissions committee. There are seventy-eight private schools within twenty miles of the Stanford campus, along with over twenty-five public high schools. Our average freshman class is around seventeen hundred. That means that even under this new policy, if we were to accept only one deserving student from each of the schools in our area, that would still be six percent of the total incoming class."

While my classmates watched, stunned into silence once again, Parson explained that Stanford wasn't the only school taking such action. Harvard was doing it in Boston, and even smaller schools like Amherst and Pomona were taking the same approach. It was the wave of the future.

"Stanford is a global university," he said, "and as much as it pains me to deliver the news to the students of my alma mater, we hope this action will ensure our ability to attract a diverse student body from around the state, the country, and the globe. Now, can I answer any questions?"

Hands shot up like jack-in-the-boxes.

Geoff asked if what they were doing was even legal, and Parson assured him that it was. Keegan Schroeder asked whether it was more important for kids to be really good at one thing or pretty good at a lot of things. I thought it was a stupid question, considering that Keegan was really good at everything, including throwing massive parties when his parents were out of town. Not only had he already been recruited by at least a dozen Division I soccer programs, but he was also a National Merit Scholar, and he'd even modeled for a regional department store catalog when he was younger.

"Yes," Parson said, "you in the back."

"How does the new policy affect early admission?"

I turned at the sound of Vanessa's voice. She'd put on a pair of silver-framed glasses, which made her look even older, smarter, and more out of place than normal. Ellen sighed, and I recognized a note of resignation. If Vanessa was the competition, her sigh seemed to say, what chance did any of us have?

"It would certainly behoove you to get that application in early, otherwise the spot might be gone without your ever being considered," Parson said.

Ellen huddled over her notebook, the pages full of tips and reminders. Her Vanessa-inspired insecurity aside, she had a legitimate chance, even under the new policy. She was president of the Oak Fields chapter of the National Honor Society, had volunteered at a local homeless shelter since the sixth grade, and was the one most responsible for convincing the administration to revive a school-wide recycling program. Plus, she had the pogo stick record. Her parents—co-owners of Peninsula Life Coach, Inc.—had prepared her well.

In closing, Michael Parson relaxed his shoulders and scanned our faces, establishing a deep and personal connection with each of us. "Stanford is indeed a wonderful place," he said solemnly, "but it's not for everybody. Before you apply, make sure you're ready for the rigors, the pressure, and the excitement. If you do decide to choose us, and we choose you, then I promise that we'll provide you with an education that will prepare you to be successful for the rest of your life."

He thanked us again for our interest, and then he was gone. We all sat there for a few moments, processing. I felt like I'd just watched a commercial for the Marines. Did I have what it took to be one of the few, the proud?

For the first time, I found myself thankful for the distraction of my upcoming audition. Sure, Juilliard was stressful, but at least it beat the whole every-man-for-himself thing that Parson just laid down for us.

It wasn't enough to be a well-rounded student with intellectual vitality. We knew we had to be more well-rounded and intellectually vital than everybody else in the room. If one of us made the all-district team, the next guy would have to make all-state. If one of us got all A's, the next guy would have to load up on summer classes at some institute for Gifted Youth. If one of us volunteered for Habitat for Humanity, the next guy would have to convince his freaking parents to donate their home to charity.

This was the reality of our situation. The administration prided itself on the cultivation of an environment that bred healthy competition between the students. A rising tide lifts all boats, so to speak.

Unless it doesn't, of course. Unless the tide comes up too fast. Then what do you have?

3

I knew I was in trouble when I walked through my front door and the first thing I saw was my dad at the kitchen table, his reading glasses propped atop his thinning crew cut and his arms crossed, with short stacks of papers spread across the table in front of him.

"Do you remember the Jenkinses?" he said. "Who used to live down the street?"

I opened the fridge, but the carton I went for was too light. I put it back and turned to my dad. "Didn't we buy milk yesterday?"

He closed his eyes and pinched the bridge of his nose. Wiry and intense, my dad is put together like a Doberman and wound just as tight. Most days he takes down an entire pot of coffee before my sister and I even wake up. He's great with numbers and code; not as good with people.

"Their daughter, Allison, just got back from two years in Hollywood." He sounded relieved, as though she'd been serving in the military overseas and hadn't been expected to return in one piece. It took me a moment to realize that this was a conversation and I was expected to participate.

I rested against the doorjamb and went for noncommittal. "Wow."

"She was featured in a pornographic film." He paused, letting whatever he was trying to say sink in. "Can you believe that?"

My first thought, admittedly, was not that I couldn't believe it, but that I had to find out the title. She was one of those hot neighbors you see on TV sitcoms, about five years older than the poor puberty-ravaged protagonist. I'd always wondered what she looked like naked, and now, lo and behold, there was actual film! "Is that what made her come home?"

My dad threw up his hands, frustrated, as though I hadn't been paying attention. "She couldn't make any money as an actress, David, so she resorted to prostituting herself for the camera."

I took another look at the papers in front of him and understood that our conversation was in fact going to be another in a long series of "discussions" we'd had about the wisdom of my supposed "career" choice.

"I have to set the table," I said. "Can we move that stuff?"

"I came across some figures I'd like to share with you." He nestled his glasses onto the bridge of his nose and shuffled through the papers until he found his lead item. "According to the Screen Actors Guild's own calculations, only five percent of union members make more than five thousand dollars from acting in any given year."

"That's not a lot," I said.

"And it only includes union members, you understand, not the thousands upon thousands of people like poor

Allison Jenkins who don't even make enough to join the union."

I pulled out a chair and eased into it. "The numbers are daunting," I said as if conceding a point.

"They get even more so. In order to qualify for union-sponsored health insurance, a SAG member has to make at least seventeen thousand dollars. That means that ninety-five percent of so-called union members—and probably more—don't even qualify for their own benefits!"

I checked the clock on the microwave. This being Friday night, it was Mom's turn to cook, and she hated when the table wasn't set in time.

"Look at me," he said, and then he gestured to the table, where he grabbed a stack of printed-out articles and held them up like Moses and the stone tablets. "This is reality, right here. These are real numbers."

"I get it." Then I had a flash of inspired logic. "But I have some numbers, too."

He palmed the stubble on his chin with his left hand, surprised by a tactic I'd never shown him before.

"Let's say I'm better than fifty percent of the people who try to make it. Is that a fair baseline?"

Dad said, "I'm willing to accept that number."

"I'd like to think I'm more talented, but we'll stick with fifty percent," I said, fishing like an idiot for a compliment I didn't really think would come. "Okay, so let's say the one thing I *can* control is my willingness to work, and let's say I work harder than fifty percent of the people who are more talented. The numbers start to look better, right? Now what about if I work harder than seventy-five percent? Than ninety percent?"

"I see where you're going with this, David. And I understand your desire."

"So let me show you my monologues. They're really coming into shape, you'll see—"

"Even if I gave you your ninety percent, these decisions aren't made in a vacuum. College is expensive, and you know we're going to take out loans to pay for it. I know you think you'll work hard at acting, but I want to be sure that what I'm paying for is of *value*."

Ahh, the value card. His trump card, every time. As excited as he'd been for the money I earned from the Sparkles campaign, he'd always figured that acting was a phase I would grow out of soon enough. I looked at my shoes. One of my laces had come untied, but now wasn't the time to retie it. "Juilliard has a liberal arts program," I said.

The drone of the freeway traffic two blocks away. The sheet of paper rustling in his hands.

"Juilliard." The word burned like acid on his tongue.

I slowly brought my head up to make eye contact with him and asked a question I'd always been too defensive to even consider. "What do you want me to do? Am I supposed to be a doctor? A lawyer? An engineer like you?"

He seemed almost taken aback. He'd fought for so long to convince me that my problem existed in the first place that he seemed unprepared to offer a solution. There was the sense that something significant was happening between us. A step forward, so to speak, in our relationship. He cleared his throat and mumbled to himself, something about my decisions being important.

A car door slammed outside, followed shortly by the jingle of keys. The front door opened.

"Thai food's here!" my mom said, propping the door open with one elbow.

"I need to set the table," I said to my dad.

"Lisa, dinner!" Mom yelled as she hefted a large to-go bag onto the table. Ginger chicken and curried shrimp, courtesy of her favorite restaurant, ThaiRiffic. She pointed to my dad's printouts. "What's this?"

"Dad was just doing some research," I said and pushed back from the table. I opened the dishwasher and piled a short stack of clean plates on the counter above it.

Mom shrugged off her sweater and hung it on the back of the chair before unpacking the bag. Her energy isn't artificially produced like my father's; she's strictly decaf. Just a whirl of flailing arms and sharp sighs and raised eyebrows. "Lisa!" she yelled. "Lisa!"

My sister wandered into the kitchen with one headphone still stuck in her ear. "I heard you already. Jesus."

"Don't say 'Jesus,'" Dad said.

"We're religious today?"

Mom said, "It's getting cold."

"No music at the table," my dad said.

Lisa made a big show of removing her headphones and tossing her player onto the couch in the living room.

"Mother, Father," she said, "I am eager to consume this carefully prepared meal and to participate in the nightly dining ritual like the dedicated family member I am."

I snorted to myself and jammed a spoon into the white rice. We got along fine—as well as you could expect from a senior and a freshman—but we didn't have much in common. Lisa took after my dad, with her pipe cleaner arms and legs and her intimate relationship with code. When she was twelve, she hacked into Coca-Cola's Ultimate Dreamz Sweepstakes with a tiny program that allowed her to enter as often as she wanted—a total of over 1.5 million times—which yielded her a tidy 13.7 percent of the prizes until a Coke executive and an IRS agent appeared at our doorstep and notified her that she'd violated the spirit, and quite possibly the terms, of the competition. Much was expected of her.

We piled food onto our plates—my mom to my right, Dad to my left, and Lisa across from me—settling into the comfort of routine. Nobody ever spoke until we'd all had a chance to down at least three or four bites. It was our version of a mini-vacation.

Lisa eventually pointed her fork at me. "Was Sophie really topless in the pictures?"

"What?" I said.

"I heard she was." She leaned forward. "I heard she was smoking a bong and flipping off the camera and naked."

My mom said, "What are you talking about?"

Lisa looked at both of our parents before continuing.

"So there's this guy who calls himself The Artist, and yesterday at school—"

"She wasn't topless," I said.

Lisa said, "Why are you defending her?"

"I'm not—"

"Flipping off the camera?" Mom said.

Dad cleared his throat. "This happened at school?"

"Doesn't bong mean marijuana?" Mom said.

Lisa nodded. "I heard she was naked."

I dropped my fork on the table. "Mom, yes, there was a picture of her flipping off the camera and smoking what appeared to be marijuana. Dad, it was put on a school bulletin board, but Mr. Edwards took it down right away. And Lisa, you don't know what you're talking about, so shut it."

"David!" Mom said. A gasp.

Lisa smirked at me.

There was a short silence, and then my dad turned to my sister. "I don't understand what you mean by The Artist."

"He's, like, an artist, you know. And he does collages with photos and stuff, and there were all these pictures of Sophie Meyers topless—"

"She had a bra on!" I said.

"And he wrote, 'This is what a Citizen looks like' underneath it."

"What does that even mean?" my mom said.

"It was, 'How well do you know your Citizens?'" I said.

"Well, whatever." Lisa shrugged. "I think it's one of the seniors. Someone mad at Sophie for something. Do you know who it is, David?"

My parents both looked at me expectantly.

"Didn't Sophie Meyers win the Oak Fields Prep Citizen Award last year?" my mom said.

Dad nodded. "That must be what 'look at our Citizens' refers to."

"Yes, that's the whole—" I dropped my hands with enough force to rattle the fork on the table. "Here's the deal. The award goes to the junior 'whose outstanding academic achievement and personal integrity most indicates the promise of greatness,' so clearly whoever did it was making a point."

"I don't know why you're so upset," Lisa said.

"Because you—"

"That award must look good on a college application," my dad said. "That's probably why they give it to a junior?"

"Yeah, it looks less good if you have to explain why the school rescinded it." I shoved a bite of chicken into my mouth, disappointed with myself for letting Lisa press my buttons like that. Yes, she was three years younger, but shrewd and distant will defeat overly emotional every time. I tried one of my relaxation exercises—breathe in on a three count, out on a four count.

Lisa waited a few seconds and then broke the silence with a conspiratorial stage whisper. "I heard there's a huge party at Keegan's house tonight," she said. "Are you going?"

"Can you pass the water?" I said.

My mom stopped her fork an inch from her mouth. "Keegan Schroeder? Will his parents be there?"

Lisa said, "It's supposed to be crazy."

"Who'd you hear that from?" I said.

"Like it wasn't all over school."

"Ellen's coming over," I said to my mom, doing my best to ignore Lisa. "We're going to work on my essay."

"How did the Stanford meeting go today?" Dad wiped the corner of his mouth.

"Unexpected. Oak Fields has only one spot."

Mom said, "What does that mean?"

"They're taking one student, max, from each of the schools within a twenty-mile radius. It's like affirmative action but in reverse and based on location instead of race and ethnicity."

"What?" Dad said. "Can they even do that?"

"Supposedly it's the wave of the future, at least among private colleges and universities."

"Is that going to be a problem with you and Ellen?" my mom said. "With you both applying?"

"Both applying?" Lisa snorted. "What's he going to do—no offense—monologue his way in?"

"Don't listen to her," Mom said.

Dad came to my defense. Dad, of all people. "David's scores are on par with the majority of his classmates. GPA, ACT, SAT, all well within range. There's no reason to think he shouldn't apply."

My mom patted me on the arm. "You can get in if you try hard enough."

The doorbell rang.

"I wish you'd told me she was coming," Mom scolded playfully. "I'd have ordered a veggie dish."

I pushed back from the table, for once grateful that Ellen showed up early to everything, and opened the front door. Her backpack was slung over one shoulder, and she wore pink flip-flops and a short beige pleated skirt that showcased most of her legs. We were definitely going to Keegan's later.

"You're still eating," she said, peering over my shoulder.

"Come in, come in," my mom practically leaped up from the table, her arms wide and welcoming. "Are you hungry?"

"No, thanks, Mrs. Ellison." She smiled politely. "I had a—"

"You can nibble on some veggies. Have a seat with us."

My sister and dad made space for Ellen between them, and I pulled out another plate. "I'm fine, thanks," she said, but my mom motioned for me to set some food in front of her anyway.

"David told us about the meeting." Dad angled his head toward her as though sharing a miserable secret.

Ellen shrugged. "We all just have to work that much harder, I guess."

Mom waved her index finger at Dad. "Oh, honey, they don't want to talk about school."

"I like your earrings," Lisa said, resting her chin reverentially on her open palm.

Ellen shot a grin my way as her hand tickled the small

chain of polished bamboo squares hanging from her left ear. "David gave them to me—"

"He did not!"

"Oh, he's a pretty thoughtful guy," she said and reached hesitantly with her fork, picking out mushrooms, bell peppers, and onions from the pile of ginger chicken.

The rest of the meal was quite lovely. Not only was I no longer the focus of conversation, but I was also showered with kind smiles and proud glances from my parents, a reward for bringing into our home a girl so attractive and put together as Ellen.

When they finally freed us from the table, Ellen and I went back to my room and sat on my bed. Multiple aborted drafts of my essay outline were spread out before us, many of them peppered with slogan-filled Peninsula Life Coach sticky notes. The red pen in Ellen's hand hovered over my most recent attempt, taunting me.

"You okay?" I said. "About the Stanford thing?"

"Whether I'm okay is irrelevant. Doesn't make much sense to ask the cow if it's okay with becoming a burger."

I laughed. "Colter called it a feed lot this morning."

"Colter Stern?"

"Hmm?" I said, feeling the sudden urge to stall. "Yeah, he and Vanessa are kind of funny together. I wouldn't be surprised if one of them was adopted."

"I haven't really spent much time with them."

"I'm just saying . . . Forget it. Let's do this."

"Let's do this, indeed." She licked her lips and uncapped the pen. "First off, you can't list your Jefe Pizza delivery job as a life-changing experience."

"They offered me assistant manager. I would have been in charge of people. Enrique was the first person who saw leadership potential in me. I was honored. I started to look at my life in a different way."

"And?"

"And nothing," I said, a bit defensively. I searched through the essay until I found the right sticky note. I peeled it off the page and read the preprinted life coachism at the bottom. "Our character is shaped by our reactions to the opportunities before us."

"You didn't take the job."

I paused. "Fair point."

"Damn it, David—"

There was virtually no time between the quiet knock at the door and my mom nudging it open and peering through. "Dessert?"

"Mom, we're working. Please."

"Thanks anyway," Ellen said.

"I could make some tapioca? Or—"

"Mom!"

She nodded as she closed the door, saying how proud she was of us and of how hard we were working and to let her know if there was anything we needed. Then she was too far down the hall for me to hear.

"Where were we?" I said.

Ellen gestured to the papers on the bed and waved the one in her hand. "Um, here?"

"I know. It's just that with the audition in less than

three weeks, my mind is a little . . . Maybe you could watch me run my monologues? And then we can get back to it?"

"Are you even going to try with this?"

"But I haven't *done* anything. I act. I hang out with you. When I'm bored, I go to the mall and watch people's mannerisms. How awesome a college essay would that make?"

She capped the red pen and tucked it behind her ear, considering me. Finally: "So."

I cocked my head at her. "You don't want to be doing this any more than I do."

Her face softened a bit and she rolled her eyes. "You're like a mind reader."

"Then why—" I stopped myself as I understood. She was there because she believed in me. She wanted the best for me, and she really thought that I could get into Princeton or Penn or even some place like Amherst, and the world would be my oyster. And seriously, how could I not love her for that?

I tossed a draft to the side and turned to her. "I'm sorry," I said.

"What does David Ellison want?"

"Before we can go after what it is we want, we first have to determine what it is we need, remember? You told me that." I snuck my arm between her back and the wall.

She laughed. "Oh, he wants action?"

"No, he needs it. Just a little. To take the edge off. Then we'll get to all this, I promise." I leaned in and planted a small one on her lips. Then another. "You find me irresistible."

She cupped my face with both hands and jiggled my head. "Not exactly the word I would have chosen."

I fell backward and pulled, and she squealed as she collapsed on top of me. Papers crumpled beneath us, and we both motioned for the other to be quiet as we turned our heads to the door, holding our breath and waiting. A minute of silence proved that we were safe. I felt her heartbeat against my chest as my hand found its way to the small of her back, and then lower.

4

The houses on Page Mill were set way back from the road, with winding tree-lined driveways and sign-covered fences alerting us to the privateness of the property. We parked my white Subaru station wagon—known to all as the White Horse—just off the street and walked up to Keegan's house, by clusters of future CEOs smoking weed or passing around bottles of the hard stuff. The moon was full and the sky cloudless, so the walk through the trees had a Hansel and Gretel fairy-tale quality: pale light and dim shadow as we followed a trail of empty cans and bottles toward the front door.

I'd been to Keegan's before, once last year for a party and a few times when I was a freshman dabbling in the Young Californians Community League. Always planning ahead, my parents thought membership in a civic-minded organization would look great on my college application, but after seven meetings that consisted entirely of discussing the limitless possibilities available to us as community volunteers, I figured I didn't need the YCCL; I could tell myself how awesome I was on my own time.

The house boasted a new addition since last year's party: a series of ten-foot-high aviaries in a side yard. Five or six girls in tight jeans and short skirts surrounded one of them, protecting it from some guys who were pleading for the girls to let them through with vodka-soaked birdseed.

Ellen followed my gaze as we walked by. "Don't."

"You're not curious? Not even a little?"

We opened the heavy wooden door, and then my legs went out from under me and I was falling. My right foot kicked out straight as though I'd hit a patch of ice, and then I crashed hard to the floor. I tried to push myself up, but my hands slipped on the cold marble and I fell backward again. A sharp pain spread across my whole right side.

"Cut him off," I heard someone say. A few other people whistled and clapped. Ellen knelt at my side as I lay groaning.

"I don't even know if that was on purpose or not," she said before helping me to my feet. "What do you suppose that says about you?"

Her best friend, Amber, intercepted us just as we reached the living room. She must have broken up with her boyfriend again; her white shirt was tight and spaghetti strapped. "I guess that counts as an entrance."

I cracked my neck and bowed theatrically.

"Sorry we're late," Ellen said.

Amber gave me a mischievous smile. "How goes the tutoring?"

"It's just me helping out," Ellen said.

"And me appreciating it," I said. "Who's thirsty?"

Amber held up a cider. "I'm good."

"Make it the usual," Ellen said.

I pushed into the kitchen, rubbing at the dull pain on my right hip as I wove to avoid sloshing Dixie cups. In the backyard a bean-shaped swimming pool was connected to a long narrow lap pool, and behind the pools, the lawn sloped downward for about a hundred feet to an ivy-covered fence, with one of the country club's fairways on the other side.

The beverages were in a cluster at the bottom of the hill—a keg and a few huge coolers filled with various bottles and cans. I grabbed a Bud Light for myself and a hard lemonade for Ellen, and on my way back I had to dodge a frenzied barrage of drunk classmates having roll-down-the-hill competitions.

"This place is ridiculous," Amber said. "I bet Keegan doesn't know half these people."

Ellen said, "I bet half these people don't know Keegan."

"I used to come here for YCCL meetings," I said.

Amber raised her eyebrows. "Oooh, did the Young Calis make it into your essay?"

"Did the Dumb Beavs make it into yours?"

Ellen elbowed me and pointed the opening of her clear bottle at Amber. "Where's Brad?"

"Wait, we were talking about Sparkles here."

I made my face all innocent. "But your love life is so much more interesting."

Amber shrugged. "No Brad."

"If your boyfriend is on a train leaving from Cleveland going twenty-eight miles per hour, and you show up at a party without him, how long does it take to figure out that he's off somewhere with Cindy Saunders?" I smiled. "My math skills are wicked, see? That's going in the essay, too."

"You guys haven't had to find a date to anything for the past two years," she said, ignoring me. "You can't relate."

"You should ask Iggy," I said. "That dude thinks you're hot."

I pointed toward the hot tub, which was surrounded by a kind of grotto with soft yellow floodlights shining up from within the ground. Iggy Rockwell—our very own all-district power forward—held court with the other jocks, all practicing their flexes, leaning forward with their fists together and growling like The Hulk.

"Wow," I said with reverence. "You need to get on that, Amber. That guy is ripped to shreds."

"What's wrong with him?" she said, poking her head at me.

"Ahh, the million-dollar question," Ellen said, laughing.

Amber gestured over my shoulder with her chin. "Vanessa Stern and her brother just showed up. Look at her hair. I love her hair. No, don't look!"

I pretended to stretch my back, turning around in one direction and then the other, each time catching a glimpse of Vanessa and Colter by the back door. Vanessa looked fantastic, and it wasn't just her hair. Everything I thought before about how she wasn't sure whether she wanted people to recognize her for her body went out the window. Her shorts would have been tiny even if she hadn't rolled up the cuffs, and she wore a tight red T-shirt with the word ANGEL stretched across her chest. She looked around anxiously and when she saw me, her face lit up, and she waved.

"Could you be more obvious?" Amber said. "She's coming over here."

Vanessa and Colter scooched into our circle. "Hey guys."

We all said hi back, and then there was a small pause.

"I love your skirt," Vanessa said, pointing.

Clearly pleased, Ellen did a little turn from side to side. "Oh, this old thing?"

I wondered if there was something I was supposed to be doing to reassure Ellen that I wasn't at all interested in Vanessa. At the same time, Vanessa and I had spent the last two days rehearsing a scene that would eventually require actual kissing, and I didn't want to be a jerk and completely ignore her. I took a drink.

"Hey, Chief," Colter said.

I nodded. "Hey, Weird New Guy,"

Colter turned to his sister and jumped up and down like he was going to Disneyland. "He called me Weird New Guy! He called me Weird New Guy!"

Just then, Keegan stumbled by with his pink plaid shirt half unbuttoned. "Settle down, settle down," he said. "You're scaring my guests."

Colter stopped jumping and looked away.

"There can be only one," Keegan toasted Ellen and

Vanessa with an overflowing Dixie cup. "And I . . . will be looking forward . . . to knocking your cute little asses out of El Stanford."

"Keep dreaming," Ellen said.

"You know how I know I'm not dreaming?" His eyelids lowered halfway and he leaned in to her. He slurred a whisper: "'Cause you're still *dressed*."

"Hey!" I stepped between the two of them and thought about pushing him back. As for what I would do next, I had no idea. I'd never been in a fight before—not a real fight, anyway, one that wasn't choreographed for the stage—and I didn't want to get my ass kicked in front of Vanessa and Ellen. Even still, I had to at least *look* like I was ready to go.

"Easy, now," Keegan said, dismissing me as though I offered no challenge at all. "Tonight's a party, and I'm a lover, not a fighter." Liquid sloshed over the rim of his cup as he serpentined toward the grotto. "Rockwell!" he shouted.

Christina Guerrero, Keegan's girlfriend of six months, appeared in his wake and offered us an apologetic smile. There was something in her eyes, though—embarrassment? regret?—that made me wonder if she'd heard the rumor that Keegan was cheating on her with one of the sophomores. "He's just drunk," she said on her way through.

"Well," Colter said. "I should probably go get caught up."

"I'll go with you." Vanessa included the three of us in a general wave. "See you guys."

"You're my hero," Ellen said to me when they'd gone.

"I'm pretty sure he would have killed me."

She laced her hand around my arm and tiptoed to kiss me on the lips. "Yeah. Me too."

"I didn't know you and Colter were buddies," Amber said as she watched them go.

"His sister's in the play," I said. "Daisy Buchanan."

"So you're using him to get to her?"

"Yes, Amber, that's exactly what I'm doing." I gave Ellen a little nudge with my elbow. "Because this whole long-term relationship thing is a drag."

I brought my bottle up to my lips, and something smacked me hard on the back and I stumbled forward, spilling a hefty splash of my Bud Light onto Amber's chest.

"What's up, bitch?" The voice was low and rough, and I recognized it instantly.

Jake Starr was the most experienced techie in the theatre department. He'd do lights and sound, but he really liked to make things go BOOM, mostly to try to throw me off my game. Last year when we did *Godspell*, he created a crazy pyrotechnic display for my entrance as John the Baptist that had the fire department threaten to shut us down.

The night of Keegan's party, he wore black boots, black jeans, and a ratty black T-shirt. I give him a hard time about embracing the stereotype of the theatre freak, but he always said that his wardrobe and bald head were more about convenience than style.

Ellen and Amber glared at him, but he didn't seem to notice. He scanned the party over my shoulder, bouncing on his toes like a boxer before the fight. "Nice place. I bet they film porn here."

"Jesus Christ," Amber said.

"Hi, Jake," Ellen said.

Jake rubbed his hand over his scalp. "Ladies."

Techies tend to regard performance as some sort of torture, and actors wonder how techies can be so close to the stage without wanting to take it over, but we both realize that we couldn't exist without each other, so we make it work. Our real-world dynamic, however, is less well-defined.

"Where'd you get the beverage?" Jake said finally.

I pointed down the hill, and Jake slapped his hands together. "Mmmboy, delicious!" he said, and we watched him go.

"He totally hijacked Corky Cheung's presentation on the Spanish-American War the other day." The disdain on Amber's face was caked on thicker than her foundation. And as an actor, I knew all about foundation. "He kept asking questions about Mexican food and—"

"Hey, what about Julius Chu?" Ellen said. "Didn't he and Corky just end it?"

Amber's face lit up. "Ooh, Julius Chu. He's a hot one."

"You could catch him on the rebound," I said.

But they were already off. I had nothing more to offer the conversation, so I stepped away from them and avoided the rolling idiots as I walked down to Keegan's back fence, eventually stopping next to a small birdbath. The column was chipped to hell on one side, as though someone had taken potshots at it, and the little reservoir pool was dry.

"You're not stroking that fountain, are you, Sparkles?" The voice belonged to Francine Cardenas.

I turned and smiled at her. Francine was still as cute as she'd been in the sixth grade when—right at the height of my Sparkles Tea fame—we spent a brief and nondescript period as a couple.

"It's good to see you out," I said.

"I figured, might as well. Senior year and all." She shrugged. "When's Juilliard?"

A bolt of unease shot through me so hard that I may have even staggered back a bit. I tried to mask it with a drink of beer, but no amount of alcohol would have chased away the nerves. "Nineteen days, give or take, and thanks for bringing that up."

I looked up at the party. Ellen was still talking to Amber. She waved down at me, and I waved back. Francine and I nodded for a bit.

"You want to practice?" she said.

"Now?"

"Please don't insult my intelligence. I know exactly what's going through your head." Francine was one of the few people at Oak Fields who could relate to my situation. She'd played the accompanying music for our shows the last two years, and a recent contest had crowned her the best high school pianist in northern California. She was dead set on Carnegie Mellon.

Corky, self-proclaimed costume queen of the theatre department, came down and handed Francine a cup of punch.

"You okay, Corky?" I said. "I mean, with you and Julius—"

She squealed. "Ewww! Run quickly and rinse your mouth out! That word makes it taste like poop."

"You seem to be holding up okay."

"Blah, blah, blah. Enough about me. What are you guys doing down here?"

Francine took a sip. "David was about to show us his monologues."

"I was not."

"Sure you were," Corky said. "Come on, let off a little steam."

"I've got four of them—"

Corky held up her hand. "How about just one?"

"And you're sure you want—"

"What else are we going to do tonight? Roll down the hill?"

Of my two classical monologues, my non-Shakespearean one was my favorite, from the Ben Jonson play *The Alchemist*, about three con men who set up shop in an abandoned town house after the owner flees London because of the plague. My character, Tribulation Wholesome, is a Puritan minister who wants to use alchemy to fund his ministry. He's kind of like the students of Oak Fields—someone who believes he's one of God's chosen people and is therefore slated for salvation no matter how he behaves.

I imagined stepping into a spotlight, presenting my hands as if holding a Bible.

"Where have you greater atheists than your cooks?
Or more profane or choleric than your glassmen?
More anti-Christian than your bell-founders?
What makes the devil so devilish, I would ask you—
Satan, our common enemy—but his being
perpetually about the fire and boiling
Brimstone and arsenic? We must give, I say—"

Francine's laughter interrupted me. "I have no idea what you're saying. Good enunciation, though."

"Enunciation is important," Corky said.

"Relax, Sparkles," Francine said. "You're going to do fine. Nice-looking young man like you?"

I looked back up the hill, where Ellen and Amber were heading to the cooler for a refill. Vanessa and her brother hung out by the edge of one of the pools, both looking around uncertainly. Someone should go up there and keep them company, I thought.

"Would you look at us," Corky said, raising her glass. "Three little theatre geeks such as ourselves, at a party such as this."

Francine took a sip and followed my gaze. "So this is what high school parties are like."

"I'm glad you came."

Corky said, "Of course she came. I needed a wing-woman."

"You haven't missed much," I said. "Nothing new ever happens at these things anyway. Doesn't matter where they are."

We looked at each other almost long enough to make the pause meaningful, and then, for the second time that night, I was on the ground, flat on my back and gasping for breath.

5

wheezed. I clutched at my chest. Something was weighing me down, and that something was Iggy Rockwell. "Day-VID!" he said, pounding his own chest like an ape. The alcohol on his breath was nuclear. "Yeah, boyee!"

"Iggy, you're sitting on me," I croaked.

"No, man, you're bein' sat on by me," he said, pushing himself to his feet. He kneed me in the chest as he tried to gather his balance.

"We're going to leave you guys to it," Francine said as she and Corky disappeared.

I groaned and rolled over onto my stomach, grateful for the cool grass on my cheek, the smell of nature scouring Iggy's tequila breath from my nostrils. I pushed myself up on all fours and concentrated on getting air into my lungs. I opened my eyes, and the next thing I knew, Iggy was coming after me with a golf club.

"FORE!" he said, and I realized that he was holding not one but two clubs over his head, and in the other hand a bucket of balls. "I foun' these in Keegan's room!"

"I can't—"

"We're hittin' balls tonight!"

It's a strange thing when the biggest guy on campus takes an interest in you. On the one hand, it's nice to be noticed. On the other hand, when the dude is 6′6″ and 225 pounds of lean, mean, rebounding machine, it's not as if the dynamic between the two of you is ever going to be even.

"Iggy, I suck."

"Hold this," he said, lifting me up and handing me the bucket.

"No, really—"

He grabbed me by the back of the shirt, spun me toward the golf course, and marched me straight ahead like I was a human shield. A gate appeared between the bushes, and we walked through it and onto the course. I fought the urge to crouch down and creep along the grass, cat-burglar style.

He stopped in the middle of the fairway, in full view of the party, but I didn't want to get busted for trespassing so I convinced him to keep going until we were squarely under the moon shade of a large oak tree.

"Eight-iron, six-iron." He held out a club in each hand. "Pick your poison."

"I told you, I don't hit—"

"I'll take the eight." He tossed the six on the ground and started to loosen up with practice swings.

This was my relationship with Iggy. Every couple of months he'd blow in, usually with a tackle or a punch or some other physical greeting, and before I could weasel away from the situation, he'd take me completely out of my comfort zone. Last year I found myself in his cousin's strip club because, according to Iggy, I needed to do research in case I ever had to play an underage guy who sneaks into his friend's cousin's strip club.

I always went along with it as a form of self-preservation: make the big guy laugh, live another day. It was a one-way street, though. Iggy probably never thought, Whoa, if I'm not careful, this dude could bust a Brooklyn accent on my ass.

He took a huge looping swing and nearly came out of his shoes. The ball popped high in the air but settled no more than fifteen feet in front of us.

"Harder," I said, chuckling.

"Jus' warmin' up." His next swing was furious, although this time he actually made solid contact with the ball, which disappeared into the night. He struck a pose with his club on his shoulder, covering his eyes as though shielding them from the sun.

"You're going to hurt your back."

"Screw my back, Day-vid," he said. "Your turn."

The thing about doing anything athletic in the presence of an athlete is that you're constantly judging yourself. My swing felt disjointed and pathetically slow, but I somehow managed to hit the ball. I smiled even though it dribbled out to the right.

He said, "Good backswing." I couldn't tell if he was being sarcastic or just drunk.

Up at the party, Ellen was talking to some guy I didn't recognize, probably one of Keegan's friends from another school, and they were both laughing. She ran her hand across her forehead and tucked her hair behind her ear—he must have given her some sort of compliment. We were so far away, and with the whole party in front of us, that it was like watching a silent movie, but with deep bass instead of piano music as the soundtrack.

"Do you know who that guy is up there with Ellen?" I said.

"Some dude, I guess. She's looking especially toasty tonight, bro."

I grunted. He swung again. Divot again.

"Not to toot my own horn, but I do a lot of chicks. That's why I don't have to toot my own horn!" He laughed to himself as though pleasantly surprised by his own wit. "You wanna know why?"

"I'm dying to."

"'Cause chicks dig the Ig, that's why!" He leaned backward and rotated from side to side, stretching. "No offense, but you don't ever get curious? Like maybe you want to get with someone else just to see what you're missing?"

"Who says I'm missing anything?"

"They charge much rent in the land of make-believe?"

There didn't seem to be much point in explaining my relationship with Ellen to someone like Iggy, especially as drunk as he was. The bottom line was that we were good. Ellen was a good influence on me. And Iggy was right: she was hot, too. Toasty, even.

"When you're ten years old an' you're six-foot, the lady at the grocery store asks if you play baske'ball. The mailman asks about your jumper. Maybe I wanted to play golf instead, right?"

He stopped and looked at me. Then he gazed over my shoulder up at the party. "You know what I like about you, David? You listen to me. People don't listen. We're friends, right?"

It felt like a trick question, but what choice did I have? "Sure."

He dropped the club and wrapped his massive paw around my neck, pulling my head closer as he leaned down to whisper in my ear. "I hate baske'ball." And he followed that with a giggle.

He held me there for a moment longer, then squeezed and released me. Then he bent over and picked up the club again. I watched him hit balls for a while, carving out chunks of earth the size of cereal bowls with every swing.

I cleared my throat. "You're not quitting."

"I'll let you know," he said without looking at me.

"Well, I think it's great," I decided to say. The bass beating from the house, the clear night, the full moon. If Iggy Rockwell could turn his back on basketball, then anything was possible. "Why do we have to explain ourselves to anyone, right? Why can't we be free to do what we want?"

"I could've been pretty good," he said as he watched a shot disappear. I wasn't sure if he meant golf or basketball. "Pretty good."

Something like shame slapped me in the face; he hadn't heard a word. I nudged a ball out in front of me. "Twenty bucks says I can hit it farther than you."

"Look at you gettin' all feisty." He laughed a deep one. "A theatre freak an' a cement-head. Playin' golf. Who'd-a-thought?"

Iggy rolled his shoulders back and took his cut. It wasn't one of his best—the club dug into the earth so deep that he could barely finish the swing—but he was so strong that the ball still shot forward. He shrugged. Given what he'd seen out of me, he probably figured he was home free. "Your turn, Sparkles."

I stood over the ball, squeezing the grip's cool rubber. I gave the club a little waggle. For some reason, I was so sure I was going to crush it that I almost swung with my eyes closed, and as soon as I made contact, I knew I'd won. The ball exploded off the club.

"Damn," Iggy said, and pride swelled deep within me. I had beaten him. At a sport.

And then it happened. As the ball disappeared into the moonlight it made a hard, slicing right turn. I lowered my club. Nerve-racking silence for one second, then two, then—

The distant yet unmistakable shattering of glass. A dog barked.

Iggy and I immediately dropped our clubs and sprinted through the trees—we couldn't find the gate, so we hopped the fence—and rejoined the party. When we reached Keegan's backyard, everyone was already rushing toward the direction of the crash. People jostled with each other, fought to get through to the other side of the house.

Iggy and I exchanged a look and then he crushed his

bulk into the crowd, clearing a path that I followed, and shouted over his shoulder, "My lips are fuckin' sealed."

"Shut up," I said.

"Nobody would believe you could hit it that far anyway."

"Dude, shut up!"

We reached the front yard, but nobody was worried about a broken window because Keegan and my techie friend Jake were rolling around on the grass, cursing at each other and punching.

I spotted Ellen and Amber and pushed my way through, yelling over the crowd, "What's going on? What happened?"

"Where were you?" Ellen said. "I was looking all over."

"Who was that guy you were talking to?" I said, hoping it sounded casual.

"I asked you first."

"Iggy made me hit golf balls with him."

"Iggy Rockwell?"

"Is there another Iggy?"

"You suck at golf."

"Not tonight." She didn't need to know about the window.

A couple of Keegan's friends rushed the circle and pulled Jake away, then Jake broke free and took off at a sprint, knocking a trio of cheerleaders backward into one of the aviaries as he wove toward the backyard. Keegan leaped to his feet and darted after him.

That was the last I saw either of them until Monday morning.

6

The setting was the senior hallway, outside the college counseling office. The mood was one of excitement mixed with disbelief. About fifteen students jostled for the best view of a photo collage tacked to a bulletin board. From time to time, we looked over at Christina Guerrero, who seethed with anger. The murmurs quieted down when Keegan appeared at the end of the hallway.

He walked toward us, looking puzzled, but nobody said a word. We backed up to a respectful distance and let him experience the artwork for himself.

The center of the collage was an 8×10 photo of Keegan passed out on the floor of his bedroom, wearing only the pink plaid shirt from the other night and his boxer shorts, cuddling a fifth of vodka with one arm and a girl who was clearly not Christina with the other. Arranged around the 8×10 were small action photos of Keegan and the blond sophomore, and written in block letters on the bottom of the page were the words HOW WELL DO YOU KNOW YOUR FELLOW MAN? It was signed THE ARTIST.

Keegan grabbed the top of it and ripped his arm down, leaving the top two corners stapled to the bulletin board. "What is this?" he said, looking at the pictures in his hand.

Someone answered: "That's some good action is what it is."

Keegan turned around slowly, his blinking eyelids hammering a staccato beat. He held the collage in an outstretched hand. He tried to smile, but his voice was a whisper. "Who did this?"

Christina stepped out from the crowd, and Keegan's face flashed an instant red. The paper drifted to the ground like a fallen leaf. It was like watching a horror movie through our fingers—our instinct was to turn away, but at the same time we couldn't resist the impending carnage. Keegan opened his mouth to say something, but before a word came out, Christina's hand fired across his face, the sound like a gunshot. Then she huffed away.

I kept my eyes on the train wreck but leaned down and whispered to Ellen, "Looks like karma went ahead and kicked his ass."

"Saved you the trouble."

Christina's slap had given the crowd permission to pile on. Everyone pushed forward, all shouting at once. "Now that's what I call rock-hard abs!" "I didn't know you were modeling again!" "A sophomore, Keegan?" His red face was stoic, but his right eyelid twitched, and he gripped the strap of his backpack so tightly that his knuckles spread white across his fist. He'd been blindsided and was desperately trying to catch up, and that mental state no doubt led to what happened when Jake Starr and his black boots stomped by.

Jake glanced at the picture still lying on the floor and

muttered something under his breath. It must have been bad, and Keegan must have heard it, because he dropped his backpack and launched himself at the techie.

"Son of a bitch!"

Jake knelt down immediately, lowering his shoulder, dipping forward and using Keegan's momentum to somersault him forward, where Keegan landed hard on his back. The hallway exploded into shouting as Keegan lashed and squirmed and flailed at Jake.

This lasted only five seconds before good old Mr. Edwards shot through the doorway of the college counseling office as though the building were on fire. In the four steps it took him to reach the fight, he managed to shed his tweed sport coat (with elbow patches) and loosen the knot of his orange and yellow striped tie. He was way more agile than his potbelly suggested. He grabbed Jake by the collar of his black T-shirt and pulled him off.

Keegan jumped to his feet. "I'm going to kill you."

Mr. Edwards stepped to Keegan and pointed a jittery index finger. "We treat one another with respect." The bell rang, and Mr. Edwards said, "To the dean's office, both of you."

Jake looked around in disbelief. "I was minding my own busine—"

"Both of you. And everyone else, get to class. Show's over."

We milled around just in case Keegan and Jake decided to go at it again, and there was an odd sense among the crowd. Some wonderment, some respect, some fear. If this

Artist guy had the guts to take on Keegan and Sophie, he'd go after anybody.

I gave Ellen a squeeze and a kiss. "See you in History?" Keegan and Jake picked up their backpacks and walked down the hall, taking opposite paths to the dean.

Mr. Edwards turned back toward his office. "I need your essay, David," he said, hardly breaking stride. "Perhaps you have time to chat right now?"

I wanted to get out of there as quickly as possible, so I mumbled that I was late for class as I spun away. I kept my head down, and, because I only really cared that I was going *away* from Mr. Edwards, I wasn't paying attention to where I was going *toward*. The moment I turned the corner I drilled Colter Stern square in the chest with my shoulder. He flew backward and splayed out on the ground as I stumbled to the side, losing control of my backpack, which skidded to a stop between us.

"'Morning, Chief," he said through gritted teeth. He clutched his chest and wheezed a bit. He wore a simple white T-shirt and a skullcap pulled low over his unwieldy mane of hair. A couple of small square sheets of colored paper spilled from the pockets of his cargo shorts.

"Weird New Guy." I helped him to his feet, and he handed me my backpack. "You okay?"

"I'm a tough little man," he said, waving me off.

I picked the red and orange squares off the floor and gave them to him with a laugh. "What are you, into origami or something?"

His eyes lit up. "You're a folder, too?"

"Stop it."

"Best form of meditation there is," he said, smoothing the bent corner of one and replacing it in his pocket. "Give me a square, a quiet place, and twenty minutes, and I'll give you low blood pressure and a Japanese peace crane."

"You are a strange human being."

He shrugged. "Did I miss something?"

I replayed the highlights as we walked toward the end of the hall, and he rubbed his hands together like a cartoon villain relishing his devious new plot. "What was the look on Keegan's face? Can you do it, like an impression?"

"I'll walk with you," I said. "Where are you going?"

He shrugged. "I don't know. It's the one in the room with all the motivational posters. 'If you aim at nothing, you will hit it' is one. 'Reach for the stars.' History? English, maybe?"

"'It doesn't make sense to ask a cow if it cares about becoming a burger,' is that it? Footnote, Ellen."

"That's my kind of lady. And she's right. The cow's better off enjoying the breeze, feeling the sun on its back. That way when the spike rams through its brain, it has no regrets about the life it could have lived."

By this point the hallway was deserted. I stopped him at the bottom of the stairwell. "Can I ask you something?"

"You—"

"Don't say, 'You just did.'"

"But you did just did."

"You really don't care? I mean, not at all?"

"Look, man," he said. "Vanessa's the firstborn. By six minutes, but still. I read somewhere that the firstborn is always striving to be the best to impress everyone, always trying to be perfect. And then the second one comes along, and perfect is already taken." Colter clapped his hands. "I saw that and, boom, all the pressure disappeared. It's not like I'm ever going to get as good grades as V anyway, so why even worry about it?"

"You're basing this on six minutes?"

"Six minutes, six years, whatever." I turned to climb the stairs, and he followed. "V had a good time at Keegan's. We wanted to say good-bye, but we didn't know where you were. Your lady looked excellent, if you don't mind the feedback. Maybe if things don't work out, you can put in a word?"

"What?"

"Kidding, wow."

When we reached the landing, I said, "Amber told Ellen I wanted to be your friend in order to get close to your sister."

"Do you?"

I stopped halfway up the second flight, my foot poised on the next step, and looked at him.

"She's hot," Colter said. "She may be my sister, but . . . Come on, don't look at me like I'm her pimp or something."

"I have a girl—"

"Not judging; just saying."

I noticed a tingling sensation at the back of my neck.

"Ellen is awesome." I said. But was I telling him or reminding myself?

"I never said she wasn't." He shrugged that little blasé shrug of his, as though we were talking about the weather.

I checked the clock at the top of the stairs. "I have to get to class. Firstborn and all."

Dean Donaldson interrupted History after lunch with a plea for witnesses to come forward regarding the mysterious posting of scandalous and unsanctioned material on the school's bulletin boards.

"We take great pride here at Oak Fields Preparatory School in providing our students with the supportive and nurturing environment necessary for the realization of every ounce of potential within them. These recent incidents are a threat to the very fabric of that environment and therefore a threat to each and every one of us."

I stole a peek around the room. The dean had not managed to put the fear of God into any of us. Iggy sat in the back row with his head turned to the side and resting on his hand, a telltale white wire snaking out from the cuff of his sweatshirt. Corky may have been asleep. Ellen and Vanessa sat politely, their fingers laced on the desks in front of them.

The Dean spread his spindly arms as if he could impress upon us the importance of the matter solely by demonstrating his tremendous wingspan. "In my experience, it is best to nip these situations in the bud, as it were. I hereby offer amnesty for anyone who comes forward."

Then his eyes narrowed and he slammed his open palms onto the polished wood of the lectern. It was a bit too calculated and obviously theatrical for my taste, but at least three of the girls in the room squeaked in surprise. "I will not allow the nurturing environment of this fine institution to be sullied by this self-proclaimed Artist."

I looked at Ellen and Vanessa again, and I found myself with little fireflies in my stomach. One ten-minute chat alone on the catwalk and this is where my mind went? There's nothing there, I told myself. Even if I could choose between the two of them—which was ridiculous to consider—there was no reason not to choose Ellen. We were the only constant in the uncertain chaos of high school. We had what everyone wanted, and besides, if it ain't broke, don't fix it, although Ellen would have been justified in killing me for describing her that way.

And yet, there was Vanessa. I would see her at rehearsal after school, and we'd have to run the kissing scene again, and how would I react to that?

Ellen glanced back at me, and damn if I didn't look down at my desk. Idiot.

7

With just under four weeks until opening night, a manic energy had begun to seep into rehearsal. Actors worked onstage or waited just off, costume people were in their little section of the greenroom, poring over magazines and books on the Roaring Twenties and comparing sketches of wardrobe possibilities. Francine practiced her jazz piano. Jake and the other techies hung lights on the catwalk above; set guys were testing their budding power-tool skills in the parking lot just outside. Even people who had only one or two lines were there, scattered in the audience doing homework while they waited for their scenes.

It was just about the point of Vanessa's and my big kiss—the first time, by the way, that we were actually going to go "live" with it—when a high-pitched clink came from somewhere to my left, followed by another. I heard, "Oh, sh—" and then what sounded like hail on a tin roof. Coins were everywhere—pennies, dimes, quarters—careening off the stage and into the audience.

I was hovering over Vanessa when it happened, and I instinctively crouched down and brought my hands up to cover my head. When the noise stopped, there was a moment of stunned silence. Francine poked her head through the backstage doorway.

Vanessa stared down at me. "My hero," she said dryly.

Big Pro burst onstage and pointed up to the catwalk. "What are you, the Salvation Army?" he said, arching his neck to the point where I thought he might tumble onto his ass. His name was Mr. Prokov, but everyone called him Big Pro. He was the faculty version of the theatre freak: mismatched clothes, thick plastic-framed glasses, a spotty awareness of the outside world. "Who carries around fifteen dollars in pennies?"

"My bad," Jake said. The soles of his work boots bowed the mesh almost directly above me.

"I can see it was your bad with my own two eyes. You and your goddamn piggy bank up there." Big Pro went around the stage kicking unsuccessfully at the coins. After a while, he stopped and pointed to Jake. "In case you forget, the audience doesn't care about your lighting, dumbass, no matter how great it is. People come to see the actors. The audience wants to see Nick lay a wet one on Daisy, but they can't really see that if Nick and Daisy happen to be dead thanks to your little demonstration of gravity, now can they?"

This was clearly a rhetorical question, and we all waited nervously to see if Jake would hit back with sarcasm. Mount Pro had erupted. The important thing was not to say something or do anything that would keep the lava flowing.

They say that those who can't do, teach, but Big Pro had been in at least a dozen movies, either as the violent

Mafioso in the dim corner of the restaurant or the romantic lead's portly and jovial uncle. There was no middle ground with Big Pro, on screen or in real life.

Jake squatted on the catwalk so that I could see his face. He waved at us. "Sorry, David. Sorry, Vanessa. It won't happen again."

"Damn right," Big Pro said. "You're carrying bills from now on."

The chuckle that spread across the room seemed to mellow him out a bit, and he closed his eyes and took a moment for himself. When he opened them, it was as though he'd never raised his voice. His skin had lost its redness; his eyes were relaxed behind his glasses. He stepped toward Vanessa and me with his arms outstretched, and when he spoke, his voice was resonant with concern.

"You're both okay?"

I nodded. Vanessa said, "Mmhmm."

"I'm sorry you had to experience that," he said, as though we were the only two people in the room. "Would you like to take it from the top, or do you need a break?"

Vanessa and I both said we were ready, and Big Pro patted us each on the shoulder before hitching up his cargo shorts and retaking his seat in the front row. He glared up at the catwalk, then smiled and motioned for us to continue.

Unfortunately for me, his tranquility was short-lived. Vanessa and I were only a page into the scene by the time he'd leaped onstage again. "Ellison!" He put his hands to his forehead. "Please tell me you know how important a scene this is."

I said nothing, unsure whether he was actually expecting a response.

"Hello?!"

I swallowed. "Yeah, it's really important."

"Then let me see some damned unease! Why do you suppose Nick is uneasy at this point?"

"He's having a fantasy about kissing his cousin," I said.

Vanessa piped in: "Second cousin once removed."

"Which makes the unease even more important, doesn't it? And Tom's in the next room as this is going on. Tom?" he yelled over his shoulder. No response. "Tom Freaking Buchanan?"

Still no response. We waited while Big Pro nibbled on the tip of his tongue.

I said, "Do you want me to see if I—"

"So Tom's in the other room," Big Pro said, dismissing my offer with a flick of his fleshy wrist. "You're in his house! The man already gave his mistress a black eye, for Christ's sake."

"I just don't think this scene makes that much sense, is all."

"It's an adaptation, David. Christ Almighty, we're after feel here. Tone."

I struggled to keep the blood from rushing to my face. Big Pro was treating me like some freshman, like we hadn't done almost a dozen shows together. "But there was a reason this scene wasn't in the book, right? So what's my motivation here?"

He waddled to me and made his voice all high. "Motivation, motivation," he said, mocking me. Mocking *me*. "This isn't paint by numbers. Sometimes you have to dive the hell in and . . . um . . ." He looked at the ceiling as if searching for the right word. "ACT!"

I felt my voice threaten to waver, but I had to hold my ground. "Yeah, but what does Nick have to gain by going after Daisy? Why would he even be attracted to her?"

"Come on, Ellison, get some stones." He pointed to Vanessa. "How could he not be?"

This was not supposed to be happening, not to me. I was the lead. Big Pro never yelled at the lead. And I'd played Brother #2 in a three-month campaign for the country's sixth-largest bottled tea manufacturer! I sensed that everyone around me was scooting backward, millimeter by millimeter, as Big Pro laid into me. I rubbed my chin and nodded, trying to give the impression that I was deep in thought, that I was taking his criticism stoically and professionally, when the truth was that my heartbeat rang so loudly in my ears that I could hardly hear him anymore.

"I got it," I made myself say.

"This isn't the first time you've had to kiss onstage—"

"It's not that—"

"I need the unease to come from *Nick Carraway*, not David Ellison. So get over it." There was a pause. He raised his eyebrows.

"What . . . Now?" I said.

"If that's what's holding you back, then let's get on with it."

I glanced over at Vanessa, hoping to gauge her reaction to all this, but she was focused on Big Pro, squinting as though she were trying to decipher a foreign language.

"Fine," Big Pro said. He turned to the rest of the cast, waving his arms in a huge gesture of frustration. "We're staying as long as it takes for Dilweed Carraway here to muster up the stones to kiss his second cousin once removed."

The moan of protest was both collective and instantaneous.

"Oh, stop with the sob stories. Another hour in the theater isn't going to keep your pampered asses out of Princeton." He pointed at me and waited. "Go on, kiss her."

Vanessa flashed her eyes at him. "Kiss her? What the hell am I? A prop?"

"Spare me the lecture on how far our society has come. You're supposed to be 'p-p-paralyzed with happiness.'"

"It's not about the kiss," I said meekly, and it really wasn't, or at least not all of it. My mind was on other things, too, on Keegan and The Artist and Mr. Edwards and the essay I was supposed to already have written. "I just wasn't focused."

Big Pro couldn't have backed down even if he'd wanted to. It was a power struggle now, and he was the authority figure. "You'd better start focusing."

"Come on," someone said from the shadows. "I have SAT prep tonight."

Another voice: "There's a calc test tomorrow."

Vanessa stepped to me, her eyes still clouded with anger. It was a look she had from time to time, one that I'd so far been unable to muster, a glimpse into what Big Pro calls the "dark zone." I'd seen it on the first day of rehearsal, when the entire cast sat around in a circle and read the play together. It was the way she looked at her script, I think, in the moment before reading her first line, like a raptor.

"We don't have to do this," I said to her.

Someone whistled.

"Screw them." Her face was only inches from mine, so close that I could see the tiny flecks of amber in her green eyes. Quietly, so that only I could hear, she said, "Let's put on a show."

I had never felt so insecure onstage. Her lips were softer than Ellen's, cool against my own, and for the first few seconds, it actually felt like a kiss. The theater melted away, and I could have convinced myself that we were alone, but there was another whistle, and someone else clapped, and then it was as though we both remembered where we were and why we were doing this. That's when the kiss turned ferocious.

"That's enough," Big Pro said. We ignored him, pawing at each other in a grotesque caricature of affection.

Generally a stage kiss doesn't need to involve tongue, but there we were. I wrapped my arms around her, my fingertips rubbing up and down the accordion of her spine. She cupped the back of my head and pulled my face even tighter to hers.

Big Pro's voice boomed. "I said, that's enough!"

Vanessa and I stepped away as though we were strangers who'd bumped into each other on a crowded street. No recognition, no acknowledgement. The theater had gone silent, and I could feel the shock in the room. We turned to Big Pro and waited. Still rattled, I wiped the corner of my mouth with the tip of my index finger.

"Okay," he said. "See you tomorrow. Good work today."

That was all. He grabbed his production binder, tucked it under his arm, and left the theater without another word.

Books slammed and zippers zipped. Someone whispered, "This version is way better than the book."

I sat in the audience and stared at the stage, trying to figure out what had just happened, why Big Pro had jumped on me like that. Doors creaked open and closed. The theater cleared out, people said good-bye.

It's easy to think you have thick skin when criticism is theoretical. Only ten minutes before, my mind had been all over the place—the scene, Vanessa, Ellen, even the sound of Christina's palm on Keegan's face—but now a single thought had forced its way into my mind and spread like a virus, overwhelming everything else:

What if I wasn't as good as I thought I was?

Dread oozed from every pore of my body. If I wasn't

good enough to make it through rehearsal without Big Pro going after me like that, then no way was I getting into Juilliard. And if that was the case, what was I supposed to do? My mind flashed forward to my ten-year reunion, with me all fat and broke and wondering where it all went wrong, a community college dropout surrounded by young millionaires.

"Hey," Vanessa said, plopping down in a seat across the aisle. "You okay?"

I took a deep breath and summoned a smile to my face. "You had a good time at Keegan's?"

"What happened to you? I was looking all over for you, but you disappeared."

I felt an incredible gratitude toward her for embracing my change of subject so naturally. "Yeah, Iggy basically kidnapped—"

"Iggy Rockwell?"

"Is there some other Iggy out there I'm not aware of?" This time my smile was genuine.

"No, I just . . . I tutor him. I don't think people give him enough credit for being a nice guy. They see how huge he is and assume he's an asshole, but he's really a big teddy bear."

For some reason I started thinking of Iggy as competition, but that was ridiculous. How could there be competition for something I wasn't actually competing for?

"Are you guys going out?"

"Nah," she said. "Big guy like that isn't my type."

Naturally, I had to wonder right then and there what

her type really was. The specter of our kiss hovered over every word. I struggled to come up with something to say. Finally: "You're a tutor? Like, a real tutor?"

She shrugged. "For some extra cash now and then. I got an eight hundred on the English Lit SAT." We sat in silence for at least a minute. "You think Jake did it?" she said. "The Keegan/Artist thing?"

I shook my head. "Collage isn't his style."

"What is?"

"Straight up elbow to the temple."

She gestured to the coins still scattered along the edges of the stage. "Or a piggy bank to the back of the head."

I still needed an essay in case I didn't get into Juilliard, and thanks to Big Pro, I felt a newfound sense of urgency. But Ellen and I had already proven that we couldn't get anything done. That wasn't Ellen's fault, or mine either, only the simple fact of our relationship: Ellen wasn't my tutor; she was my girlfriend.

"I have an idea," I said. "What are you doing tonight?"

8

My parents were both working late, and Lisa had her weekly meeting of the Young Hackers Crew, so the house was empty when I got there with Vanessa and her brother. Vanessa had agreed to look at my essay so she could get a sense of where it was and how many sessions we might need to whip it into shape, and since Colter had nothing else to do, he came along to keep us company. Or was it to chaperone?

"So this is your place," Colter said as we walked into the living room. "Nice. Homey."

"It's not as fancy as Keegan's," I said. "No grotto. But if you close your eyes, you can pretend that the freeway sounds like a babbling stream."

"Or wind rustling through the trees," Colter said. "I dig it."

Vanessa wandered over to the framed photos opposite the front door. She pointed to the one of me in my pajamas, about three years old, pushing Lisa around in a yellow plastic toy shopping cart. "This is cute."

"All sisters twenty percent off," I said.

I retrieved the latest draft of the essay and came back to the living room to find them sitting on the couch, with Vanessa in the middle and Colter at one end. I tossed the essay on the coffee table and came around to sit next to Vanessa. "There's the masterpiece," I said.

Colter said, "Are your parents behind you with the acting thing?"

"My mom is, in the 'we love you because you're our son' kind of way. But my dad doesn't really know what to do with me. He comes to my plays and says he's supportive, but he's always brainstorming new ways to talk me out of it. I don't think he can actually comprehend that someone would want to choose the theatre as a *profession*."

"And yet you're still going through with it," Colter said. "That takes *pelotas*."

"I think you mean *cojones*," I said. "I took AP Spanish last year."

"Are you writing about acting? For your essay?" Vanessa said.

I laughed, and then it occurred to me that she might be serious. "Why?"

"Don't you love it?"

"Of course I love it."

"You could write about exactly what you just said, about how you've devoted yourself to theatre even in the face of what your father wants. That shows dedication, initiative—"

"It's boring," I said. "And it's a little 'cry me a river' isn't it? I mean, admissions committees probably read essays all day about people who have overcome actual challenges. I'm not sure my complaining that daddy doesn't support me would come off as anything but self-centered whining."

"Dude," Colter said, pulling a wrinkled piece of origami paper from his back pocket and smoothing it flat on the coffee table. "I appreciate the self-awareness and all, but you can't judge your own issues against other people. Just because some other guy out there has a shattered femur doesn't mean your broken nose doesn't hurt."

"Seriously," she said. "If I hadn't written my essay already, I would totally write about acting, about memorizing lines and escaping into another character. I love being onstage, and we haven't even had a performance yet."

"You should see Vanessa since she started doing the play," Colter said without looking up. "It's like a light went on or something. She's totally different."

"I am not," she said, though I could have sworn I saw a little color come to her cheeks.

"This is really your first time?" I said.

"I never auditioned for anything because I didn't think I would be any good and I didn't want to get rejected."

"You're very good," I said, "but I think you already know that."

"Oh, stop," she said, making a *keep going* motion with her hand.

"Let's have a look at this bad boy," Colter said, picking up my essay and taking no more than three seconds to scan each page.

"So you're okay now?" Vanessa said. "After today?"

Colter looked up. "What happened today?"

"Mr. Prokov was a little rough with the feedback in one of David's scenes."

"Was that before or after you guys macked it like you were getting paid?"

I glared at Vanessa but couldn't suppress the little spark of giddiness that flashed in my chest. "Is that what you told him?"

"I told him it was the most passionate passionless platonic kiss in the history of Oak Fields Prep theatre."

"Big Pro goes off sometimes." I shrugged. "You just have to figure out how to deal with it. Turn the page. Make it to another day."

I was talking a big game, but I still hadn't completely recovered. It was like so much of my self-worth was predicated on being an actor, the best in my class—the best the school had ever seen—that to have *that* challenged was not something I could get over in a couple of hours, no matter how much I wanted to.

Colter crumpled up the origami paper and took a piece of my essay and started folding. "You don't need this, do you?"

"Why would I?"

"I love all the warm-ups before rehearsal, too," Vanessa said. "The breathing exercises and vocal exercises and all those 'exhale the tension from your fingertips' exercises."

"Have we done the rocking chair yet this year?"

Vanessa shook her head.

"It's a doozy," I said, jumping to my feet. I motioned

for them to do the same. "Help me move the coffee table."

Colter groaned but put the half-folded sheet of my essay on the table, and we moved it to the side of the room. I knew how we'd look if someone walked in on us, but Vanessa said she liked the exercises, and this one was my favorite.

"Spread out and lie down on the floor," I said. "And audience participation mandatory, Colter. You're the one who wanted to hang out with us."

"Everyone makes mistakes." Colter sat cross-legged in front of the television.

"Okay, so put your feet flat on the ground and your knees raised like you're about to do a sit-up."

"Sir, yes sir!" Colter said. I ignored him.

"You're going to rest your arms at your sides with your palms up. Now close your eyes and breathe, in through your nose, out through your mouth, and when you exhale, pretend you're pushing all the stress from your core out through your extremities."

"You're not going to hypnotize me, are you? I don't want to wake up in the middle of the street with my underwear on my head."

Vanessa said, "Shut up, Colter."

"Not relaxing, guys." We breathed for a minute. "Now. You're going to lift your pelvis up, then ease it back dow— Colter, you're not humping the air. It's more gentle."

"It's the motion of the ocean," Vanessa said. "Not the size of the wave."

I chose to ignore that one, too. "Imagine curling your

pelvis back up toward your head; imagine you're rolling your spine up around your coccyx like you're rolling a napkin."

Colter giggled. "You said 'coccyx'!"

"Guys!"

"Sorry."

"And now, roll it back down. And up, and back."

"What is this doing, exactly?" Colter said. "I mean, aside from potentially becoming the most viral video in the history of mankind."

"We're circulating the cerebrospinal fluid. Enhancing your ability to concentrate and focus. You can do this before your next test."

"It *is* almost like sitting in a rocking chair," Vanessa said. "Not bad."

I was dimly aware of the sound of a car door slamming shut, and by the time I realized it, the front door was open and Lisa was standing over us with her eyebrows raised.

"I was wondering whose Benz that was out front," she said.

For some reason, none of us got up. Perhaps it was being caught the way we were that we didn't want to draw attention to the absurdity of our positioning. Yes, David's Sister, we've moved the coffee table aside, and we're all lying on the ground rolling our pelvises slowly up and down. What of it?

"Lisa," I said, "you know Vanessa and Colter?"

"What's up, Lisa?" Colter said.

She nodded, still uncertain. "What are you guys doing?"

"We were just talking about David's essay," Vanessa said.

Colter was the only one still moving his pelvis. "And then one thing led to another. You know how theatre people can be."

Lisa slid her backpack off her shoulder until it dangled from her right hand. "David's essay?"

"If you need help with English, Vanessa got an eight hundred on the SAT II," I said.

"No, I'm good." Lisa looked warily from me to Vanessa as she stepped backward toward the hallway. "I'm going to go ahead and leave you guys to . . . whatever it is that you're doing."

Vanessa raised her hand and waved. "Okay, it was good to meet you."

"That wasn't awkward at all," Colter said when she'd gone.

Their phones buzzed at the same time, and Colter watched from the ground as Vanessa sat up to open hers. "That's Dad," she said. "Matilda made flank steak tonight. He wants us home in five."

"Matilda is the best," Colter said. He pushed himself to his feet and stretched his arms above his head. "You should come over some time. Do you like osso buco?"

"Is that a dessert or something?" I said. "I like dessert."

"We'll have you over," Colter said. "For sure, okay? And soon. Then you and V can do lines or whatever actors like to do."

I laughed. "It's called running lines. Doing lines means snorting coke."

"As I said. Whatever actors like to do."

I walked them out and waited on the doorstep until Vanessa's green Mercedes disappeared around the corner. Lisa was leaning against the wall in the hallway when I went back inside.

"I thought Ellen was helping you with your essay," Lisa said. She uncrossed her arms and went to the kitchen.

"She was," I said. "But we never seem to be able to get anything done, and I'm already way behind, so I figured it might be good to try someone else."

She opened the fridge and pulled out a yogurt and went for the silverware drawer. "And you hired Miss Cover Girl Eight Hundred on the SAT II?"

"Vanessa tutors other people, too. She's a professional. She actually charges a fee."

"I see, so now you're paying for it."

"You should give her a chance."

"And you," Lisa pointed the tip of her yogurt-covered spoon at me, "should open your eyes."

"She's just a friend. There's nothing to open my eyes for."

"Right."

"I think Ellen would really like her if they ever spent time together. We should do something, like double-date or something."

"That is just a terrible, terrible idea," Lisa said over her shoulder as she walked back down the hallway. "In all your history of terrible ideas, I think that one just jumped to the front of the line." The door closed, and she yelled from her room, "It's even worse than the necklace-making business from fourth grade."

"Hey," I called out after her. "I made a lot of money before all the strings started breaking!"

Later, as we sat around a dinner table of take-out lasagna, my dad said, "I have news. And I think you'll like it."

Uh-oh. My mom shook her head. "Honey, let him eat his dinner first."

"Why wouldn't he want to know right away?"

"Right here," I said, waving my fork. "Sitting in the same place I've sat for the last ten years."

My dad folded the napkin on his lap and crossed his legs underneath it. "I've—*We've*," he said with a glance at my mom, "hired an independent counselor for you."

"Like a shrink?" Lisa said. "David's not crazy, he's just a theatre geek."

Mom said, "Lisa."

"A college counselor," Dad said. He cleared his throat. "To help you with your essay. She comes very highly recommended."

"She blew us away in the interview."

I was struggling to keep up. "You interviewed someone—"

"College narrative coach is what she calls herself. I think you'll really like her."

Lisa had a mouthful of lasagna, but that didn't stop

her from saying, "David already hired someone."

"Who?" my dad said.

"Lisa, stop talking."

"Oh," she said innocently, "did you not hire someone?"

"Who is it?" my mom said.

I closed my eyes and shook my head and imagined Lisa bound and gagged and stuffed in her closet for the rest of the night.

My dad cleared his throat again. "Your first session is Wednesday after school. On the Stanford campus."

"That's only two days from now. I have rehearsal."

"You'll need to skip it."

"I can't just skip—" I caught myself starting to yell.

Dad said, "This is a commitment to your future."

"What about the commitment I've already made?"

"I know it comes as a surprise," my mom said, "but your father and I think it's best for you to cover all the bases, just in case the Juilliard audition doesn't go as well as you think it will."

"We believe in you," my dad said as though reading from cue cards. "We support you. But even you have to understand that it's a long shot."

"And hey," Lisa said, "if it doesn't work out, there's always Stanford."

"Lisa!" This time my parents and I all said it in unison.

9

I spent most of the next day trying to figure out how to finagle Big Pro's permission to miss rehearsal, and by the time History rolled around, I'd pretty much settled on fake appendicitis. Halfway through class, Mr. Nadlee said something about the Ottoman Empire, and there was a knock at the door. It swung open tentatively, and Dean Donaldson poked his beak inside. "I need to see David Ellison, please?"

Class came to a halt and everyone stared at me. I closed my notebook and cleared my throat and smiled. "Oooh, busted," I said under my breath. It was a performance, of course—what you're supposed to say in this scenario. I hadn't actually done anything wrong. My appendix wasn't even supposed to fake burst until after lunch the next day.

We crossed the quadrangle, passing a simple fountain—representing the Oak—and a small reflecting pool—representing the Fields. I couldn't help wondering what the dean had on me, even though I knew it was nothing. "I'm working on my essay, okay? It's not like I haven't been giving it a lot of thought."

Mr. Donaldson didn't answer as we reached the administration building. He opened the door and ushered me inside. The school's great seal occupied the center of the lobby floor: the Latin motto, *Scientia potestas est*, in calligraphic script on a scroll wrapped around the stout trunk of a leafy oak tree. We walked in a wide circle so as to avoid stepping on it. Knowledge Is Power.

The dean pointed to a single chair outside Headmaster Lunardi's office. "Wait here, please?"

As if I had a choice. I typed out a quick text message to Ellen, making sure we were still on for a bubble tea after she got off work, and waited with my arms crossed, listening to the squeak of sneakers on the floor until a secretary called me inside.

The headmaster was firmly entrenched behind his sparkling mahogany desk, with Dean Donaldson perched on one of the two large leather chairs across from him.

I sank back in the other chair to the point where my forearms were almost above my shoulders when I laid them on the armrests. I tried keeping my hands in my lap, but that was even worse, with me hunched over like I was in a beanbag. I'm sure my fidgeting only made them more suspicious that I was hiding something. Eventually I scooted up to the edge of the chair and kept my posture straight.

"Should my parents be here for this?" I said. Whatever this was.

The dean leaned across his lap, his eyes steady on mine. When he spoke, his voice was almost gentle. "How old are you, David?"

Headmaster Lunardi glanced at a file on his desk. "Seventeen."

"You're one of our finest thespians," Dean Donaldson said. "A real talent. We have high hopes for you."

"And you're auditioning for Juilliard. Isn't that something?" said the headmaster.

"Am I in trouble?"

Lunardi clicked his pen a couple times. "Tell us about Friday night."

Silence all around. In cop shows, when the interrogator lets the perp stew until he cracks because he can't take the silence anymore, it comes off as contrived. If the idiot criminal would just keep his mouth shut, the cops would have nothing on him.

"You seem like a smart guy," the dean said.

Lunardi read from my file. "3.57 GPA, 1260 SAT, PSAT 87th Percentile, 4 on the Spanish Language AP."

The dean said, "And a smart guy doesn't pretend he wasn't at Keegan Schroeder's illegal house party on Friday night."

What? "I wasn't going to pretend—"

"The reason we've come to you, David, is that you're visible. You do plays. You've hosted homecoming ceremonies, you MC'd the talent show—"

"That bit you did with the fractals last spring? Pure genius." Lunardi chuckled. "How did it go?"

I shook my head as I tried to process whatever was happening in front of me. "I . . ."

"You vant fwacktals?" the dean said, bouncing his head slightly back and forth and attempting a German accent. "Ya? You vant zem?"

"Zat's chaos!" they said at the same time.

I laughed with them, nodding like a moron but at least starting to relax now that it didn't seem I was in trouble. That didn't necessarily explain why I was there, but it was something.

"So," Donaldson said. "You're visible. And we figure you've got your finger on the pulse of the student body."

"How is that, exactly?"

The dean smacked his lips as he inhaled. "Quite frankly, most of the theatre kids tend to spend all their time with one another. You have friends outside, in the real world, so to speak. We've seen you interact with people. Ellen Conroy is a wonderful student; she has a chance at valedictorian."

"Would you have called me in here if I wore more black?"

Lunardi rested his elbows on top of my file. "Look, David. We're not completely blind to what's going on out there. We know that Stanford's regional admissions policy has ruffled a few feathers."

"You could say that."

"It's a legitimate issue," Donaldson said. "I don't know if you're aware that one of your classmates has brought suit against the university."

I was not aware, and I didn't manage to keep the surprise off my face.

"Indeed," the dean said.

Lunardi continued, "And we know that this is a very sensitive time for young people. Hormones, college choices, we've been there ourselves."

"Boy, have we."

"Which brings us back here." The headmaster again. My eyes bounced back and forth like I was watching live tennis. "We wondered if perhaps you might have any information about this Artist character."

"The Artist?"

"You're not the only one we're talking to about this, you should know. We'll bring in others we think might be attuned—"

"Who?"

The dean looked at Lunardi. "We're going to keep that information private."

"You pulled me out of history class in front of about twenty people," I said. "If you're aiming for privacy, you might want to consider a new strategy."

"Nevertheless." Donaldson nibbled his bottom lip. "Back to The Artist. We're interested in the connection between Sophie Meyers and Keegan Schroeder. We know that Keegan was involved in a series of fights with Jake Starr."

They were going to pin this on Jake? "Wait a minute—"

"Both in the senior hallway and at Keegan's illegal house party."

"Who told you that?" I said. Silence. They looked at me, waiting. "Is this about The Artist or about the fight?"

"Is there a difference?" Lunardi said.

The mood in the room had somehow taken on a decidedly accusatory turn, and it was like the headmaster and dean were trying to out-overreact each other.

I said, "How can this be worth your time—"

"Illicit material was posted on school-sanctioned bulletin boards, Mr. Ellison," said the headmaster.

"Okay," I said. "If I have my finger on the pulse, then let me tell you—maybe The Artist is on to something." I tried to make it sound offhand, like maybe I didn't really believe what I was saying, like I was trying to help them come up with explanations. But I was rattled, and I could feel myself getting carried away. "I mean, this school is called Oak Fields, and it doesn't have any oak trees on campus. Please tell me it's because of the soil, the pH or something, and not because you don't want to diminish the symbolic importance of the fountain in the quad—"

"I don't appreciate your tone," the dean said.

The headmaster said, "I fail to see where you're going with this—"

"The school is called Oak Fields and it has no oaks! Maybe asking if we know ourselves is a valid issue. How did we get here, right? And where I'm going with this, if you don't mind me saying so, is if the school were helping us answer that question, there might not be a need for someone like The Artist."

"You think there's a *need* for The Artist?" Donaldson said.

"I'm just saying—"

"We're in the education business. Anything that interferes with the education of our students is very much our problem."

"Understand this, David," said the headmaster. He capped his pen and placed it on the desk next to my file. "It's a well-known fact that serial killers tend to start off small, with animals, say, before moving on to actual humans."

I smiled, but he wasn't joking. "Did you just make the leap to serial killers?"

"It's just slogans and collages for now, but who's to say it stays that way?" Donaldson said. "We know how you kids can be. Retribution, escalation. Honor fights and the like."

"We just want to make sure it doesn't get to that point." Headmaster Lunardi took a sip of his coffee and then snapped my file closed. He stood, and so did the dean.

The dean smiled coolly. "Thanks for your time, David."

I found myself thanking them, waving as I walked backward out of the office, and then somehow I was standing in front of the Oak fountain.

There was no escort back to History; I was on my own, free to wander the deserted campus as I saw fit. With fourteen minutes before my next class and no desire to spend them in the Ottoman Empire, I headed for the parking lot. I needed to clear my head, and the White Horse was as good a place as any.

"Excuse me," said a voice. Female, important, unfamiliar.

I turned, and a microphone appeared.

"Are you a senior?"

I froze. The camera, the microphone in my face. A news reporter. I was going to be on TV.

"Are you an Oak Fields senior?"

My only answer was a tentative nod, so she turned to the cameraman and made the throat slashing gesture with her microphone. The blinking red light turned off, and the ponytailed cameraman brought the camera down from off his shoulder.

The woman was tall and thin, with a mannish jaw and a helmet of black hair. She asked my name, and I gave it.

"Look, David," she said, her voice suddenly soft and friendly. "I'm just going to ask you a couple of questions about Stanford's new admissions policy, okay? You want to try that again?"

"How does my hair look?" I was going to be on TV, after all.

The reporter smirked. Her black hair was styled big for California. "David Ellison, you said?"

I nodded, and she stepped next to me, turning us both toward the camera with the recently remodeled football stadium in the background. "Roll it," she said, and the light snapped on.

"A policy? Changed. Dreams? Shattered. And a prep school scandal in the making. This is Trinity Stampede reporting from the prestigious Oak Fields Preparatory School. With me here is David Ellison, a senior."

Her voice was different now that we were on camera—harsher, sharper. She gripped the microphone so hard that the tendons strained against the skin of her right forearm.

"David, how are people taking the new admissions policy?"

"Not well," I said.

"What went through your mind when you heard the news?"

"Wave of the future, I guess." My voice sounded off; there was a little knot in the back of my throat. I was constricting my soft palate, not allowing the air to escape properly, and that made my voice slightly nasal. I powered through. "To tell you the truth, it doesn't matter too much to me. I mean, I'd love to go to Stanford and everything—"

"Cut," she said, making the throat slash movement again, and the cameraman lowered the camera. "Thanks for your time, David."

She made to walk away, but I stepped back in front of her. "Wait, wait. You don't really need to talk to someone who *actually* cares, right? You just need to talk to someone who *says* he cares. Give me another chance. I can do it."

"You'll pretend to care?'

"I'm an actor. I'll just think of it as a role I'm playing. I'll be good, I swear."

She turned to the cameraman, who shrugged. "Okay, we'll give it one more shot."

"Great," I said. "Anything to work on my craft, right?"

Trinity chuckled and arranged us side by side again. "How's the background look, Reuben?"

"Good," the cameraman said. "The uprights are over your left shoulder."

"Roll it." The red light came on, and she did the intro again, and this time when she asked what went through my mind when I heard the news, I tried to picture my audience. If it was my classmates, I'd have to admit to being disappointed, but I'd still need to keep my cool. My parents, on the other hand, would want me to really care, especially my dad.

"I thought it was horrible," I said. I relaxed my soft palate and let my voice come from my diaphragm. It was richer and more confident than before. "I mean, Stanford is *right there*, and if you grow up anywhere near it, you know it's the only place you want to go to school. And then to find out they place an arbitrary cap?" I shook my head.

"What do you think of the legal challenge brought by one of your classmates?"

I couldn't tell her the truth—that I thought it was kind of a whiny douche-bag move and I could pretty much guess who was behind it—so I gritted my teeth and raised my eyebrows and said, "It may be worth exploring legal action, you know? It doesn't seem fair, and maybe the courts will agree."

Trinity was impressed with me, I could tell. There was a twinkle in her eye as she asked her next question. "And how would you respond to those who say that a student such as your classmate, someone of such privilege, shouldn't have to resort to the courts to get ahead? That a legal challenge is not only frivolous but offensive?"

I smiled. She was testing me. This was like improv, where you feed off the other people in the scene, building on what they've contributed, and where the cardinal rule is never to say *no*.

"It's a valid point," I said, stalling for an extra split-second. "And I understand. At the same time, just because someone else has a broken femur, that doesn't mean your broken nose doesn't still bleed all over your face."

The corner of her mouth danced up as if to threaten a smile, and then she turned to the camera. "Oak Fields Headmaster Joseph Lunardi has expressed great pride in the maturity with which the students have handled the policy change. This is Trinity Stampede reporting from Oak Fields Preparatory School."

The microphone across the throat again, and the light dimmed to nothing. "Thanks, David," she said, still stifling a giggle.

Reuben shook my hand. "I don't know what the hell you meant by that last thing about the broken nose," he said, "but I bought it. And I like what you did with your voice. Nice."

The bell rang, signaling the end of my reprieve. "Gotta go learn stuff."

He pointed to the towering brick buildings, the elegantly manicured grounds. "Hard to believe that's just a high school."

"That's no high school," I said. "It's a *preparatory* school."

I was halfway to my next class before I realized that I'd forgotten to ask when the interview was going to air.

10

I was supposed to meet Ellen for bubble tea downtown after she got off work, but I'd gotten caught after rehearsal talking with Vanessa about the interrogation with the dean and headmaster and the interview with the reporter. I'd lost track of time, and when I found my phone in the White Horse, there were seven missed calls from Ellen but no voice mails, and I hadn't yet mustered up the courage call her back.

Now Ellen's Audi was stuck against the curb outside my house like an accusation. If I tried to explain why I hadn't dialed her number, it would just seem like I was making excuses, which I was, of course, even though I preferred to think of them as reasons.

I tasted a familiar cocktail of embarrassment and remorse as I sat in the driveway. Every once in a while, in an effort to change my ways, I would announce that New David was coming on to the scene. New David was a doer, a follow-through type of guy. New David was the type of person who wouldn't forget the date he'd made with his girlfriend. He was also no match for Old David.

"Must have been an interesting conversation," was the first thing Ellen said to me when I walked inside. She sat in the living room with Lisa, a bowl of popcorn on the coffee table, textbooks spread on the couch next to her. And she was smiling.

"Rehearsal ran late," I said, but with less conviction than I'd been planning. There was something odd about the way Lisa and Ellen were looking at me. Then, because I didn't know what else to do, I said, "You're off the hook. My dad hired a college narrative coach. I have my first appointment tomorrow afternoon."

Lisa narrowed her eyes at me but, miracle of miracles, didn't say anything about the night before with Vanessa.

"Hold on," Ellen said, pinching the shoulder of her polo shirt and bringing the fabric up to the corner of her eye. "Let me just shed this one tear."

"I think she has a crush on you," Lisa said.

"Clearly." Ellen tossed a piece of popcorn into her mouth and munched it daintily.

I swallowed hard. Were they talking about Vanessa? Had Lisa already told her? "What do you mean?"

Ellen pointed a remote control, and it dawned on me that they were talking about something on television. I followed her gaze, and there I was on the screen, standing next to Trinity Stampede, the image of me paused with my eyes half-closed and my mouth in a half O.

"I thought the camera was supposed to add ten pounds," Ellen said. "But you look pretty good."

"Except for right here," Lisa said.

"Yeah, here it looks like you're stoned."

Lisa laughed. "Or taking a poop."

"Amber saw a promo," Ellen said, probably noticing

my confusion. "She called me at work and told me I had to watch. So here we are."

I sat next to Ellen, keeping my eyes on the TV. I was still nervous, but now it was like the nerves you have before opening your report card or going out onstage. I reached for a handful of popcorn and started eating.

"Does this station go all the way up to San Francisco?" I said. "Or is it just the Peninsula?"

Ellen hit me with the remote. "Could you be more predictable?"

"Sparkles is in town!" Lisa said.

In my defense, at least some of my curiosity came from the fact that my audition was in San Francisco and maybe some of the judges might have seen the newscast. Maybe they might have thought I looked good, and maybe when they saw me, there'd be something that seemed familiar.

"Well," I said, "how did I come off?"

Rather than respond, Ellen pressed a button on the remote, and the images sped backward to the beginning of the segment. There was an intro from the anchor about a "controversial" new policy and the "turmoil" it had caused at Bay Area prep schools. A graphic highlighted the bullet points of the new policy, and then the anchor threw it to Trinity Stampede, reporting from Oak Fields Preparatory.

My onscreen demeanor was pretty good, considering how unprepared I'd been for her questions, and although my recorded voice sounded predictably strange, I don't think I embarrassed myself with any of the answers. It looked like I cared enough, but not so much that it seemed forced. I did have a tendency to shift my weight from side to side, though, which was disappointing.

Ellen paused it again when they cut to commercial. "Well?"

"Not bad," I said.

Lisa grabbed some popcorn. "Why was your voice like that?"

"I was projecting," I said. "From my diaphragm. Using my vocal register."

"You were pretty convincing," Ellen said.

"I'm a heck of an actor."

"Any way we could get some of that fake passion into your essay?"

"Baby," I said, giving her my best Barry White, "ain't none of my passion fake."

Lisa made a big show of stacking her books one on top of the other and scurrying away. "Is that my phone I hear ringing in an entirely different room?"

"You're a disaster," Ellen said to me as she tossed the remote onto the coffee table and scooted close. "Rehearsal ran late?"

"I was going to call."

"You had other things on your mind. Apparently." Ellen bounced back and tucked one foot underneath. "So?"

"What, so?"

"So, you were on TV again!"

"I wish I'd been more comfortable. Was my voice really that bad?"

"Forget your sister," Ellen said. "What was she like? Trinity Stampede."

"Intense."

"I think the camera added ten pounds to her hair."

"No, it was that big in real life." I patted her just above the knee. Her skin was warm and soft. I left my hand there to see what would happen. There was no objection. Then I moved it up a little further. And a little more.

"Excuse me?" Ellen was not fooled by my stealth.

"My parents are both working late."

"Not with your sister here."

"I'll be quiet, I promise. You won't even know I'm there."

"So tempting." Ellen swatted my hand away and jumped to her feet. She smoothed her skirt down. "Come on. There's a tapioca passion-fruit tea with my name on it, and you're buying."

I picked up the remote and pointed it at the TV. "Let me just watch this one more time?"

Ellen groaned and spun around.

"Kidding," I said, at her side before she got to the door. "I was kidding."

"We're taking my car," she said, twirling her Stanford keychain as she gave me the eye-roll head shake. "I don't want you to get a ticket for Driving While Narcissistic."

11

"We need to do this more often," I said. "Just get away from school. Be together."

Ellen and I walked along the jogging path next to the railroad tracks. From time to time, a Caltrain going to or from San Francisco would rumble by, and we'd both turn to it and watch, feeling the vibrations against our bodies until it passed. The sun had dipped below the horizon, and nearby streetlights shone through the sparse trees and onto the path.

"I've missed you," she said.

"Missed me? What are you talking about?" Ellen's passion fruit was too sweet for me, so I'd gone for iced coffee with large tapioca.

"I don't write you notes on little heart-shaped Post-its, and I don't demand flowers all the time or presents, and I have no interest in wearing a bracelet with your name etched on it."

"Thank God for that," I said, feeling the need to brace myself. "Besides, your Post-its are inspirational."

"I don't want to be that girlfriend who always wants to be told she's loved. I hate that girlfriend. And usually I don't even think about it, because usually you're the one who's all romantic—"

"That's because I do love you."

"But in the last couple weeks, it's like you're not even here. Even when you're here, you're not here." She stopped walking and nudged a stick to the side of the path.

"I'm sorry," I said. "You're probably right. It's the audition, I think."

"It's not the audition."

"What is it?"

"Do you remember what you said the morning of our first anniversary? When I asked if you had anything special planned, what did you say?"

The memory brought a smile. "It's a surprise."

A glimmer of amusement appeared on her face. "That's right. But I knew—*knew*—that you'd totally spaced it. I tried not to show it, but I was so pissed at you all day. And then I come out of AP Bio, and there's a trail of rose petals leading from the classroom to my locker and then all the way to my car. I still remember the note on my dashboard: 'Surprise not over. Follow the path.' There was a long-stemmed rose taped to every stoplight, every stop sign."

We basked in the memory together. A southbound train roared by. "I skipped a lot of classes that day," I said when the train had disappeared.

I'd bought a rusted pogo stick at an antique store two weeks after we started dating, but I hadn't given it to her right away out of fear that she would think I was moving too fast, so I tossed it in the back of my closet, where it disappeared under fifty weeks of junk. I remembered just in time to have it waiting at the end of another trail of rose petals at the park near her house where we first hooked up.

She shook her head. "I really don't want to be high-maintenance. And I hate the fact that I'm even saying this out loud. But do you think you're even capable of that anymore?"

"I am," I said reflexively. "When we're together, like right now, there's nowhere else I'd rather be. And I *want* to think about you all the time, I really do, but it feels like there's only a limited amount of space in my mind, and when I'm dealing with Big Pro, or school, or my family—"

"I'm not asking you to think about me all—"

"Am I wrong about the mental space thing? That doesn't happen to you?"

She nodded and started walking again, and I couldn't tell whether I'd given her an answer she could be happy with. We sipped our tapioca bubbles in silence until she said, "Where did you get that thing about the bloody nose? What you said to that reporter about the femur and the broken nose. That didn't sound like one of my dad's Life Coach-isms."

"Colter."

"Ahhh," she said.

"What does that mean?"

She gnawed at a tapioca ball with her front teeth before answering. "There's something about . . . I kind of can't stand him."

"How can't you stand Colter? He's like a big monkey. Everyone likes monkeys."

"Yeah, but he's a lazy monkey, and lazy monkeys get feces thrown at them by other monkeys."

"You want to throw feces at him?"

"It's hard not to resent people who have so much but work so . . . I mean, don't we kind of have a responsibility to ourselves to maximize our opportunities—"

"Now *that's* one of your dad's Life Coach-isms—"

"To whom much is given, much is expected, and all that?"

"Yeah," I said. "But even you have to admit that sometimes we can take it a little far. Isn't that the whole point of someone like The Artist, for example? To show us how ridiculous this façade of perfection really is?"

"You sound like a fan."

"I actually defended him to Lunardi and Donaldson today, after they pulled me out of History. They're worried he's going to become a serial killer."

Ellen had just taken a sip but couldn't swallow quickly enough, and she laughed, spitting a mouthful of passion-fruit tea, complete with tapioca balls, onto the gravel path.

I sucked in through my teeth. "If those had gone out your nose . . ."

"What did you tell them?"

"That they were out of their minds. But I don't think The Artist is some grand social warrior critic. For all the thought-provoking captions, he's probably just jealous or vindictive, simply picking off the people who've pissed him off. Any one of us could be next. I'd watch out if I were you."

"I have nothing to hide," she said. "And it's not like he's going to find a picture of me doing something stupid."

"Unless I give you a roofie at Keegan's next party."

"You really know how to make a girl feel special," she said, eyes rolling. "So, Vanessa and Colter. What's their deal? You seem to be hanging out with them a lot—"

"Not too much—"

"Oh, come on," she said.

"I know what you know. From Boston, moved here. She drives a Benz; I'm not even sure he drives at all. But he does make origami stuff a lot."

"Is she going out with Iggy?"

"Why do you say that?"

"I see them together from time to time."

He's not her type, I caught myself almost saying. "She's tutoring him in English."

My phone buzzed. I pulled it from my pocket. "Speak of the devil," I said, showing Ellen a text message from Vanessa: *bleed all over your face? ;-) WTF?*

A thin smile bisected Ellen's face as she nodded, but she didn't say anything.

"You guys would be good friends," I said. "She's smart like you. She has her shit together like you. Yeah, you're both applying to Stanford, but so is everybody else. It's not like that should stand in the way."

"Do you text a lot?"

"She's in the play," I said, hoping that explained it.

The way Ellen narrowed her left eye at me told me it did not.

"We kiss," I said. I was barely able to keep myself from blurting it out. "In the play, there's a scene where we kiss. I wanted to tell you earlier, but I didn't want it to be a big deal, and then I thought you would be thinking that I was trying to keep it from you, and so I thought it would be best to say something now."

"Oh, I heard about it." Ellen considered me a beat before the thin smile reappeared. "Our school is not large."

That made sense then, why she was acting all insecure. She could have said something already, instead of making me jump through hoops. But I knew better than to tell her that. "I thought you might have."

"Did the playwright even read the book? Nick and Daisy getting it on? That's disgusting. They're cousins."

"Second cousins once removed."

"I don't even know what that means."

"There's evidence for it in the text," I said, and quoted one of my lines. "'The exhilarating ripple of her voice was a wild tonic in the rain.' Anyway, it's one person's interpretation."

"This kiss, it's like a peck on the cheek? Or is it a kiss kiss? I've heard conflicting reports."

She's going to see the play eventually, I thought, so it makes no sense to lie to her now just to make this particular moment easier. "It's supposed to be a fantasy," I said. "So it's more than a peck on the cheek. Quite a lot more. But it's acting. It's not for real."

"Is your real tongue in her real mouth?"

"Come on, Ellen," I said. "This isn't the first time we've had this conversation. *Romeo and Juliet* was a thousand times worse. Besides, I'm not even myself—"

"Spare me the 'lose myself in my character' nonsense. By that argument, I could just go around banging guys left and right as long as I didn't get emotionally involved."

"We're not banging each other," I yelped, and then, lowering my voice again, "and we're not emotionally involved."

My phone buzzed in my pocket. Ellen crossed her arms and raised her eyebrows.

"She's a friend, okay?" I said.

Ellen kept her arms crossed and nodded to my pocket. Our relationship may now have been riding on an unread text message. I removed the phone, and a small raindrop hit the screen. I wiped the moisture away to reveal a message. *U look good on tv but don't shift from side to side.*

It was from Francine. I showed Ellen, trying to keep the relief off my face.

"I swear to you that there is nothing going on between us. I would never cheat on you," I said. I even held her underneath her chin and brought her lips to mine and kept them there until hers relaxed and she finally kissed me back.

"I've never been jealous," she said, pulling away. "I don't know how to handle this."

A light rain had begun to fall. We turned around and started back toward her car. I couldn't take the silence anymore. "Now that we're admitting things . . . may I?"

She smiled. "That so depends on what it is."

"I'm terrified of my Juilliard audition."

"Terrified?" The surprise in her voice seemed genuine. "You've been working toward this since before we were dating."

"That's why." I didn't know how to explain that not only was I scared, but I was also embarrassed for *being* scared. I took her free hand in mine and squeezed it gently. "And it's worse the closer it gets. Like my whole self-worth is riding on me achieving this ridiculous long shot, and now that the audition is moving from the theoretical to the actual . . . I don't know."

"You're preparing, right? Rehearsing your monologues, all that?"

"Every day, but that doesn't matter. Every time I imagine myself not getting in, I see my dad's face, the I-told-you-so look in his eyes. I should have based my self-worth on getting into Stanford like everyone else. At least then if it didn't happen he could be proud of me for trying."

"I didn't know you cared so much about what your dad thought."

"I didn't know, either," I said. "Surprise!"

"Have you talked to Mr. Prokov about it?"

"Not really. He's got so much on his mind about the play, and—"

"Talk to him. You're David Ellison. He loves you."

"Not for long," I said. "I have to miss rehearsal tomorrow for the narrative coach thing."

"You're going to be fine."

I squeezed her hand again. It was a thunderless storm, but the occasional drops quickly became constant, and then huge. Ellen squealed, and we ran for shelter under the thick branches of a pine tree.

Rainwater had plastered her brown hair to the sides of her face. She smiled up at me. "What do you think the thematic importance of the rainstorm on our conversation is?"

"Literary analysis overload." I laughed. "I'm going to go ahead and vote for 'cleansing' and 'new beginning' over 'trouble on the horizon.'"

"Of course you are."

"Vanessa and I are friends," I said, meaning it with every synapse in my brain. "That's all. And I can promise you that if I had an antique pogo stick lying around, I would still be capable of ditching school and leading you to it with a bunch of flowers."

I took a sip of bubble tea, and a chunk of tapioca got caught in my throat. I pitched forward and hacked while Ellen smacked me on the back. I didn't even want to consider the thematic importance of that one.

12

Seeing as how I'd never faked appendicitis before, I decided maybe it wasn't such a good plan after all. I scarfed my lunch down the next day and ducked through the back entrance of the fine arts center and down the hallway to Big Pro's office. I took a deep breath before I knocked on the open door. "Got a minute?"

His chair creaked a protest as he arced backward and swiveled around to me. He motioned to the ratty old couch across from his desk. I sat and, as was my habit, scanned the walls, which were covered with posters advertising over two decades of the plays he'd directed. A plaque above his desk listed the names of each year's "Most Outstanding" actor or actress. I was a near lock to be the first student to have his name up there two years in a row.

"How're the monologues going?" he said.

I shrugged. "Good. Working on them every day. They're good."

"You're lying. What's going on?"

The springs in the cushion dug into the back of my leg, and I tried to make myself more comfortable. "Do you think it's possible that someone can be privileged, like with a normal family life and stuff like that, and still be a real artist? A real actor?"

He made a show of checking the calendar on his wall. "Is this Feel Sorry For Yourself Wednesday?"

"Never mind." I was halfway out the door before his voice stopped me.

"Sparkles, get your ass in here."

I tossed my backpack on the floor by the couch and collapsed back down. Big Pro stood and lumbered to close the door. He came back and sat against the edge of his desk. "Out with it."

I took a deep breath and closed my eyes. I opened them and said, "What if I'm not as good as I think I am?"

His smile was immediate and genuine. "Let me tell you a little secret. None of us are as good as we think we are."

"Yeah, but what if I don't get into Juilliard? What does that say about me? About everything I've been planning on and working for?"

"You know what the worst part about my job is?" He tongued the inside of his cheek and gestured to the plaque on the wall. "Year in and year out, kids so convinced that they're the special ones. And I have to be the one to tell them . . . You're no more or less special than any of the hundreds of kids who've already sat on that couch, or the hundreds who'll do it in the future."

I whistled through my teeth. "Hello, Mr. Sunshine."

"That's no insult. Come on, David, we can stop pretending, can't we?" He continued before I could answer.

"You think talent and drive has something to do with it, but I guarantee someone is going to pass you over because your voice is too high or too low, because your eyes are too blue or not blue enough, because your features aren't symmetrical. People are going to tell you that you suck—to your face. You have no idea the number of times you're going to be rejected."

"My features aren't symmetrical?"

"Your right eye is almost a centimeter lower than your left, and the lid is just a touch lazy. I saw your little thing on Channel Four last night. You're telling me you've never noticed?"

I opened my eyes wide, trying to sense if he was telling the truth or not. I brought my hand up to my face and pinched my right eyelid. "I have a lazy eyelid?"

"That's not the point," he said, reaching over to knock my wrist away. "Everybody has something. I weigh three hundred pounds. My point is that the second—the *second*—you start basing your definition of success on what other people think, you've lost. If you know what you want, and you're doing everything you can control, then it doesn't matter who tells you that you suck or how privileged you are or how normal your childhood was; your self-worth is safe no matter what happens."

"I guess."

"Don't guess. Know," he said with an emphatic grunt. "What do you want? What do you *really* want?"

"I want to do important art. Important work." A comment like that was exactly the same thing one of his "idealistic kids" would say, but I meant it. I also wanted to be famous, of course, but I wasn't about to admit that.

"Then find a cure for cancer. Don't pretend that putting on a costume and regurgitating someone else's writing is going to get you the Nobel Prize. But, and this is key, don't think that there's anything inherently wrong," he said, "with not doing something 'important.' Because honestly, Sparkles, how many of us really get to do something important in our lives?"

The bell rang, but I made no effort to get up. "What about you?"

He opened his arms wide. "I inspire young people."

"And, boy, are you good at it."

"You just get tired after a while, tired of the assemblies and the conferences and the 'go get 'ems.' I'm supposed to tell you that you can change the world, but wouldn't you rather I tell you the truth?" Big Pro lowered himself into his chair and rolled it toward me. He propped his heels on the couch's armrest. "So, tell me about your monologues."

"I need to miss rehearsal today." I'd been meaning to ease into that one, but I didn't want to talk about the audition any more.

Big Pro's face went slack. "Fuck me, Sparkles."

"I normally wouldn't ask—"

"You're the lead."

"I know, and—"

"Are you going to tell me why? Or will I just have to take your word that it's more important."

"It's not more important," I said. "At least I don't think so."

"Anytime you want to start making sense is fine by me."

"My dad hired a college counselor." I couldn't even look Big Pro in the eyes when I said it. "And because it was so last minute she only had one slot to squeeze me into."

His belly jiggled with a silent laugh. He wheeled backward and picked a pencil off his desk. He inspected the tip, then tapped the eraser against his thumbnail. "It's either let you go this afternoon or not have you for the show at all, am I right?"

"Something like that."

The bell rang again, meaning I was already late for Humanities. I took my keys from my pocket and removed one from the ring—the one Big Pro had given me toward the end of last year. "Here," I said. "You can have this back."

"Would you stop with the melodramatic nonsense already?"

"I know you're disappointed in me. And you should be. I don't deserve—"

"What am I, the mayor? I didn't give you that as some grand symbolic gesture. I just got tired of letting you in before school all the time. Not everything has to be packed with meaning. The sooner you realize that, the better off you'll be."

"Thanks," I said as I put the key back.

"Always here to help." He saluted good-bye. His voice stopped me as I reached the door. "Hey, Sparkles?"

I made myself turn around.

"Good luck today. College is important and all that."

13

Palm Drive leading into Stanford is both a continuation of Palo Alto's University Avenue and a completely different road. Sixty-foot palm trees begin lining the street the moment it crosses the campus border. After almost a half mile, the road circles around "the oval," a vast grassy area where students play volleyball and Frisbee, host picnic study groups, and take in the sun. I parked at the oval and hustled past the stone cathedral, where a bride in her flowing white dress was posing for pictures with a dozen members of her wedding party.

I jogged up the side street toward the University Coffee Shop but started walking to catch my breath as soon as it came into view. Most of the tables outside were occupied by groups of students, some laughing, some studying, others hunched over their phones, their thumbs flying.

A woman in an olive polo shirt and khaki slacks sat alone under a red umbrella. She was watching me. I appreciated her posture immediately: shoulders square, knees together, hands resting on the table. Her brown hair was pulled back by the sunglasses propped atop her head. On the small table in front of her was a manila folder. I smiled and wiped my forehead with the sleeve of my shirt as I moved toward her.

"You're five minutes late," she said, extending her hand, and then, before I could summon an excuse, "I'm Stephanie Blair."

"Do you work on campus?"

She shook her head. "I thought it would be a good idea for you to get a sense of the place. You'll need to feel the ambiance if you really want to craft a story."

"Did my dad tell you I want to go here?"

"You did," she said. "On television last night. I think you told everyone in the Peninsula. You were quite persuasive, even though you were clearly lying—"

"How did you—"

"A word of advice? When you've really got a whopper, try not to glance up and to the left so much." Stephanie dismissed any further response of mine with a little laugh.

She opened the folder and removed individual sheets of paper, which she then spread across the width of the table. I noticed my résumé, my last two years of grade reports, and the results of the questionnaire all Oak Fields students take at the end of their junior year.

"Your college counselor, Mr. Edwards, forwarded me your file." She put her elbows on the table and rested her chin on the knuckles of her right hand. "But all this is just paper. Why don't you tell me about yourself. Who is David Ellison?"

I've always hated that question. My answer usually depends on who's doing the asking, but I was having a hard time reading Stephanie Blair. The way she leaned in to me suggested that she was curious and open and maybe even interested in what I had to say about myself—whatever that might have been. I couldn't come up with anything to tell her, so I tried laughing the question off, like it'd only been a joke.

"You're interested in theatre, I see."

I knew she was just trying to get me to participate in the session, but whether the dismissiveness in her statement was actually present or only projected on my part, I took it as a challenge. "I have the lead in this fall's play."

"Is the theatre something you'd like to pursue? As a career?"

"Would you mind talking a bit about what we're going to be doing together?" I said. "You and I?"

Her smile disappeared, and she pulled a sheet of paper from the bottom of the pile and slid it toward me. It was a simple list of big-name colleges and universities: Harvard, Yale, Princeton, Stanford, etc., plus some of the higher-tier small schools like Williams, Amherst, and Middlebury. Next to each college was a double-digit number.

"I've had thirty-seven clients in the last four years, and every single one of them has gotten in to at least one of their reaches. Twenty-six of them have ended up matriculating at their top choice. My success rate for the Ivies is over seventy-eight percent. So, you ask what exactly we'll be doing together?" she said, a hint of confrontation in her voice. "We're getting you into college. I'm going to tell you exactly how to craft your story and exactly how to write it."

She stood up and reached for her purse. "Do you

want anything? I was waiting to get some coffee until you showed up."

Put it on my dad's tab, I almost said. What the hell was wrong with me? "No, thanks."

I watched her disappear into the coffee shop. I slapped my thighs and leaned back, gazing out over the campus. It wasn't her fault I was here, but Big Pro was right: I was the lead. Every second spent here made me resent my dad even more. He wasn't at the table, though, which left her to take it out on.

"I'm sorry I was late," I said as Stephanie sat back down. "And I don't mean to be defensive. It's just that I'm missing rehearsal, and I'm auditioning for Juilliard in two weeks, and—"

"No apology necessary. I know we're all under a lot of stress these days. Now, if we're going to make things happen, we have to get started." She gestured to my portfolio. "We don't have a whole lot to work with here."

"Excuse me?"

"You want to be an actor, so when you receive criticism, you know it's not personal, right? I'm just saying that while the grades are solid and the scores won't be an issue, the extracurricular material we have to shape is a little less robust than what I'm used to seeing from my clients."

"We rehearse late," I said, doing my best not to be distracted by the warmth wrapped around my throat like a turtleneck. "There's no time for the other stuff."

She rested an index finger on the temple of her sunglasses

and pushed down until the frame bounced onto the bridge of her nose. "I understand that. The trick is making sure that it comes through in your essay without sounding like an excuse."

"I don't have to defend myself to you."

"You're right about that. I work for your parents, and if you knew how much this session was costing them, you might be a little more cooperative. So if there's something you may have, I don't know . . . forgotten to list here, now is the time to remember."

"You want me to lie?"

"Not lie, exactly, although that might help." She winked. "I do have an MFA in creative writing."

I was missing rehearsal for *this?* "My parents said you blew them away with your pitch."

"People just like me are meeting with your competition all over the country. Why would you *not* want to level the playing field? I suppose that's noble of—"

"Is that what you told them? That you could level the playing field—"

"What you're feeling is very common, just so you know." Not only did Stephanie refuse to match my energy, she actually seemed bored with me. The tilt of her head and the way her cheeks puffed out slightly as she exhaled seemed to say, *Blah, blah, blah.* "I call it rich kid guilt. And I understand where you're coming from, I do. You think of all the kids on the other side of the tracks, kids who can't afford tutors or SAT study classes or independent narrative coaches. It's not fair, you think."

"Well," I said, "what *about* the kids who can't afford all those—"

"I didn't make the rules, David, I'm just playing by them. I'd help out a scholarship kid once in a while if I could—really, I would—but you know what the cost of living is here." She spread her arms out as if gesturing to the sunshine. "So, yes, I provide a service. And for that, I happen to be well-compensated."

"How well-compensated are we talking?"

"Maybe you could look at it from your parents' point of view. Here they are, both working their tails off in order to send you to private school, and how do you repay them? By spending all your time in plays? By not taking all of the AP classes available to you? By working at," she sifted through the small pile of papers spread in front of her, "Jefe Pizza for a summer?"

"I was very good at that—"

She held up her hand to stop me. "Okay, let's take it from the beginning. What do you think is your biggest weakness?"

Oh, boy. Only one?

14

I dropped Lisa at the freshman lot early the next morning and opened the theater to run my monologues. I could practice in my bedroom all I wanted, but there was nothing that compared to the sensation of being onstage. With a few minutes before the beginning of school I headed to the senior hallway and checked the bulletin board outside Mr. Edwards's office for something new from The Artist.

That's where I ran into Iggy. It was the first time I'd seen him since Keegan's. He stood in front of the bulletin board with his backpack at his feet. The thin fabric of his workout shirt stretched against his massive shoulders. He gave me a nod and turned back to the board. According to the college-visit schedule, Yale was today, Princeton and Williams tomorrow, and Pomona before school on Monday.

"I think you owe me twenty bucks," I said. He just grunted. "How's your back?"

"They ever find out that you were the guy with the golf clubs?" he said, his eyes trained on the bulletin board. His voice was mellow as could be, but the threat underneath was impossible to miss: My back is none of your business, theatre freak, and I'm not quitting anything. I was drunk, so keep your mouth shut.

Colter walked by and patted me on the back. "Chief," he said. "You okay?"

"Yeah, I . . ."

"You free tomorrow night?"

"Sure," I said. I couldn't take my eyes off Iggy. Whenever we did something together, I'd let myself get suckered into thinking that we were friends, and the next time I saw him it was like I hardly existed.

"Dinner, my place. My folks are psyched to meet you. Think of it as an interview to be my dad's son's friend."

"What?"

"Just pretend you're smart. He'll like that." Colter cleared his throat. "Are you sure you're okay?"

"Yeah, sure," I turned to him. "Fine. Tomorrow night. I'll be smart."

"All right, then," Colter said as he walked away. "Good talk."

The bounce, bounce of a basketball echoed in the hallway, and starting point guard Felix Gutierrez came over. He cradled the ball beneath his arm. "Ignacious!"

"What's up, brother?" Iggy's face lit up, and he gave Felix a man-hug.

Felix nodded at me; I nodded back. They smalltalked each other for a bit and then—after a borderline-threatening nod from Iggy—disappeared down the hall, Felix's basketball once again pinging out a rhythm.

Before I could do anything stupid, like call out after him, someone covered my eyes from behind. "It's The Artist," said an artificially low voice.

I took a deep sniff. "I don't think The Artist would smell like jasmine."

"So perceptive," Ellen said. She dropped her arms, we gave each other a quick school-kiss, and she came around to stand next to me. "Anything new?"

"Just that." I pointed to a small sign at the top of the bulletin board. THIS AREA RESERVED FOR OFFICIAL COLLEGE COUNSELING INFORMATION ONLY!

"Oooh, that'll teach him." She gave my ass a little squeeze as though marking her territory. "What were you and Iggy talking about? He didn't say anything about our History presentation, did he?"

"The subject didn't exactly come up."

She groaned. "Why am I the one who does all the work in these so-called group presentations? If you see him again—"

"It will be the first thing on my mind. Promise."

"So, I was thinking. Tomorrow night? You. Me." She tiptoed up to whisper in my ear, "The back of the White Horse."

"My trusty steed," I said with a smile. "Not you—the car."

She hit me playfully on the shoulder "Pick me up at seven? I have an Amigos meeting at six, but I'll be back home in time."

"Crap," I said, remembering. This was not good. "I have something tomorrow."

"What?"

That was the one question I didn't want her to ask. I

shrugged into the lie. "My dad and I are talking colleges."

"Look at you, all focused on your future and everything. Dare we welcome New David back into our lives?"

The genuine delight in her eyes was almost enough for me to tell her the truth about my Friday night plans, but before I could make a decision on that, Geoff Cronyn appeared over her shoulder.

"Do you have a second?" he said. To me.

Ellen gave me a look, like *What the heck does Geoff Cronyn want a second with you for?*

I kissed her on the cheek. "Saturday night. The White Horse."

"Geoff," she said warily, and then she disappeared down the hall with a little pep in her step.

"What's up?" I was as hesitant as Ellen had been. Geoff was Keegan's friend, belonged with that crew. Even at rehearsals he kept to himself, as though he thought he was better than the rest of us, just slumming with the theatre geeks.

"Did you mean what you said the other night on TV?" he said. "About the lawsuit?"

"I figured that was probably you," I said.

"Did you, though? Mean it?" His brown hair was disheveled just right and set in stone with gel, and his skin was spotless, and yet there was insecurity on his face. That threw me. Geoff Cronyn was not supposed to show weakness. Geoff Cronyn was one of the chosen ones.

"Sure, Geoff. I meant it."

"It's not like I asked my parents to make a big deal of

it. All I did was tell them what that Parson guy told us in the meeting."

"You could have told them not to—"

"They know what's best for me." He shrugged me a that's-the-way-it-is. "These are people who leave me a drawer full of medications for anthrax and radiation sickness when they go out of town. Every base covered, no stone unturned, etcetera, etcetera."

"Are you all right?" I said. I couldn't wait to tell Ellen that I'd actually asked Geoff that question.

"I just wanted to thank you for . . . you know, for sticking up for me."

I nodded. He and his leather flip-flops shuffled away, leaving me in the hallway, still in front of the bulletin board, wondering what in hell this world was coming to.

15

I was the only dinner guest, but they'd brought out the good china, set it on freshly ironed linen place mats, and put a small purple orchid in the center of a long table that would have easily sat twelve. The parents were on opposite ends, with Vanessa and Colter across from each other about halfway down. My chair was next to Colter's. An older white woman named Matilda brought dinner to the table plate by plate.

It's not like my family didn't have any money, but there's money and then there's *money*, and I always felt like I was an impostor around *money*, like at any moment I was going to take a sip from the wrong glass or cross my legs the wrong way, and the game would be up. Some of my best performances have been at the dinner tables of my friends' houses.

And after seeing the Stern *money* with my own eyes, I had to laugh when I thought of us moving the coffee table in my living room so we could all lie on the floor together.

"This is fantastic," I said as Matilda spooned a thick sauce over the veal on my plate. "Thank you."

Matilda nodded and shuffled back into the kitchen.

My mom's egg burritos or home-cooked take-out Thai didn't even deserve to be called food in comparison.

Matilda's osso buco—"awesome buco," according to Colter—was on an entirely different level. I barely touched the meat with the tip of my fork, and it literally fell off the bone.

Colter tried to inject a little levity into the evening with a prayer: "Rub a dub dub, thanks for the grub, yaaaaay God!"

I caught his dad shoot him a little glance, and Colter looked down at his plate and stabbed a sautéed portobello mushroom.

Mrs. Stern's blond hair was pulled harshly against her scalp and wound into a tight bun, like she was wearing a yellow swim cap. Wrinkles seemed terrified of both her skin and her clothes. "Colter so rarely invites friends over. I'm thrilled we have the chance to get to know one another."

"So, David," Mr. Stern said. "Tell us about yourself."

At least there'd been no audience with Stephanie Blair. I'd come off as an ass, but the only other person who noticed was the stoned guy with the backward hat and the unopened copy of *Madame Bovary* at the next table. Now there was Vanessa, and even Colter. How do you describe yourself to parents in terms that won't sound ridiculous to their kids?

What little I knew of them was enough to assume that any mention of theatre or plays or acting was going to get me a flat smile, a shake of the head, maybe even an "isn't that interesting." So I went for a joke to start off.

"I'm a Pisces," I said.

Silence. Joke falls helpless to the polished hardwood floors.

Mrs. Stern said, "You're interested in astrology, then?"

Why was I even nervous? What the hell did I care what the Sterns thought of me? It must have been the size of the table, the polished wood and inlaid glass. Or Colter's pained slouch. Or Vanessa's reluctance to look at me as I floundered.

It was time for the History Channel version: forget being interesting and try to make myself sound as boring and simple as possible in order to head off any more questions. "I grew up here, in the Bay Area," I said. "I have a younger sister. Lisa. She's kind of a genius when it comes to computers."

"She's in the right place, isn't she?" Mr. Stern said.

"And your parents?" said his wife. "What do they do?"

"My mom is an account manager. Have you heard of SpeakEasy?" Thin-lipped head-shakes. "They do voice recognition. Like when you call a toll-free number and it asks you to state your preference? That's them."

Mrs. Stern nodded. "That's so much more convenient than pressing numbers on a keypad."

"My dad's an engineer with Cisco. Been there forever."

Mr. Stern pulled out the frown nod. "Good company."

Colter was making more sense to me. His goofiness, his baggy wardrobe, his apparent lack of desire, even the leisurely way he strung words together made him the polar opposite of his father. You always hear about people defining themselves against the people they hate, but you almost never actually get to see it happening right in front of you.

We ate in silence for what had to be ten of the most awkward minutes of my life. Matilda came in periodically, offering seconds, refilling the bread plate, bringing another bottle of wine for the parents. As excruciating as it was for me, it had to be even worse for Vanessa. She was chewing with a determination that would have been hilarious in any other setting.

Finally, Mrs. Stern cleared her throat again. "What's your best subject—"

"David has the lead in the play," Colter blurted.

Mr. Stern narrowed his eyes. "Is that right?"

Vanessa winced as if offering an apology. Colter probably couldn't help himself. But then it struck me that he'd engineered this whole thing for a reason. I was his little dancing monkey. He probably wanted his parents to see that there were people like him—unconventional people, creative people—at Oak Fields, and now that he'd outed me, I had little choice but to go along. "Yep."

"Vanessa, is that the same one—"

"They kiss," Colter said for some ridiculous reason.

I could feel every one of the pores on my forehead. I said, "I have a girlfriend."

"Good for you," said the father, unimpressed.

"What I meant was—"

Vanessa leaned forward. "David's going to Juilliard next year."

"Not exactly," I said. "At least not yet, fingers crossed.

The audition is next Wednesday. Not this coming, but next. Just twelve days away." This was the Lifetime Channel, not the History Channel; I tried to shut my mouth, but the words kept coming out. Vanessa's dad rested the prongs of his fork atop the meat, waiting. "I've got four monologues to deliver, two classical and two contemporary. One of the classical ones has to be Shakespeare—"

"And what happens if you don't get in? Do you have a backup plan?" Mr. Stern peeled the meat away from the bone in thin, tender strips. "A safety school?"

Colter said, "Can we not talk about college tonight?"

"Honey," his mom said. "We're just trying to get to know David a little bit, is all."

"I have a number of schools on my list," I said, though I didn't really. I'd thought that even making a physical list of other schools would open the mental possibility to me not getting in to Juilliard.

His dad tucked a forkful into the hollow of his cheek. "I don't know what your family's philosophy is, David. But our core principles here are hard work, dedication."

I took a sip of water to stall. "We don't have an actual, you know, stated philosophy, but dedication is—"

"It's one of the reasons we moved. Sometimes you need a change of scenery, and Palo Alto . . . You feel it, don't you? The future is happening here. People are looking forward."

This was a game, I finally realized, a game of platitudes bounced back and forth. He didn't care what my answers were, he just wanted me to play along. Okay, I could do that. "It's funny you should mention that, sir, because I just started working with a college narrative coach."

"Vanessa tutors," her mom said. "She has that basketball player— Honey, what's his name? The real big one?"

"Iggy—"

"If there's one thing my family has taught me," I said, going for self-aware, "it's that I can always use more help. This woman, Stephanie Blair, I met with her for the first time two days ago. She's quite something. Over the last four years, all thirty-seven of her clients have gotten into at least one of their reaches. Her Ivy acceptance rate is almost eighty percent."

"I can respect that," said Mr. Stern. "Would you feel comfortable giving us a referral? I have a feeling that Colter might benefit from a conversation."

The way he said it made it seem like an exclamation point. Sentence ended, topic complete. Colter shrank in his seat.

We powered through dessert—a spectacular lemon tart with homemade whipped cream—and then we were excused. I thanked everyone for a wonderful meal and started to carry my plate to the kitchen, but Mrs. Stern waved me off. "Matilda will get that."

"Jesus, Colter," I said when we'd been excused. "Fight your own battles. I'm not a freaking show pony."

"Sure you are." He smiled. "Like a Shetland."

"Come on, let me show you the backyard," Vanessa said.

"I've got my own crap to deal with," I said. But I threw

him a little laugh so as not to add to the tension.

"Clearly," Colter said. "You guys go ahead. I'll catch up."

Vanessa and I wandered onto a vast lawn leading down toward a swimming pool with an attached spa. Potted fruit trees lined the cemented flagstone path toward a small hut-like building where a large gas grill shone under an overhead light.

There were two wooden lawn chairs across from a small table in the center of the grass. We sat. Had Colter left us alone on purpose? Was this his plan all along? Was the dinner with his parents a red herring? Was I possibly overthinking this?

I couldn't handle the silence. "It's nice out here," I said. Lamely.

"Sorry about my parents. They can be a little intense."

"Just a little." I thought *my* dad was bad. I didn't know how Colter forced himself to sit at the same table night after night with someone who so clearly despised him. "They just want what's best for you guys, right?"

She rolled her eyes at me. They were gorgeous eyes, even when rolled. "Right."

"How are they dealing with your newfound love of the stage?"

"I think you know the answer to that."

"Maybe we could set up a man date with our dads. Take them up to the city for a musical or something. You think we can count on the magic of the theatre to soften their hard edges?"

Vanessa laughed. "Everything we do, from middle school on, is geared toward getting into the best college. What if that's a joke? What if we want other things? What if we just want to get into an okay college?"

I motioned to the swimming pool, the pavilion. "I don't think an okay college is an option."

She chuckled. "Poor us, right? We have to go to private school. We have to apply to Stanford and Princeton."

"What's your essay about?"

"Oh, the usual stuff. Family dynamics, expectations, desire. The move. You're not trying to cheat off me, are you?"

"Like that would ever work," I said.

She rubbed her hands along her thighs and slapped her kneecaps with a kind of finality.

"So what happened to your accent?" I said, trying to lighten the mood. "You know: Paahck the caah."

"I still have it when I want to." She pointed to the night sky. "The staahs look wicked gaahgeous when they spaahkle."

Her eyebrows danced, and a jolt of something that I shouldn't have let go through me went right through me. I remembered our fierce, fake kiss, the sensation of her lips on mine, her back against my fingertips.

"Speaking of spaahkle," she said. "Your nickname."

"Nobody's told you?"

"I'm still the new girl," she said. "Who wants to waste time explaining what everyone else already knows?"

I told her the story, how I'd begged my dad to let me

audition after school in seventh grade, how the shoot took four days, for which I was paid—in cash—two hundred dollars per day, plus a total of over $10,500 by the time the campaign was over, how the ad aired from California to Arizona.

"My big line was me turning to the camera right after taking a sip of tea and saying, 'Mmmboy, delicious!' I couldn't actually drink what was in the glass, though, because it wasn't tea. The real Sparkles tea looked too watery on screen no matter how many packets they added. So they used glass cubes instead of ice, and motor oil instead of tea."

"Like real engine motor oil?"

"Quaker State 5W-30. I saw them pour it right into the glass. Looked good on camera, though." I shrugged. "The commercial wasn't even a day old by the time someone started calling me Sparkles. As far as nicknames go, it could be worse."

"People used to call me Right Guard back home. I was always raising my hand in class." She shook her head at the memory and then leaned back, the skin of her neck tightening against her throat.

"Where's Ellen tonight?" she said. Clearly, my mind was not difficult to read.

"Amber, I think."

"She okay with you being here?"

I said nothing.

Vanessa snorted and pressed her mouth into her shoulder. "You didn't tell her?"

"It's not like I'm hiding anything from her—"

"Oh, come on, David. Don't be an idiot. If you and I were together and you were hanging out at some other girl's house, I'd be pissed."

"First of all, this is Colter's house, too. And second of all, I'm not allowed to have female friends?"

"So why didn't you tell her you were coming over?"

"I just figured it would be easier to tell her that my dad and I were going to talk about colleges."

"Oh yeah," Vanessa said. "Way easier."

The way she leaned one arm over the back of her chair, the way her chest stretched the translucent white fabric of her shirt . . . I ignored all that and turned my attention to the pool.

"Ellen's awesome," I said. "With all the crap we have to deal with—school and parents and colleges, figuring out who we really are and what we want to do with our lives—to have the girlfriend box checked off is actually a relief."

"You should do yourself a favor and never mention such a thing as checking off the girlfriend box ever again."

"You know what I mean," I said. "And I think you guys would really get along."

"Hey, David," Colter ambled toward the chair next to Vanessa. He was holding my cell phone, and the look on his face was apologetic. "It was ringing in the living room, and my mom answered it. She does things like that."

Vanessa nodded. "She's pretty much OCD about missed calls."

"Who is it?"

He breathed in sharply through gritted teeth as if to say, "Oops."

I stood and took two steps toward the swimming pool. The lights underneath were a deep green, giving the still water the eerie look of an enchanted lake. "Hello?"

"What the hell, David?" It was Ellen, and there was exasperation in her voice. "A big college discussion?"

"Colter invited me over for dinner."

"*Colter* invited you."

I winced. Unconsciously avoiding talking about Vanessa was no way to assuage suspicions. "And Vanessa's here, yes, for the family dinner. We had osso buco. Did you know that's not a dessert? It's—"

"Veal shank on the bone, yeah."

I glanced behind me. Colter had taken my spot, and the two of them were staring up at the sky, not talking, not even moving, just staring. Behind them, through the window to the kitchen, their parents stood on either side of the large island in the center, with a glass of wine in front of each.

Ellen sighed. "Were you not even paying attention to what you yourself said the other day? It was raining. We went out for bubble tea? Any of this ringing a bell?"

"I'm sorry. I should have told you I was coming over here, but I didn't want you to get upset."

The sarcasm was in full force. "Why *on Earth* would I get upset?"

"It's not my fault Vanessa is his sister, and I know you

don't like him, but Colter's a good guy, even if he did have me dress up in a monkey suit today."

"What does that mean?"

"I'm like the token creative guy. I think he invited me over so his dad would see there are other people like him out there." I ran my fingers through my hair. "Whatever, it doesn't matter—"

"You should have just told me the truth. We can deal with the truth."

"I know. It was stupid. Vanessa even said it was stupid. I'm telling you, she has your back. She said if she and I were going out and I was at some other girl's house, she'd be pissed."

"Well, she's right about that," Ellen said. "Maybe I should be glad she's keeping an eye on you."

I lowered my voice. "Hey, I love you, okay? A little osso buco isn't going to change that."

"Are we really on for tomorrow? Or was that another—"

"My word is my bond," I said.

"Yeah, it's a junk bond," she said. "Zing!"

We hung up, and I made myself walk back toward the house to say my good-byes.

Colter winced. "Are you busted?"

"Everything okay?" Vanessa said.

"Yeah, fine," I said. "No problem. Just some last minute questions about her Spanish presentation."

Not that either of them believed me.

16

picked Ellen up in the White Horse before dusk on Saturday. The sun had just begun to pierce the horizon, and the air had taken on the golden tint of an old Western movie. I hadn't told her where we were going, but my plan was to show her how much I valued our relationship, to be present with her, and of course to make up for everything that had happened recently.

Normally I would have spent some time inside with her parents, but I was running on time rather than early. I had to keep the schedule moving, so I honked and waved at Mr. Conroy through the living room window. Seconds later, Ellen bounded out the door in a pair of plaid shorts and an orange tank top.

"You look great," I said when she got in. I leaned over to kiss her, but she'd turned to reach for her seat belt, and when she brought her head back around, her forehead hit me square in the nose.

I yelped and bent over and brought both hands to my face. My eyes instantly started watering, and I felt a dull pain at the back of my throat and in my stomach, as though any second I was going to vomit.

Ellen put her hand on my back. "Is it bleeding?"

I mumbled an I-don't-know through my hands, and

she couldn't stifle her laughter any longer.

"What a smooth operator."

"Don't laugh," I said, even though I couldn't help it myself. I sat up and blinked the tears away. "That could have been a disaster."

"I'm sorry—"

I pointed to my face. "This is my moneymaker!"

When my eyes had cleared enough for me to see, I leaned to her slowly and received a painless kiss on the lips.

"Better," I said. The White Horse's engine came to life. "And we're off."

I drove the speed limit from her house down Alameda de las Pulgas, but when we reached Sand Hill, I made a right rather than the left that would have led us to the mall or into downtown Palo Alto.

"Interesting," Ellen said. I caught myself taking a deep breath. "Are you going to tell me where we're going, or do I have to wait until we get there?"

"It's a surprise."

She must have noticed the apprehension on my face or the tension in my voice, because she said again, "Interesting."

"It's not a big deal," I said. "So don't expect a pony or anything."

"Right, okay. No pony."

"You know what I mean."

We crossed the freeway into the foothills of the Santa Cruz mountains, and the car protested a bit as the road tilted upward. I turned right again, on Old La Honda, and the road narrowed.

"Have you ever been to one of the houses up here?" Ellen said as we climbed. Ellen's family was wealthy by almost any measure, but if there's one thing the Bay Area teaches you, it's that no matter how rich or beautiful or successful or powerful you are, there's always someone out there richer, more beautiful, more successful, or more powerful.

"Mmm." I drove less than ten miles an hour, and though it was probably because the turns were so tight and the slope was so steep, it might also have had something to do with the growing sense that this maybe wasn't the best idea.

I never understood how people could play the field, or see each other casually or whatever you want to call it. I didn't want to waste energy in something that was probably doomed from the start, so I always convinced myself that the next one was *the* one, even as a freshman. Needless to say, I'd always had a hard time finding a match between the way I imagined things would work out and the probability of that actually happening.

"Watch out," Ellen said, pointing to the side of the road. "There's someone there by that driveway."

I slowed as we got closer, and I was relieved to see the look on Ellen's face as one of astonishment rather than anger. "What the hell?"

"Surprise?" I said.

Vanessa's jeans were tight but not outrageous, torn in

places, but not obnoxiously so, and she had a simple black blouse with a sash tied around the waist. She waved, and then her eyes kind of went wide as the car pulled up next to her with Ellen in the front seat. She adapted quickly and opened the rear door.

"Ellen," Vanessa said, more than a little uncertainly.

Ellen returned the favor. "Vanessa."

I pulled a K-turn to head back downhill. They were both looking at me with the same expression: eyebrows slightly raised, mouths slightly open. The mood in the car would have to have been described as one of bemusement.

"So," I said. "I thought we could hang out. You guys have a lot of things in common."

"This is like a blind play date?" Vanessa said.

Ellen made a show of looking around the car. "Where's the hidden camera?"

"My sister thought this would be a horrible idea. I had to repeat it three times before she finally believed I wasn't kidding—"

At exactly the same time, Vanessa said, "Your sister's a smart girl," and Ellen said, "You should listen to her."

They both laughed, but I was unfazed. "*My* point was that there's no reason you two shouldn't be best friends. You're like the same person."

Ellen snorted a bit, and it occurred to me that might have been the wrong thing to say. A weight settled onto the air in the car, and I racked my brain for something that would lift it. We reached the bottom of Old La Honda and turned down toward town.

"Is this the part when you tell us where we're going?" Vanessa said.

"And ruin the fun?"

"The fun?" Ellen said.

"I'm going to go out on a limb," Vanessa said, "and guess this isn't the first time David has done something like this."

Ellen laughed. "How'd you know?"

"Come on," I said.

"He's not so good at the big picture." She turned and patted me maternally on the shoulder. "Better for in the moment."

"It's an occupational hazard," I said lamely. "Makes for a better actor."

Vanessa said, "Oh my God. I dated a guy like that in Boston. Nicest guy. When we were in the same room, he couldn't have been more caring, more thoughtful, more devoted. But as soon—"

"As you were out of sight—"

"It was like we'd never met. No phone call, no text. Nothing." She took off her seat belt and scooted to the center of the backseat, resting one hand on each of the front seats as she leaned forward. "But what killed me is that the relationship was *so* good when we were actually together that I kept giving him chance after chance after chance. I thought I could change him—"

Ellen made a loud buzzer sound.

Vanessa laughed. "Exactly! Wrong answer. Thanks for playing."

"I know, right?"

"I'm kind of surprised you guys have lasted, what, two years? No offense, David."

"None taken." At least they were on the same team. If the price of getting them to bond was an evening of ripping on me, I was more than willing to pay it. We passed the mall and crossed El Camino, veering right on Alma. We were almost there.

"It's not too bad, not all the time," Ellen said. "Have you been introduced to New David and Old David?"

"This should be good." Vanessa rubbed her hands together.

"Old David is, well, David." She pointed at me with her thumb, and I tried to bow against the seat belt. "But New David is like a normal person. He remembers important dates, he's on time to things. Sometimes he actually *makes* plans."

"How often does one get to spend time with New David?"

Ellen slapped the dashboard and turned to Vanessa. "That's the thing! You never know when New David's going to blow into town! One day, all of a sudden, his homework will be done on time, a phone call will have been returned, a plan will have been kept, and you think to yourself, 'Well, okay, he's here!' And you try to ride that horse for as long as it's around."

"In Old David's defense," I said, "a lot of what New David does nullifies some of the things that make Old David so endearing. So it's not like he can totally take over. You're going to lose a lot, and you may not like all of what you're left with."

There was a silence, and then they both started laughing.

"What?" I said.

"The Two Davids need some professional help." Vanessa said.

"No argument from me," I said as I pulled into an empty parking place and turned off the car. "Here we go."

Ellen looked out the window. "You're not really making us go in there."

"It'll be great, I promise. They have decals and iron-ons. You can make—"

"My God," Ellen said.

"No wonder you and my brother get along." Vanessa shook her head as she got out of the car. "You're both such dorks."

"There's nobody inside," Ellen said. "Is it even open?"

"I'm afraid to ask how many times you've been here before," Vanessa said.

"First time for all of us." I locked the car. I'd figured that the best way to make this work would be to put them both in an unfamiliar setting so neither had the advantage, and T-Time: Self-Made Tees was the most unfamiliar setting I could think of. "It's the undiscovered gem of the Mid-Peninsula. Now keep an open mind, children, and you just might enjoy yourselves."

The single room featured four large circular tables with white power strips built into the center of each.

Surprisingly hard-core drum and bass electronica filled the room from hidden speakers. On the far wall was a display of the available T-shirts with samples tacked from floor to ceiling: beefy, fitted, baby-doll, ringer, organic, distressed, long-sleeve, tank top, spaghetti top, crew neck, V-neck, scoop neck, sweatshirts, hoodies, toddler tees, onesies. And so on.

"That's quite the selection," Vanessa said.

We were met in the center of the room by a girl in a tie-dyed apron who couldn't have been older than thirteen. "We have polos and tote bags, too, but there's no room on the wall, so . . ."

I caught Vanessa and Ellen sharing a wide-eyed look. I said, "How do we—"

"Choose a shirt style and color, and then you figure out what you want to put on it, and then you put that stuff on it. It's pretty simple. Some of our customers even like to wear their shirts out. You can use the restroom to change if you want to."

We chose our shirts—gray fitted for me, yellow scoop for Vanessa, and pink spaghetti tank for Ellen—and were each given a plastic bin filled with supplies.

"I'm Bernie," the girl said. Clear braces pushed her lips out as though she wore a mouth guard. "Short for Bernadette; not my fault. Use any of the decals on those shelves over there, but remember to keep track. You know, for pricing."

I thanked Bernie and we moved to our table and began to unload our bins: an electric iron the size of a deck of cards, various markers and small bottles of multicolored paints, a selection of generic decals. I heard Vanessa and Ellen giggling, so I motioned for them to stop.

"Be nice," I said, looking over my shoulder.

Ellen put her hand over her mouth. "Oh, don't worry, it's not her we're laughing at."

For that moment, at least, the night was working. We plugged our irons into the power strip and organized our supplies. I selected a happy face, a motorcycle, a rainbow, and a monster truck. Ellen went with an animal theme— cats and unicorns, mostly—and Vanessa sifted through the decal box for snowflakes, a sun, a few leaves, and for some reason, a leprechaun.

We worked in silence. Maybe it was because there was nobody else in the store, or maybe it was because T-Time really was the undiscovered gem of the Mid-Peninsula, but for as much crap as they'd given me, when presented with the chance to build their own T-shirts, both Vanessa and Ellen dove right in.

"Have you seen his monologues?" Vanessa asked after a while.

Ellen nodded. "A time or two."

"They're pretty good, right?"

"Yeah, but I'm not the most objective audience. I could do without the *Death of a Salesman* one, though. Too depressing."

"The play's called '*Death*' of a Salesman," I said. "And besides, it's just a play. I don't get how you of all peo-ple can complain that it's depressing when you spend so much time around things that are legitimately real-life depressing."

Vanessa chose a thick orange marker and drew a giant X across the front of her shirt. "Do tell."

Ellen shot me a glance and sifted through the iron-ons for more unicorns. "I volunteer at this homeless shelter, soup kitchen, whatever. I keep asking David to come with me, but I think he's afraid—"

"I'm not afraid. I have rehearsal—"

"Whatever it is, he's missing out. It keeps you grounded. Reminds you that no matter how overwhelming you think your problems are, there are always people dealing with worse."

"Does Sophie work there, too?" Vanessa said. "She's in my AP French class. I thought I remembered her saying something about a shelter."

Ellen nodded. "It's the same place. She's been spending more time there since the whole thing with The Artist."

"Probably soul-searching, reminding herself what's really important," I said.

"That might be giving her a little too much credit."

"Why don't you go there, David?" Vanessa said.

Ellen said, "Thank you."

"Bad stuff happens, and it helps to see how some people deal with it. Overcome it."

Ellen watched Vanessa work, and a genuine smile crossed her face. I couldn't believe it. This ridiculous plan of mine was actually going to work. Ellen said, "Real people overcoming real misfortune. That's exactly why *Death of a Salesman* is a tragedy, and the shelter isn't. The play is just fake."

"Sometimes you just have to leave your comfort zone," Vanessa said without looking up.

Ellen jumped on the thread. "Which is harder and harder to do when our whole world is a comfort zone."

Vanessa picked up her mini-iron and held her hand less than an inch from it, testing for heat. "That's one of the reasons I like acting, you know, because that's just about as far from my comfort zone as I can get."

"Could have fooled me," I said.

"You say that, but—"

"You'd never know it was her first play," I said to Ellen.

"I just don't know how you can be motivated all the time," Vanessa said. "It feels like every scene is more important than the last; it's exhausting."

"That's why you need to focus on the moment of the scene. You can't afford to let the idea come into your head that one scene or one line or even one gesture is more important than any other."

Vanessa groaned. "That's so much easier said than done."

"You'll get there," I said. "I thought you were already there."

"Who plays Gatsby?" Ellen said.

"Some sophomore named Jason," I said, then turning back to Vanessa: "You're a natural."

"Someone once told me that the worst thing is to be a

natural. Because if you start out good at something you never learn to work hard."

"Yeah," I said. "But you're a natural *and* you work hard. That's like the best of both worlds."

Ellen cleared her throat. "They cast a sophomore as Gatsby?"

"He's kind of a minor character," Vanessa said.

"But it's called *The Great Gatsby*."

"Yeah, but this is an adaptation, right?" I said. "And the playwright wanted to spend some more time with Nick and his story, rather than concentrate on Gatsby as a cautionary tale."

Vanessa said, "So there are a lot of scenes in the play that don't exist at all in the book, or are just hinted at."

"Like when you guys make out," Ellen said.

"It's more of just a kiss," Vanessa said, not breaking eye contact with Ellen. "But yeah, like that scene."

This was not good. I dropped my decals and explained to Ellen, "In this version, Nick is envious of Gatsby, right? Envious of his money and his parties, at least at first, but what really gets him is Gatsby's relationship with Daisy. Or more to the point, with the emotional connection behind it. He knows he can't compete with Gatsby, but he can't help wondering what it would be like if he could."

"And so he has that fantasy," Ellen said.

"Exactly," I said.

"That is one—how do I put this?—fucked-up adaptation. If you don't mind me saying so."

I ironed my monster truck onto the ridge of a rainbow. "Maybe. But the playwright won a Tony a couple of years ago."

Bernie asked from across the room if we needed anything, and we shook our heads. She said the store closed in twenty minutes but would we please try to finish in fifteen so she could get the place cleaned up by the time her mother came by to lock up.

"Hey, Ellen," I said, scrambling to avoid the awkward silence that was no doubt headed our way, "tell Vanessa about Amigos de las Américas. Vanessa, you're going to love this."

Ellen breathed out her nose. "It's like a mini–Peace Corps thing for high school and college kids. They have programs all throughout Latin America. Community service, youth-to-youth initiatives, cross-cultural exchange, things like that. I spent eight weeks in Ecuador last summer repairing a school classroom. Laying concrete, painting, the works."

"Isn't that awesome?" I said.

Vanessa said, "Is that what your essay is about?"

"It's a component," Ellen said. "Part of a larger theme of service and leadership development."

"I bet Stanford is going to eat that up."

The house beats thumped while Vanessa and Ellen smiled at each other. This was like a shootout at the OK Corral. High noon. And guess who was standing in the crossfire?

"I hope so," Ellen said. "What's yours about?"

"Overcoming adversity. Life's many challenges, things like that."

Ellen smirked as if to say that the idea of Vanessa overcoming adversity was a joke.

"You know, personal issues," Vanessa continued. "A component, by the way, that David would do well to explore more deeply in his essay."

"You've read it?" This seemed to take the bravado away from Ellen, if only for a moment. She turned to me.

"Remember," I said quietly. "I told you she and Colter came over after rehearsal the other day?"

"You read it." Ellen pointed the tip of her mini-iron at Vanessa, and the cord rattled against the table. "So, what do *you* think he needs to do?"

"Let's leave my essay out of it," I said.

Ellen pressed the iron down onto the decal of a smiling purple narwhal. "No, I'm interested in her professional opinion. As a tutor. Pretend David's not right here. What did you think of the essay?"

"It was okay," Vanessa said. She looked at me for some indication as to how she should respond, but I had nothing. If there'd been an eject button on this conversation, I would have pressed it long ago. "A little cold, actually, which is strange coming from someone like David, who clearly cares deeply about a lot of things."

I took this as a gesture to my relationship with Ellen, but I'm not sure she was in the mood to see it the same way.

"Guys," Bernie said. "We're closing, okay? Can you wrap it up?"

Saved by the preteen, I thought. I pulled out some cash and motioned for Vanessa and Ellen not to move. "Don't worry about it. This is my treat."

Ellen held up her shirt—a mythical zoo from hell. "We weren't exactly reaching for our wallets."

At least Vanessa laughed. At least that was something. It may have even been something to build on. I held out hope that school the next week would be better, that me being the common enemy once again would, against all odds, bring them closer together.

17

ggy Rockwell punched me on Tuesday at the beginning of lunch period. I had been minding my own business, as the saying goes, when he met me at my locker, spun me around, and delivered a knuckle sandwich directly to my stomach. He wasn't helping me with research, either, in case I ever had to play a guy who got hit in the gut; it was the real thing. I doubled over and collapsed like I'd been shot.

I coughed on the floor and pushed myself to my hands and knees. "What the hell, Iggy?"

He squatted like a catcher and whispered into my ear. "Coach calls me into his office this morning. Says there was a note waiting for him when he got there. From me. Telling him I was quitting."

"What?"

"I'm trying to talk to him, but he gets in my face about how the way a real man communicates."

The hallways weren't exactly deserted; it was lunch, after all. I could tell by the shuffling that more than just a couple people had gathered to watch. Yet nobody was helping.

"This is none of anyone's business," Iggy said. "Move along."

I coughed again. "Why would I tell him?"

"It doesn't make sense, does it?" Iggy kicked my arms out from under me and my face smacked to the floor. Sharp pain spread from my cheekbone in all directions, wrapping my face like a mask.

"Iggy!" a voice called out. It was Geoff. My buddy, good old Geoff Cronyn. I thought he was going to come to my rescue, but apparently all he wanted was a front-row seat.

"Iggy, I swear—"

"Don't swear, David. Makes you look weak."

"You were wasted that night. I bet you told a hundred other people."

"And this?" He pulled a folded piece of paper from his back pocket and slid it on the floor beneath my face.

It was another collage, from The Artist, with action shots of Iggy on the basketball court surrounding a blown-up copy of his yearbook headshot. Stamped in capital red letters across the yearbook picture was the word QUIT-TER, and below it was the caption: TO THINE OWN SELF BE TRUE. THE ARTIST.

I recognized Felix's voice before his high-tops appeared in my field of view. "Mr. Edwards is coming."

"I had nothing to do with that," I said, pushing myself to a kneeling position.

He pointed to the collage. "That's Shakespeare, and you're a theatre freak. You do the math."

I looked up at him from my knees. He had me if he wanted me, execution style. I didn't know what to say.

And then Colter Stern burst onto the scene from out of nowhere and pushed a surprised Iggy back a few feet.

"Step away from the theatre freak," Colter said.

Iggy's massive shoulders bounced in rhythm with his laugh. "You don't want a taste of this."

"Come on, big man, what are you going to do, kick my ass?" He tried to sound nonchalant, but Colter's voice betrayed a hint of the fear that had to be just beneath the surface. You just didn't push Iggy Rockwell in the chest. "I'm like a hundred and thirty pounds. Where's the fun in that?"

"You might be surprised."

"Edwards," someone said.

My head was ringing, and I wanted to help Colter, but I couldn't make myself do anything other than sit on my heels. My stomach churned, and the muscles around it throbbed and twitched. It felt like a bomb had gone off inside me.

Colter picked up The Artist's collage, keeping himself between me and Iggy the whole time. "You're going to cry because someone put your picture on a bulletin board? Are you really a quitter?"

"This is my *life*," Iggy said. "You don't fuck with people's lives."

Felix grabbed a handful of Iggy's shirt and pulled him away. "Let's go, man. Edwards is coming."

And they were gone. Colter crumpled up the collage and threw it down the hall after them. He helped me to my feet and walked me to a spot on the stairs. There were varied murmurs of concern from the people who'd gathered, but I didn't pay attention to them, the cowards. It was easy to show support after the danger was gone. Mr. Edwards appeared at the end of the hallway, but there was no longer a fight to break up, so he just stood with his hands on his hips as the crowd dispersed. There was innocent whistling.

"Can I get you anything?" Colter said. "Bag of ice? Kevlar vest?"

I sat with my legs spread and my elbows on my knees. "You were like an avenging angel."

"Yeah, well. I think I might have peed myself a little."

"Don't tell anybody that," I said. "You had witnesses. People will think you're a badass."

He patted me gently on the shoulder. "Come on, let's get you some lunch."

I tried to stand, but the pain dropped me right back on the steps. I waved him off. "I'll just hang out here for a while."

He laughed. "I'm starving. Call me if you change your mind, and I'll bring you a veggie wrap or something."

"Deal," I said. "And Colter?"

He stopped about four steps above me. "Yeah?"

There was something I wanted to tell him, but I didn't know how to say it or even exactly what it was. Something about never having had a friend who would do what he did. About being grateful. But every time I thought I had the words, I became embarrassed by how inadequate they seemed, and how cliché.

"My pleasure," he said.

I don't know how long I sat alone at the foot of the stairway after he left, but it must have been most of lunch. I leaned my head against the wall and closed my eyes and felt the throbbing where my cheek had slapped the floor, and I prayed that whatever was going to happen to my face would disappear before my audition, only eight days away.

I could tell before I opened my eyes, before she said a word, that Ellen had settled down next to me. It was the jasmine. At least my nose still worked.

"Hey," she said. "I heard. You okay?"

I touched my cheek and winced. "I've never been in a fight before."

"Oh, sweetie." Ellen brushed the hair from my forehead and cupped her hand behind my neck. "I don't think that qualifies as a fight."

"Don't make me laugh," I said. The muscles in my stomach screamed at me. "Iggy thought I was The Artist."

Ellen pulled her hand away. "Are you?"

"I said don't make me laugh, remember?"

She had her hair in one of those big clips, so that it was pulled back but not too tight, kind of intentionally messy, and she looked and smelled so good, I could hardly stand it. What with all the rehearsals and homework and club meetings, she and I hadn't seen each other but in passing for the last couple days. This was as good a time to apologize as I was going to get.

I said, "I'm sorry about the other night."

"David Ellison, did I detect a quaver in your voice just

then? Are you manipulating me with your current pitiful condition?"

"That depends on if it's working."

"I don't know yet. I wanted to kill you after you dropped me off—"

"I deserved it, I know—"

"Let me finish." She patted her knees and stood up, hovering over me. "But then Amber encouraged me to look at it through your point of view—"

I winced again.

"Is it your stomach?" she said. "Maybe we should get you to—"

"That one wasn't from the pain. You told Amber?"

Ellen laughed out loud. "You expected me to keep that one a secret?"

"And Amber stuck up for me?"

"So to speak. She reminded me that your idea, while foolish and irrational from any objective point of view, probably at some point made sense to your pea-size Neanderthal imbecile brain."

I grasped the handrail and pulled myself to my feet. Now standing, my stomach hurt less. As long as I could keep from laughing. "So, you're not mad?"

It was her turn to wince. "I didn't say that. Only that I'm willing to give you the benefit of the doubt regarding your monumentally stupid plan to make BFFs out of Vanessa and me."

"Let's go see a movie," I said.

She stepped back a bit, shook her head slightly as

though confused by the direction I'd gone. She recovered after a slight pause. "Okay, I guess. Friday or Saturday is—"

"No, right now."

"You mean ditch the rest of the day?"

"Don't worry," I said. "We'll come back right as school gets out—that way you can still go to your Amnesty International meeting, and I'll go to rehearsal. You don't have any tests today, right?"

"Two quizzes tomorrow. And I have to cover the desk at my parents' office tonight."

"Can't you study there?"

It was a long shot; I knew for a fact that she'd never skipped out on even a single class, let alone an entire afternoon of them, but it seemed like the only thing to do. I'd get her off campus, and we could talk more about the Vanessa thing.

I put my arm around her and whispered in her ear. "Maybe we can even sit in the back row."

"Okay," she said, almost giggling. The skin of her neck grew warm against my arm. "Okay, let's do it."

She could still surprise me, after almost two years. I loved that. "What do you want to see?"

A siren's slow wail filtered into the hallway from outside. Then another one, higher-pitched and faster. Maybe an ambulance and a fire engine? A police car?

Amber came up to us just then, right on cue for the character of Annoying Third Wheel. "Get a room," she said.

"Get a boyfriend."

"Touché. I heard you kicked Iggy's ass."

It hurt when I shrugged, but the moment demanded it. "He let me win."

My phone rang. The caller ID said it was Vanessa, so I quickly replaced the phone in my pocket. Talking to Vanessa, even if it was just a phone call, would make Ellen reconsider.

"So," I said to Ellen. I pointed at Amber with my eyes. I smiled real wide.

Amber groaned. "Would you guys stop it with the telepathy already? If you want to say something, just say it."

"Fine. Amber, would you please leave us alone? I would like to make out with my girlfriend—"

Ellen snaked a quick backhand against my chest. I yelped.

"Oops," Ellen said.

"Harder," Amber said.

I said, "Whatever happened to honesty being the best policy?"

My phone rang again. Again it was Vanessa.

"You going to get that?" Ellen said.

"It'll just be a second, I promise. And then we can make out for sure." I answered the phone. "Hello?"

"I don't know who else to call." Her voice came through sobs. "They almost killed him."

"What? Wait, Vanessa, slow down."

Amber and Ellen whipped their heads up and stared at me. Ellen said, "What—"

"Shh," I said to them, finger to my lips.

"I'm going to go to the hospital," Vanessa said.

"What's wrong? Who's hurt? Killed who?" There was silence on her end. "Hello? Vanessa?"

"It's Colter. Will you meet me there? Please?"

When the line went dead, I turned back to Amber and Ellen, who were both waiting with eyebrows raised. "She said Colter was attacked. He's going to the hospital."

"Why?" Ellen said.

Amber shrugged. "He *is* kind of annoying."

"The thing before lunch," I said. "With Iggy—" My heart sank. "It was because of me. Because he stood up for me."

Ellen said, "And you're going?"

"What does that mean? Colter's my friend."

"Are you getting defensive?" Amber said.

The back of my neck was starting to itch. I pulled Ellen to me and gave her a nice, firm kiss on the cheek. "Rain check on the movie?" I said. Then I got the hell out of there, Amber and stomach pain be damned. I knew it was risky, but it was better to leave the two of them talking about what an idiot I was than to stick around and prove it.

18

The nurse was a three-hundred-pound Asian woman with pens lining the pockets of her teal scrubs like a war hero's medals. "He's ready to see the rest of you," she said, stepping onto the maroon carpet. Mrs. Stern stood behind her and stared straight ahead.

We sat in the Stanford University Medical Center waiting room. Vanessa, her dad, and I clustered around a small coffee table piled high with back issues of *Vogue* and *Highlights for Children*. Nobody had said much in the three hours we'd been waiting. At least one of the nurses had given me an ice pack for my cheek.

"He wanted to take karate," Mr. Stern had mumbled at one point. "When he was seven years old, but I told him it was a waste of time."

I hadn't called Ellen yet, mostly because I hadn't yet figured out what to tell her, but also because my phone got no reception in the waiting room, which seemed impossibly stupid. If any place needed to have phone reception, it would be the hospital waiting room.

We all stood and walked toward the nurse, but Mr. Stern glanced at me and shook his head uneasily. "Do you mind if we . . . family."

Vanessa handed me the calculus textbook she'd been studying. "Wait for me?"

The three of them and the nurse all looked at me, as though challenging me to duck out now, after we'd come this far together. "Of course," I said. "I'll be right here."

They disappeared through the doors. I shuffled back to my chair. The thick textbook bounced off the cushion when I tossed it, and I left it on the floor, cover splayed and pages bent like a jumper on the sidewalk.

I couldn't afford to spend my whole day here; Big Pro was going to kick my ass if I was late to rehearsal. My audition was a week away. And there was the little issue of coming up with the best way to explain to Ellen why I wasn't making out with her in the back of a movie theater.

I eased down and leaned back, putting my hands to my forehead. I couldn't use my phone in the waiting room, and I didn't want to duck out in case Vanessa came back quickly. I took a deep breath of stale hospital air, and all the thoughts jockeying for space in my head started to come together. Vanessa and Ellen and my audition. My monologues. Tribulation Wholesome.

You've brought this on yourself, he'd say to me. How do you expect to withstand temptation when you've surrounded yourself with it?

"Thank you, David."

My eyes snapped open. I sat up straight and rubbed the blur away. Had I fallen asleep? The waiting room was still quiet. Vanessa's mom sat on the chair across from the small table, looking at me but not really looking *at* me. The clock above her shoulder said they'd been gone for almost an hour. I was officially late for rehearsal.

"You were there for her, for Vanessa. When she needed you." It sounded less an expression of gratitude than an accusation or a statement of disbelief. I felt the odd urge to justify myself.

I said, "She's my friend." So lame.

But I almost said, "I already have a girlfriend," which would have been even lamer.

Mrs. Stern crossed her legs and pressed against the top kneecap with both hands. "We raised our children to respect others," she said without looking at me. "Why would someone do this?"

I chose not to tell her why; I didn't want to see accusation in her eyes. It's horrible to admit, but in my mind, I actually pulled back from our conversation like a movie camera, seeing us in wide angle. I thought, "This is what grief looks like." I noticed the positioning of her head, the tone of her voice, the way she seemed to be crying by so clearly struggling not to cry. I'd have to remember all of that if I ever had to play a character in her situation.

"I'm really sorry," a character in my situation would have said. So I did.

She looked down and picked a piece of invisible lint from her skirt. She spread an invisible wrinkle from the fabric and shook her head. "After everything we went through in Boston."

She'd said it more to herself than out loud, so I didn't

know if she expected me to respond. I waited for more: a word, a glance. Something.

"What hap—" I stopped myself, caught between the desire to satisfy my curiosity and my instinct to show consideration for what she was going through.

"That was not awesome," Vanessa said as she collapsed next to me. She noticed her text on the floor and leaned over to pick it up, tenderly smoothing out the pages as though it were an ancient and fragile document.

Her eyes were red and puffy, and her face still had the sheen of water on it. The doctor said Colter had suffered from contusions, cracked ribs, and a slight concussion. They'd been worried about internal bleeding, but he was okay. Out of the woods, so to speak.

"I really should go," I said.

She nodded and put the calculus book on the table. Her mom startled when Vanessa patted her on the shoulder. "I'll be right back."

I said good-bye to Mrs. Stern and let Vanessa lead me toward the elevator. "He doesn't blame me, does he?" I said.

She managed to keep it together until we were alone in the elevator, when suddenly she had her head on my shoulder and her arms wrapped tight around me. "Vanessa," I whispered, "the doctor said he's going to be fine."

The elevator doors opened at the ground floor, but we held our embrace, and after a moment they closed again.

"He's going to be okay."

"I know."

"One thing's for sure," I said, patting her gently on the back. "Iggy's going to have to find himself a new tutor."

She slapped me on the shoulder and wiped her tears away through the laughter. The doors opened again, and we stepped out of the elevator as a cluster of white-coated doctors took our place.

"I'm sorry about the other night with Ellen," I said. "I thought maybe you were mad at me because you haven't worn your T-shirt yet."

"You mean my psychedelic representation of the four seasons?"

"Oh, is that what that was? Anyway, thanks for understanding. I just wanted to show her that you weren't a threat."

Vanessa stiffened. "No threat?"

"You know what I mean."

"Wait a minute," she said. "I have nothing to do with whatever problems you're having with your girlfriend, and—"

"Vanessa—"

"*You're* the one who took me up to the catwalk, *you're* the one who wanted me to read your essay, and *you're* the one who came over to my house and told Ellen that you were with your dad. Don't you dare try to pin any of that on me, not here. Not now."

"Vanessa, wait!"

She showed me her back and pressed the elevator button once, then five times. Tired of waiting for the doors to open, she stalked off down the hall and disappeared into the stairwell. I waited for a few minutes, just in case she came back down, but she didn't. Of course she didn't.

I showed up to rehearsal over an hour late. We couldn't run any of the Daisy/Nick scenes we'd scheduled because Vanessa was still at the hospital, and I stumbled my way through the car scene with Tom so badly that Big Pro yanked me off stage and decided to run the Gatsby/James Gatz flashback instead. I was invited to watch, sit tight, and get my head "out of my ass."

I'd been steaming in the audience for about five minutes when Geoff Cronyn sat down in front of me. He turned around, resting his elbow on the back of the seat.

"Vanessa going to be okay?"

"I don't think it's Vanessa they're worried about."

He was quiet for a while. Then he looked back at the stage, where Big Pro was demonstrating proper rowboat technique for the freshman playing the young Gatz.

"They're taking the suit to court soon, my parents. Expedited schedule, or something like that. Early admission is just over a month away, so they're going for a temporary injunction."

He was telling me this because I had pretended to care, but I didn't want to talk about it. I didn't want to talk about anything. "Geoff—"

"Are you applying?" he said.

"Do you mind if we don't—"

"No, that's cool. You don't have to tell me."

"It's a rowboat!" Big Pro leaned forward and grabbed

at the air. "You have to pull if you want to go anywhere. Christ."

Geoff scooted forward on the seat and turned around to face me with both hands holding the backrest. "Cast parties are cool, right? I mean, I've heard some stories. My parents are going to Mendocino this week for their yearly Zen retreat, and the house will be empty. I thought maybe we could have a kind of cast party dress rehearsal. I wanted to ask your—"

"You don't need to ask me. I'm sure—"

"Sweet," he said, facing the stage once more. There was silence, and then he said, "I'm sure Colter's going to be okay."

"He'd better be."

"Hey, dumbasses!" Big Pro yelled at us. "This place? Where you're sitting? With the lights and the stage and the seats all around it? It's called a theater. They do plays here. You want to shut up for just a second?"

We left it at that.

19

Administrative outrage is the best. Deans and advisers reach deep into their bags of rhetoric; teachers pretend they've never done anything irresponsible or illegal. Everyone older than eighteen hits us with the ridiculous combination of dour expression and disappointed nod. This was a college preparatory school, for goodness sakes, not a reality television show!

"It's because we are a community," Headmaster Lunardi was saying. "We strive together, we fail together, and we pull each other up when we need it."

A lectern had been placed center stage, and with the play just over two weeks away the set was rounding into shape. Various scenery flats leaned against the upstage wall: Gatsby's mansion, the Wilsons' garage, the distant shore of East Egg. Ellen and I sat stage left in the audience about halfway down. She looked fantastic today, her shorts showing off that natural tan, her hair set back with a swath of green ribbon and a bow that tickled her neck. Given how early it was, we hadn't been able to talk much yet. Amber was to her left as if acting as chaperone. At least I had a little theatre geek backup; Jake Starr was on my right.

Vanessa sat on the opposite side of the audience, staring straight ahead, her jaw set as though steeling herself;

nobody had expected her to be at school, given what had happened the day before, and I think everyone had been counting on at least a day of unfettered gossip about Colter.

"As I'm sure many of you are aware," Lunardi said, official as can be, "one of your classmates was attacked yesterday in what appeared to be an act of retribution for the recent series of anonymous postings on the senior bulletin board. And Iggy Rockwell has been suspended from school indefinitely, pending a thorough investigation."

A collective gasp spread through the audience. Our basketball team was supposed to be good this year—last year we made it to the regional semifinals, and we only graduated a bench guy. But Iggy was the best player in the league. Without him, Oak Fields wouldn't stand a chance.

"It is not currently known who was in fact responsible for the aforementioned postings, though I would ask those of you with any knowledge of such to please come forward." Here the headmaster paused while he ran his glowering eyes across the width of his audience. "However, violence is not an appropriate response."

Lunardi nodded to the dean as he stalked offstage, and Donaldson rose from the front row and took his position behind the lectern. "I want to thank you all for gathering here on late notice," the dean said. "I don't enjoy shortening classes at such an important time in the school year, but this can't wait. As Headmaster Lunardi has just indicated, life at Oak Fields has grown increasingly . . . complicated recently. We've invited Dr. Frank Dudley here today to address this with you." The dean stepped back and motioned to a wiry man well over six feet tall, probably closer to seven. "Dr. Dudley?"

The doctor shook Donaldson's hand and stepped onstage, hunching over as though to avoid a low ceiling. "Good morning." His voice was almost entirely nasal, like the words were terrified of his bushy chin beard and were trying to sneak out through his nose. It was hard to imagine anyone taking him seriously long enough for him to become a doctor. "I'd like to talk to you today . . . about stress."

A low chuckle from the audience.

"Ladies and gentlemen!" the dean said.

Ellen leaned in to me and whispered, "I'm sorry about your friend."

"Thank you. I appreciate you saying that."

"Mr. Ellison," the dean said.

I almost protested, but the dean's glare shut my mouth.

Ellen whispered again, "Do you think it was easy for me to sit across from you and Vanessa and hear you talk about acting like it was the only thing that mattered to you both?"

I glanced at her and motioned to the room with my palm open like a plea. "Here?"

"I swear to God, David. If you can't talk to me—"

"I want to talk to you."

Jake and the other people sitting nearby had to be listening in, which made me almost as anxious as the conversation itself. This wasn't the first time Ellen had tried to have a talk like this in a less-than-private setting. When she had something on her mind, she wanted to discuss it. She didn't care where she was, and she obviously didn't expect me to care either. But that was sometimes too much to ask.

Dr. Dudley, meanwhile, was going on about the importance of stress management, sounding like he was letting little bursts of air escape from an inflated balloon. Squeak, squeak, squeakety squeak squeak.

"I'm serious," she said. "And it's not jealousy—"

"There's nothing there—"

"Except for the kiss. The fantasy kiss."

My jaw was set in stone. The words squeezed out through a tiny slit in the corner of my mouth. "Are we still—"

"Mr. Ellison!" the dean said. How was it possible that he only noticed me?

"You know I can't compete with that," Ellen said. "And you flaunted it."

"Flaunted? Whatever happened to the idea making sense when seen through my Neanderthal brain?"

Amber mumbled something I couldn't understand.

"That was before you ran away yesterday," Ellen said.

"Colter was in the hospital!"

"You invited me to a movie," she said. "We were going to ditch school. Sit in the back row. Yesterday was supposed to be about us."

"I thought you didn't want to be seen as the high-maintenance type?"

Ellen breathed in sharply, almost a gasp. I felt the

warmth of her anger on my skin like a sunburn.

"You are such an asshole," Amber said.

"What the hell do you expect from me?" The words just came out.

The dean's voice obliterated the silence. "Ellison! One more time and you're in detention for a week. Now pay attention and learn how to relax!" He turned to Dr. Dudley and bowed an apology, but Dudley didn't seem to have noticed.

"Very well, then," Dr. Dudley said, moving to a small table covered with stacks of light green paper. "I'd like to use this opportunity to go over a few actionable steps we all might be able to take."

The dean assigned a volunteer from each row to help distribute the papers. I took the top sheet from the stack Ellen handed to me and passed the rest down the row.

New Horizons Stress Relief, said the paper in front of me, along with crude drawings of a balloon, a heart, and a happy face. Below the header was a space for my name, and below that a series of columns: Daily Stresses, Relationship Stresses, School Related Stresses, and Miscellaneous Stresses.

"What I'd like all of you to do right now is to list all of the various aspects of your life that contribute stress. Please organize them according to category."

"Can I get another sheet?" Sophie said, to muffled laughter.

Dudley acknowledged the joke with a slight nod. "One thing I find particularly helpful is to make a to-do list every morning of what's expected of me. That way, I can cross the items off throughout the day."

Somehow I didn't think that making lists of things that stress me out was a way to get rid of that stress. To-do lists were something that New David could handle once in a while, but Old David freaked out at the mere sight of one. Ellen was always taunting me with them. Entire pages of boxes to check, all organized by section and sub-section: school, college, home.

Amber raised her hand. "Excuse me?"

"Young lady?" Dr. Dudley said.

"Would you talk about the effect of stress on decision-making—"

"Amber, stop," Ellen whispered.

But Amber did not stop. "Specifically with regard to the area of adolescent emotions and their impact on relationships."

Ellen said, "Amber."

I could feel my heart start to thrash in my chest. Blood would redden my neck and then my face if I didn't get it under control, and soon. I focused on the sheet, but I couldn't make myself list anything. I realized that by ignoring her I was only calling more attention to myself, so I looked up. Everyone was staring at me. Not at Ellen, not at Amber, who for some unknown freaking reason was still talking. Vanessa sat with her hands neatly folded in her lap like an old lady in a rocking chair.

"I just think that's something we can all benefit from," Amber said. "You know, at this stage of our development."

The tip of Dr. Dudley's index finger got lost in his goatee. "Neurological science tells us that the frontal lobe of the human brain—which is responsible for decision-making among other things—does not fully develop until the early to mid-twenties. Consequently, the adolescent brain is more susceptible to outside forces, such as stress, that would indeed allow one's emotional state to affect the decision-making process."

Amber leaned forward. "So you're saying that stress might cause an otherwise relatively normal person to behave like a complete jackass? Pardon my French."

Everyone in the audience was paying attention for the first time that morning, some even leaning forward in their seats. Dr. Dudley must have noticed this, and he must have been unnerved by it, because he stood up straight and cleared his throat.

"I'd be happy to discuss this particular area of interest of yours after the seminar has concluded," he said to Amber. "We're a little pressed for time."

Then he held up a sheet of his own and flicked it—pop!—with his other hand. "Now, back to the checklists."

Dr. Dudley sent us off with a stress relief pamphlet and a 1-800 number for the New Horizons Stressicide Hotline. The dean glared at me the whole time I shuffled toward the aisle.

Ellen stopped me on the other side of the door and pulled me away from the stragglers.

"I'm sorry," Ellen said. "She shouldn't have said any of that."

"She's your friend. She was just trying to look out for you."

"That got a little out of control. I wish you'd talk to me."

I looked over my shoulder at the people still coming out of the theater. I thought back to our first date when—after I'd spent the whole night wondering if she liked me, if she was laughing at me or my jokes—she'd reached for my hand without even looking at me. I'd felt the strangest mix of calmness and exhilaration, and I'd known that it was all going to be okay.

"What happened?" I said. "Everything used to be so simple."

"Whatever it is, I hope we figure it out soon," she said.

I held her by both hands and pressed my forehead against hers. After a moment, she squeezed my hands and looked up, and I kissed her. It was a short one, a school kiss. It's funny, the moments that strike you as important, the moments you find yourself wanting to hold on to. They almost never advertise themselves. This is one of them, I realized, this short kiss measured in tenths, if not hundredths, of a second. Hold on to this. I tried, I really did, but then it was time to go.

20

was not in a good place. Dr. Frank Dudley might have gone so far as to argue that my stress level was in danger of negatively impacting my emotional stability. Big Pro snapped at me every chance he got. Juilliard was the following week. I'd hardly seen Ellen over the last couple of days, and people all over school were blaming me for what happened to Iggy. As if somehow I'd baited him into kicking Colter's ass and getting suspended.

Saturday night's cast party was exactly what I needed to escape from it all.

Geoff's house was so high up the Santa Cruz Mountains—almost to Skyline—that the nearest neighbor was a protected swath of land Stanford used for botany experiments. The thick trunks of ancient redwood trees guarded the property like Grecian columns, and a wide swimming pool spread across an expansive back lawn, with palapas dotting the grass at seemingly random intervals.

Because the party was cast and crew only, any differences between the two groups disappeared. We knew each so other well, had spent so much time together, that our inhibitions disappeared along with our differences. An eclectic mix of rock, hip-hop, and house music thumped from an outdoor speaker system, and the swimming pool was filled with revelers—some in their underwear and some in nothing at all.

Geoff was blitzed, and there was no escape from that. He had me by both shoulders, his arms straight like we were sixth grade slow-dancers, lolling his head so that he looked up at me through the mop of wet hair as it dripped across his forehead. He'd lost his pants at some point, and his remaining clothes—yellow polo shirt, blue and orange striped boxers, white socks—clung drenched to his body.

"You know you're like a brother to me, right?" Geoff's words came through remarkably un-slurred, but they were over-enunciated as if he'd learned only to speak phonetically, without any awareness of the meaning. "You know that. I've told you that before or if I haven't I should have because it's true."

In my experience, the best way to handle drunk sincerity was to deflect it right back at the drunk himself. "I appreciate that, Geoff. I really do. Your friendship means a lot to me."

"People think I'm some rich asshole. I know they do. Ever since my parents convinced Mrs. Moore to give me an A."

"That was true?"

"But I'm a good guy inside, I swear. I'm no asshole. And the stage knows it." Now he tilted his head back to look at me down his nose. "The stage doesn't care who you are or how much money your parents donate to the

Annual Fund. The lights don't care if you have the right girlfriend."

"Take it easy. You only have three lines."

"I know! Isn't it amazing? I mean, I can't imagine how it must feel for you, all the time out there, star of the show, line after line after line. You know what? How do you remember all those *lines*, man?"

Geoff was depressing me. I tried to remember a time when I felt that way about acting. Sure, I enjoyed it. I liked observing people and losing myself in my characters and blah, blah, blah—at least that's what I still told myself—but the joy of it was something I don't think I'd experienced in years. My audition was only four days away, and the pressure had made the whole thing feel like an exercise.

He pulled me close, and his gin breath turned my stomach. "My parents are dropping the suit, did you know that? But guess what? I don't care! Who needs Stanford? Who needs college? I'm an actor now! I can do anything!"

I raised my arms between his and brought them down, breaking his grasp on my shoulders as I grabbed his forearms. Kind of like anti-drunk jujitsu. "Baby steps, Geoff. Baby steps."

I spun him around and pushed him back toward the pool, and he flailed his arms up. "Hark! Is thateth a skinny dippeth I see before me?"

Francine and Vanessa were talking to Corky, who looked like the top and bottom half of two entirely different people. Her lower body was all Alice in Wonderland:

striped cheerleader's skirt with red knee-high stockings and purple low-top Chuck Taylors, while her upper body was Alice in Chains: black tank top, black lace bra showing underneath, black lipstick and eyeliner, pierced nose, lip, eyebrow, and ear.

"Mr. Carraway," Corky said when I wedged myself into their triangle. "You seem to be bereft of a beverage."

"I'll get there," I said. "Hey, Francine. What is this, twice in three weeks?"

"I'm a regular party girl. Next thing you know I'll be date-raping someone." There was a short pause. "Too far?"

"Do you ladies mind if I steal Vanessa for a second?"

"I think you mean does Vanessa mind if you steal Vanessa for a second." Corky laughed. "Just because the play is set in the 1920s doesn't mean you—"

"Got it." I looked at Vanessa. "Excuse me, Vanessa? May I speak to you for a moment, please?"

"Much better," Corky said.

I grabbed a bottle of Boone's Snow Creek Berry from a cooler by the diving board, and followed Vanessa just up the gentle hill overlooking the swimming pool. We sat underneath one of the redwoods and watched the party in silence. I unscrewed the Boone's and drank and offered it to her.

"How's your brother?"

She took a sip and passed the bottle back to me. "He'll be at school next week."

"Lucky him."

"As he told my dad, he'll get back to not doing sports in no time."

"How'd that go over?"

She shrugged. "About as well as you'd guess."

Vanessa picked up a dry pine needle. She rolled it between her fingers before snapping it in half and letting the loose pieces fall to the ground. "Ellen's not going to wait around for you to get your shit together, and nor should she. It's not fair to her, and you know it."

I was trapped. That's what I knew. When I was with Ellen, I wanted to be with her. I loved being with her. I loved *her*. But when I was around Vanessa, she was the one I wanted. Ellen had been right about that part all along. I didn't see it. I didn't want to let myself see it, because I thought I was better than that.

Down at the pool, a small crowd had gathered near the diving board, where Geoff and Jake were crouched and fiddling with something. From time to time, Geoff would point and give an order, and one of the guys would run into the house and return quickly, carrying something or other: a coffee can, a roll of duct tape, an extension cord.

When I said nothing, Vanessa finally grabbed the bottle and took a swig. "How's the narrative coach going?"

"There's no way I'm letting you anywhere near her. Vanessa Stern, breakout star of the Oak Fields senior class."

I thought I saw her blush. "Oh, please."

"Seriously, you're going to be that good."

We passed the Boone's back and forth whenever conversation lulled. I couldn't help feeling a juvenile thrill at the thought that my lips were touching hers, in a way. And repeatedly.

Her voice became low and far too serious for the occasion. "I think I could use her help."

"Is that a little false modesty I hear?"

She looked straight ahead as though she hadn't heard me. "How can my self-worth—my whole *family's* self-worth—be dependent on what a few strangers on the admissions committee have to say about an application that's probably exactly like a thousand others?"

"What's your essay about?"

She opened her mouth but caught herself before the first syllable escaped. She tapped the bottle on my forehead. "Are you trying to take advantage of my buzz?"

"I showed you mine. Now you show me yours. It's only fair."

She furrowed her brow. "We're still talking about the essay, right?"

"Do you really think it's the most important document we'll ever write? That stuff Edwards said about our college decision shaping our future—"

She took a deep breath, exhaling in a long, tortured sigh. "We're not supposed to die, you know? We're supposed to do great things. We're supposed to change the world."

It was a moment before I realized she was talking about her essay.

"JJ was my best friend. She was the kind of person admissions guys like Michael Parson dream about. Smart, athletic, driven like you wouldn't believe. No matter how hard I work, I'll never come close." She looked down at the spotty grass. She shook her head. "It was a car accident."

The idea of early death lingered in the night air. Neither of us seemed to want to touch it. I could hardly imagine one of my friends dying, and the only way I ever thought of my own death was by occasionally imagining myself at my own funeral. I hoped it would be well-attended, that there would be sobs of sadness at my loss, that I would have been well-liked, but you never know.

"Our college counselor promised us that a great junior year would put us over the hump." Vanessa took a deep breath. "It's hard not to blame myself."

"Why would you?"

"You know how competition is. I get an A, she has to get an A. I do activities—"

"Did you hit her with your car?" I held up the bottle. "Did you force-feed her Boone's before she got behind the wheel?"

"I told her I was coming after her, so she'd better watch out. Valedictorian was all mine. I said there was no way she could keep it up." She looked away. "Don't tell Colter you know, okay? I made him swear not to tell anybody."

I remembered the glint in Vanessa's eyes at the play's first read-through and how jealous I was that she already had the type of depth Big Pro said I didn't have. As a person and a friend I felt horrible for her. But, and I would never have said this out loud, as an actor I was still a little envious. If actors were supposed to draw upon the emotional memories of their own experiences, wasn't there real value there?

I put my arm around her and pulled her close. She hesitated for a moment and then nestled into my side like she belonged there. I felt my pulse in every inch of my body at once. Had I ever felt this way about Ellen? In the beginning? Had Ellen's touch been so powerful? It must have been, or else why would we have kept coming back to each other?

In the distance, Geoff climbed onto the diving board and motioned for people in the water to give him space. Jake stood off to the side, his attention focused on the brick-size object he had in his hand.

Geoff sprinted three steps to the end of the board and then jumped the last step as high as he could. The board bowed down, only inches from the surface of the water when it reached the flex limit. At the precise moment Geoff was launched into the air, a silent and blinding flash erupted from the base of the board, sending white light ten feet high and thick billowing plumes of smoke even higher. Geoff was silhouetted against the flash as he shot skyward, arms outstretched, before curling into a tight ball and rolling forward twice, and then knifing headfirst into the pool.

There was silence as the pluming smoke reflected off the outdoor floodlights and dissipated. Then Geoff pierced the surface with a scream of victory, and everyone around him broke into wild cheers and applause.

Vanessa started to say something but thought better of it, and I was glad she did because instead of talking, she angled her head and pushed her lips against mine. The kiss was gentle at first, tentative. We separated and looked at each other, and I thought I saw her smile. She brushed her fingers against what was left of the bruise on my cheekbone.

"Mmmm," she said.

I said, "Uh-oh."

Just then, the back door opened, and Keegan stormed through with a holler. Then came two people behind him, and then another, like roaches from a flooded drain. Crashers. It was as though they'd all bailed on another party and were arriving at the same time.

Geoff pulled himself out of the pool, waving his arms to some of his friends and pointing to the board. There was a general sense of unease among the *Gatsby* cast and crew as the newcomers multiplied. Was the cast party really being invaded like this?

"I knew Geoff couldn't keep his mouth shut," I said, holding up the empty bottle. "I'm going to get another. Don't go anywhere."

"I don't see her, if that's what you're worried about."

"See who?"

"Right," Vanessa said.

I weaved through the crowd, which had grown to at least twice its earlier size. I noticed Felix holding a beer in each hand and one in his waistband, so I scanned above everyone's heads for Iggy, but he wasn't there yet, if he was coming at all. Neither was Amber or Ellen. Jake was refilling the poolside pyrotechnics, this time surrounded by Keegan and a couple other guys, all focused on the primal joy of making things blow up.

Even the pool was crowded and, contrary to what I'd figured would happen, the theatre geeks were still swimming, some of them still naked. A few crashers had stripped and joined them. Maybe everyone would get along. Maybe just for one night the newcomers would embrace the vibe, and everyone would forget about college applications and APs and clubs and grades and The Artist.

And then Ellen walked through the back door.

"Hey," I said.

"I was hoping you'd still be here."

"Yeah, still here." I looked over my shoulder, but Vanessa had moved from our spot up the hill. I peeked down at the empty bottle for any smudges of lipstick around the rim. I felt like the guy in "The Tell-Tale Heart," whose guilty conscience makes him rip up the floorboards to expose the dead body.

"Boone's, huh?" she said. "Since when?"

"Yeah. I—"

Francine brushed by, followed by Geoff, who was still in his boxers but had ditched his shirt. "M'lady! M'lady! Won't you play a tune for us?" Now he was singing. "Franciiine, dear Franciiiine, play me a tune with those pianist's hands."

I reached after him and grabbed his wrist. "That's enough."

"Those pianist's hands! Penis hands!" He staggered to her but I came around and put my arms straight against his chest, pushing him backward. He yelled over my shoulder. "Come give me a penis hand. A hand, or a blow? A blow!"

Francine stopped by the patio furniture near the back door twenty feet away and turned around to watch. Corky and Jake appeared at her side as if for protection. For some reason, the spectators made an oval around us, with me and Geoff at one end and Francine at the other. This show was not to be missed.

Geoff offered me the wide-eyed, pleading look of a little kid trying to convince his mom to buy the extra candy. "I'm a good guy, David, remember? I swear. I just want a beej."

"You don't need a beej right now," I said.

"Everyone needs a beej!" Geoff shouted. "Come on, Francine, beej me!"

I pushed him back to the edge of the crowd, but Geoff used my own anti-drunk jujitsu move on me and broke free. He shouted into the air. "Beej me!"

The tiles were soaking wet from all the swimmers running back and forth, and that's what must have done it. When he made his move toward Francine, she stepped back and slipped. She fell in slow motion—it seemed as if there was plenty of time for me to cover the twenty feet myself—but as soon as her left arm crashed through the top of the glass coffee table, the pandemonium was instant.

The circle disintegrated; the spell was broken. Everyone yelled at once, running around like panicked yard ants. Geoff collapsed to his hands and knees and wailed apologies to anyone who would listen.

Francine splayed on the ground, with one arm still stuck in the frame of the table and shards of glass sparkling through the growing pool of blood.

Jake knelt over her. "Do we move it?"

"Someone call an ambulance," I shouted.

"I didn't mean it!" Geoff said. The emotion in his eyes was raw. Regret.

Jake pulled off his T-shirt, and we helped Francine sit forward as we wrapped her hand and arm to stop the bleeding. "It's going to be okay," he said.

She whispered, "I can't move my fingers."

Ambulance meant cops, so people were practically trampling over one another to get out the door. The swimmers gathered their clothes or, if they couldn't find them right away, simply left half-naked. Ellen looked at the mass exodus and back down at me. I knew what she was thinking—getting caught here by the cops, no matter that she'd only just arrived, would be nothing but bad.

"I didn't mean for that to happen," Geoff was howling.

"Do you want me to stay?" Ellen said.

"No, that's okay." I looked up. "But thanks. Corky, call an ambulance!"

"No, don't," Geoff said, drunk and wet and waving

his arms in the air like a surrendering soldier. "My parents would kill me. You can't call an ambulance!"

Corky froze with the phone in her hand.

Vanessa stepped forward. "I'll take her."

"You're okay to drive?" I said. "You sure?"

Ellen cocked her head at me. Everything was moving so quickly that I didn't have the time to wonder what she was thinking.

Jake and Vanessa cleared a path through the living room, past the grand piano in the corner, and I followed with Francine and Corky.

We reached Vanessa's Mercedes and loaded Francine into the front. I reached across her to buckle the seat belt, and she stopped me with the fear in her eyes. "Why can't I feel my fingers?"

Corky hopped into the backseat as Vanessa gunned the engine to life, and I said, "You know where to go?"

"Are you really asking me that question?"

"Right, sorry. But be careful." I slammed the door and slapped my hand on the top of the car. Vanessa left the driveway, and Jake and I watched until the sound of her engine disappeared. In those few moments of action, someone had turned the music off, and now the house was eerily silent.

Ellen was gone.

"You did good just then," Jake said.

"You, too—"

"No, I mean it. In control and everything. You took charge."

"Yeah, well."

Jake sat on the edge of a small fountain in the middle of the driveway. The leaves of a vine tattoo wrapped around his bare chest. "I always thought you were kind of a pussy."

"Um, thanks?"

"I figured it was my job to test you. Blow stuff around you, keep you on your toes. I would never have thought you had this in you." He leaned to the side and pulled a small silver flask from his back pocket. He unscrewed the top, took a swig, and offered it to me.

I shuffled to the fountain and sat next to him. I accepted the flask and took a swig of my own. The whiskey burned as it went down, vapors coming up and out my nose, but I didn't choke or cough. I just said, "I don't even know what I have in me anymore."

21

The first thing I noticed as I steered the White Horse into the school parking lot the next Tuesday morning was Trinity Stampede sitting in a folding director's chair beside the rear wheel of the blue NBC-TV news van. She stared off toward the stadium and tapped a pen against a small spiral notebook on her lap.

"You two have a lot in common," my sister said. I'd gotten out of the house late, so there was no time to drop her off at the freshman lot. "She was an actress before she became a reporter."

I yanked the parking brake and gave her a smirk. "Did you have an essay due on her?"

"Her bio's right there on the NBC-TV Four Web site," she said. "She went to Carnegie Mellon, spent three years in New York at a place called the New School. She had a big role as a reporter in some off-Broadway play, and a news director from upstate saw her and thought she was so good that he offered her a job as a real reporter at his station."

"My ass."

"Oh, and her real name is Marianne Wolkowski." Lisa winked. "That wasn't in her bio, though. I had to dig for that."

I waited for Lisa to get out of the car, but she sat with her hands in her lap. "What?" I said.

"Why don't you ever ask my advice?"

"What are you talking about?"

"Do you think I exist in a vacuum? Like I disappear into a void of nothingness the moment you drop me off at school? Like I don't know you got beat up the other day or why it happened?"

The dashboard clock let me know I was already late for first period; there was no reason to hurry now. "I didn't get beat up."

"I have a lot to offer," she said defensively.

"I never said you didn't."

"It's not fair what you're doing to Ellen—"

"All right." I opened the door and stuck one foot onto the asphalt. "Great talking to you."

"Would you let me finish? Get back in. Okay, now close the door."

I slammed it shut. I waited.

"Like I said, it's not fair to—"

"Lisa!"

"But I get the whole Vanessa thing, that's what I was saying. I thought I might be able to help."

"Are you going to write me a computer program? Build me a cyborg companion to—"

"I'm a girl, David. I know girl things."

I said nothing, and this pissed her off.

"Just so you know, you don't exist in a vacuum, either. Everything you do has a direct effect on me and my life."

She got out and put on her backpack and leaned in with one hand on the open door and the other on the roof. "You might want to think of that the next time you get yourself involved in a love triangle."

With that, she slammed the door and huffed away. I leaned back against the headrest. My love life was the subject of freshman gossip. And I thought things couldn't get any more ridiculous.

The senior gossip mill was grinding about Geoff and his need for beej. Word was he felt horrible about what had happened, and I didn't blame him for staying home on Monday. Big Pro was less understanding, but we'd managed because Geoff only had three lines. Francine hadn't come to school, either.

According to Vanessa, who'd stayed at the hospital with Corky until Francine's mom arrived, there was reason to be optimistic. Even still, I couldn't get the image out of my head: Francine with her bloody hand clutched tight against her chest, trying not to look at the piano in Geoff's living room as we hustled her through. I typed her a get-well text and opened the door.

Morning classes had already begun, so the few remaining students in the parking lot only had enough time to shoot Trinity the occasional curious glance as they hustled past. I took my time, then stopped in front of her and waited. She didn't seem to notice.

"Hi," I said, reflexively clearing my throat.

She smiled politely and went back to her absent gazing.

I tried again. "Slow news day?"

I don't know if I was trying to ingratiate myself with her or just make sure she remembered me, because it was clear that she had no idea who I was. "I'm David Ellison? From a couple weeks ago? With the interview?"

She stood and tapped the notebook against her forehead as if to say, Duh! "Sorry. You all look the same to me. No offense."

"What's going on?"

"Just a follow-up. Now that the legal challenge has been dropped, I'm supposed to gauge the mood of the students. See if the new policy has had an effect on application strategies. Etcetera."

"Sounds hard-hitting,"

She laughed. "Tell me about it. I'd ask you for another comment, but I'm supposed to mix it up a bit."

"I'm not the greatest spokesman anyway," I said, figuring it would be best to keep the truth about the mood of the students to myself. No need to mention The Artist or Colter or Iggy's suspension or even Francine. We were already tearing one another apart just fine without the media's help.

I took a few steps to class, then stopped and turned around. "Hey, can I ask you a question? Off the record," I said with a smile.

"This should be good." She capped her pen and tucked it into the thicket of hair behind her ear.

"Why aren't you acting anymore?"

Trinity squinted. "Well, well, well. Someone discovered the Internet."

"Do you miss it?"

She chuckled. "It's not like what I'm doing now is much different. It's all performance."

"So you don't regret it? You don't look back on what could have been?"

There was just a moment when she let her eyes wander; then she laughed again. "Sometimes, when I see one of my friends in the paper, or on some sitcom or other, yeah, maybe I wish things had turned out differently. I assume you're not just asking to be polite?"

"I'm auditioning for Juilliard tomorrow."

She crossed her arms and narrowed her eyes at me. "I remember that look."

"What look?"

"You're starting to wonder, aren't you? Wondering if everything they've been telling you in high school is true or not, wondering if you're really destined for greatness. Wondering if maybe, just maybe, you're going to end up like your parents, stuck in thirty years with a mortgage and a house full of ungrateful kids and a job you hate, with all evidence that you'd ever dreamed of something more locked in the deep corners of your mind."

She stopped, waiting for my response. I looked toward the parking lot.

"No," I said, lying poorly. "I was just curious how you lived without it. Something that was such a part of you, and all."

"Here's the deal. My friends? The successful ones? They were willing to do whatever it took to make it happen, and I wasn't. Once I realized that I didn't want it as much as I thought I did, the decision was easy."

"Your dreams aren't locked in the deep corners of your mind?"

Trinity laughed and picked up her notepad. She withdrew her pen from behind her ear. "I didn't say that. Only that the decision was easy to make once my lack of desire became clear."

"You should come to my show," I said. "Opening night is two weeks from Thursday."

"High school theatre?" She winced. "Have a good one, David."

She uncapped her pen and flagged down a cluster of juniors at the far corner of the parking lot, leaving me standing alone next to her van. Reuben the cameraman shrugged in the front seat when I caught him staring at me.

22

I dropped by Francine's house that night after rehearsal. The roar of leaf blowers filled the air as I navigated the winding stone path through her half-manicured lawn. I knocked on the door, then quickly covered the Frosty in my hand lest any stray yard clippings try to infiltrate the chocolatey soft serve. I was about to knock again when Francine opened the door. Her left arm was in a sling, and a green fiberglass cast extended from her elbow and covered her hand like an oven mitt.

"I was in the neighborhood," I said, my fist still poised above a giant brass door knocker in the shape of a musical note. "Who doesn't love a Frosty?"

"Come on in." She snatched the Frosty with her good hand, and she led me through an enormous carpeted living room dominated by a polished black piano. Three massive bouquets filled the room with an aggressively sweet aroma.

"Secret admirer?"

"Geoff," she said. "Seems like I get a new one every couple of hours."

"Imagine if you'd gone ahead and beejed him."

The hallway walls were covered with a progression of Francine's school pictures, from her senior photo of her seated at the piano in a red formal dress with her fingers delicately poised atop the keys, to all the way back to kindergarten, with her hair in wispy ponytails and half her bottom teeth missing.

"Cute pictures. It's like time travel."

Francine shrugged. "Only child."

She placed the Frosty on a small table beside the couch in the TV room and tucked one leg under as she sat down. Then she wedged the Frosty between her legs and the couch pillows and spooned a huge bite.

"Thanks for the texts, by the way."

"It was—literally—the least I could do."

A healthy dollop fell from the spoon onto her T-shirt. "I'm still heavily medicated." She wiped the spot with her thumb and licked it. There was a deliberate nature to the way she moved, almost like a stop-motion photograph.

"How are your parents dealing? Only child and all."

"My mom doesn't want me to leave the house."

"Accidents happen, right?"

"Easy for you to say." She smiled as she held up her fiberglass-encased left hand. "You can still count to ten."

"You should know that Big Pro was appropriately devastated to lose the jazz piano."

"Isn't that sweet. He'll get better sound quality with the recorded stuff anyway."

"I've been worried about you. We all have."

"You should have seen me on Sunday. Moaning and crying, the whole deal. But my dad went to college with the best hand guy on the West Coast, and I got in to see him right away. Nothing broken, some nerve stuff going on. They're pretty sure I'll be able to play again."

"Pretty sure?"

"Cross that bridge, I guess." She took another bite, and a sardonic grin crept onto her face. "This is the first week in over ten years that I haven't had to practice. I'm just hanging out at home, watching TV."

Francine pointed her plastic spoon at the big-screen television, which was on mute. "That guy right there hooked up with both of those girls last night, only he apparently forgot that they were all living in the same house, because the first girl took pictures and showed them to the second one. So now they're both pissed at him, even though they both still want to get with him because he's 'like, sooo hot.' What?"

"Someone loves her reality TV."

She shrugged. "It's been a nice break, that's all."

"No pun intended."

"Hey-oh. You ready for tomorrow? It's tomorrow, right?"

"Four minutes to determine my future."

"That sounds like the tagline from a bad action movie."

I made my voice all low. "One man. Four monologues. In the balance hangs . . . the rest of his life."

"I'd cross my fingers for you, but . . ." She went back to the Frosty and then said, "We should get you on one of these shows. You're like a real-live playa. Smooth."

"What?"

"Don't play dumb with me, Sparkles. I saw you up the hill."

I licked the dryness from my lips. "What happens at cast parties stays at cast parties, remember?"

"That's why I mangled my hand all up, by the way. Just running some interference for you when I saw Ellen."

There was a knock, and Francine's mom stepped into the open doorway. "I'm sorry to interrupt. Hello . . ."

"David," I said.

"Of course. Hello, David." Her hair was wet from a shower, and she had a slightly vacant look in her eyes, which gave me the impression that Francine wasn't the only heavily medicated woman in the room.

"Mrs. Cardenas," I said. She didn't seem to recognize me. "Francine and I were in the play together last spring? The Neil Simon one? *Rumors?*"

We weren't actually in the play together. I was in the play, and Francine played ominous music on a synthesizer offstage, but I figured her mom might remember.

"You were very good," she said.

"Thank you, ma'am. The show was a lot of fun."

She said to Francine, "I thought maybe you and I might do some scales together. I know it's been a little while. I could be your left hand?"

Francine looked from her mom to me and then scraped the bottom of the paper cup. There was enough Frosty left for one more bite. Francine's mom said nothing, just spun around and left the room with her arms straight at her sides, opening and closing her hands as if preparing for a fistfight. I had overstayed my welcome, if in fact I'd ever been welcome in the first place.

"So, what happened with Ellen? After my unfortunate exit?"

"You know how it is," I said. The truth was that I didn't have an answer. We hadn't managed to spend any time together at school, and she was working tonight. "She's busy, with the application due soon—"

"What are you doing here?" Francine said.

"I was worried about you—"

"Don't be a dick. You with the Frosty, which I loved, by the way, but seriously. Go, right now." She stood and pointed her spoon at the door. "Go to her, my son."

"Be sure to tell me how it ends," I said, nodding to the television.

Francine put the empty cup on the side table. "Don't worry, I'll be watching. And break a leg tomorrow."

I nodded at Mrs. Cardenas as I passed her in the hallway, following Francine's school pictures back to the present. I walked outside into the scent of freshly cut grass. The hedges were expertly trimmed and the leaves successfully blown and gathered into two neat bags on the curb.

A phone call wasn't going to cut it, and I figured I could catch Ellen at her parents' place, so I drove the eight blocks and jogged up the three flights of stairs to Peninsula Life Coach. The reception area included a pair of ficus trees, a floor-to-ceiling waterfall, and a coffee table featuring an impressive collection of small wooden boxes of sand with miniature rakes in them. According to the brochure on the counter, this was northern California's premiere destination for both short- and long-term strategy and support.

The front desk was empty, but Ellen's mom noticed me through the open door of her office. She waved at me as she stood and met me in the lobby. "David. What a nice surprise."

"Is Ellen here?"

She was as short as her daughter but more petite, with shoulder-length brown hair that practically glistened under the track halogen lighting. "Ahh, like ships passing in the night. Are you okay? Here, let me get you some tea. It's echinacea. Helps you stay fit in mind and body."

"I really should be—"

Mrs. Conroy talked at me over her shoulder as she filled a cup of hot water. "Ellen told us about your audition tomorrow. So exciting! How are you feeling about it?"

The other door opened a crack, and Ellen's dad poked his head out. "I thought I heard your voice."

He strode to me and extended his hand warmly. The man knew exactly who he was, and that knowledge enabled him to navigate the world with more confidence than should have been legal.

"Yeah, just looking for Ellen."

"He's nervous about his Juilliard audition," Ellen's mom said.

There were generally two reactions whenever people discovered my intention to be an actor. The first, and more common, was "What the hell is wrong with this kid?" but the other reaction, the one Mr. and Mrs. Conroy seemed to have, was something like appreciation, almost envy. As though they'd always wanted to be actors or artists or musicians but had cast those dreams aside for the stability of a more traditional job.

Mr. Conroy nodded. "He should be." There was no judgment in his voice, just a statement of fact; he may as well have just pointed out that I was wearing shoes.

I tried to laugh it off. "Thanks a lot."

"There'd have to be something wrong with you if you weren't nervous. Juilliard is a phenomenal school, and you've had your heart set on it since well before we met. If I were you, I'd be quaking in my boots."

Mrs. Conroy handed me a mug of steaming tea. I FIGHT FOR THE FIGHT, it said in big block letters. I blew gently on the liquid. "I'm trying not to think about it, actually."

He winced and shook his head. "Wrong. If you don't mind me saying. Wrong, wrong, wrong. You're nervous because there's a reason to be nervous. Ignoring the nerves just ensures that they stick around. You have to give that feeling the space it deserves."

"What he means is, honey, that it's perfectly natural to feel this way." Mrs. Conroy put her hand on my forearm.

"Have you done everything possible?" Ellen's dad said. "Have you prepared yourself for success rather than failure?"

"I think so."

"Your response to life's challenges says a lot about the kind of man you are, and the kind of man you aren't."

We all nodded, giving his advice the space it deserved. The waterfall gurgled in the background. I thanked them both for their time.

"I'd wish you good luck tomorrow," her dad said, "but you and I know there's no such thing."

"Right," I said. "Just our ability to engage fully with our opportunities."

"Would you look who's been paying attention!"

Ellen's mom took the tea from me and set it on the counter and held me by the shoulders, staring straight into my eyes until I held her gaze. "You're going to do wonderfully."

You never hear people talk about the collateral damage when a long-term relationship explodes. The Conroys had become my second family over the last two years, consistently more supportive of what I wanted than my real family, and if things with Ellen were headed the way I thought they might be, I was going to miss them.

23

A cacophony of vocal warm-up exercises echoed off the bare cinder block in the greenroom of San Francisco's American Conservatory Theater. Kids sat on the floor or leaned against the wall or paced back and forth; there were three times as many people as there were chairs. The few who weren't wearing headphones were talking to themselves anyway, running monologue lines or staring at themselves in any reflective surface to psych themselves up.

Every fifteen minutes, a frumpy woman with a headset and a clipboard appeared in the doorway. Heads would turn, the volume would drop, she'd call off a last name. We'd watch the next applicant straighten out his clothing, check her hair in the mirror by the door. I was taller than some, had a rounder face than others, had better posture than most. When the door closed again, the discordant symphony would begin again. I was up in twenty-five minutes.

One girl in black pants and a fitted white blouse wandered by where I sat on the floor. She made her mouth and eyes as wide open as possible and bellowed, "Puuuumpkiiiiiin faaaaaace." Then she squinted her eyes and squinched her nose and lips together and squealed, "Raisin face."

I stretched out my own mouth; I over-enunciated my

favorite tongue-twister—*She sat upon the balcony inimically mimicking and hiccupping and amicably welcoming them in*—but my focus was off. How was it possible that I couldn't concentrate? After so many months of preparation? After so many arguments with my dad about this being exactly what I wanted to do with my life? My inability to focus made me angry at myself, which then made it more difficult for me to focus, and that's the stuff a death spiral is made of.

My mom had left me a good luck message that morning, and Lisa, though she was still pissed at me from the day before, had given me a card. My dad must have forgotten about it. No knock-'em-deads, no we-believe-in-yous. Not even the obligatory break-a-leg.

Ellen had met me at my locker after second period. "My folks said you dropped by last night," she'd said. "You should have called."

"I didn't feel like a phone call. I wanted to see you."

"Let's not do this right now," she'd said, handing me a Peninsula Life Coach Post-it with the phrase *You are your only you!* circled in red at the bottom.

It had made me laugh. "That's a new one."

She'd cupped my cheek in her hand and locked her eyes with mine. "Remember: Juilliard should be auditioning for you."

And now, in the greenroom, I was being assaulted with, "Puuuumpkiiiiin faaaaaace."

The vibe was grimly familiar. Desperation. Desire. A craving. It was as thick in the tiny greenroom in San

Francisco as it had been during the visit from Stanford's own Michael Parson in the foyer of the Cronyn Family Performing Arts Center, and the numbers were just as bad for us here as they'd been for my Stanford-obsessed classmates. At the end of our session, the judges would post a callback list, and if my name wasn't on it, I wouldn't be considered for admission. It was that simple.

A guy about my height and weight sat down in the open space against the wall next to me. He wore designer jeans and a black T-shirt about a half-size too small. "Freaking zoo, you know what I'm saying?"

"Mmmhmm," I said.

"Patrick Jade." He stuck out his hand.

I shook it. Introduced myself. He seemed nice enough. Familiar, even, as though we might have met before. I didn't have time for small talk. I needed to get back to my preflight routine: a quick run through each monologue, a series of scales to warm up the vocal instrument. If I could find the space, I'd lie on my back and breathe relaxation into my body an inch at a time. Maybe even hit up the rocking chair, Vanessa's favorite.

I nodded to him. "I'm not trying to be rude—"

"No, of course." He sat next to me and closed his eyes.

Shakespeare would be my first, so I started there. I brought my knees up to my chest and rested my forehead as I ran the Queen Mab, mumbling to myself:

O, then, I see Queen Mab hath been with you.
She is the fairies' midwife, and she comes

In shape no bigger than an agate-stone
On the fore-finger of an alderman,
Drawn with a team of little atomies
Over men's noses—

"It's crazy to think about, isn't it?" Patrick Jade again. "Oh, sorry."

I raised my head and looked at him. "What's crazy to think about?" Was my willpower so nonexistent that I couldn't ignore some random guy on the biggest day of my life? Apparently.

"This whole scene," he said, spreading his arms in front of him. "All of us coming up here, competing, working our asses off just for the privilege of laying bare our souls to judges most of us will never see again."

"If you're trying to psych me out, it's not working."

"Psych you out, my ass. Show me any other place you'd rather be. You see everyone else at school, right? They have no idea what they want to do with their lives. They may say psychologist or engineer or whatever, but they don't know. You and me? And everyone else in here? We *know*. We already want this."

"It's a little more complicated than that."

"How? If you want this bad enough, how are you going to let someone stand in your way? Now it's all about effort, bro. Perseverance, right? Because here's the thing. You know we're all talented. Otherwise we wouldn't be here."

"Jade?" It was the lady with the headset. She scanned the room with her eyebrows raised. Patrick waved at her, and she scribbled something on her clipboard.

"I'm up. Don't feel the need to wish me luck." He smiled and dusted off his jeans, then just as he was about to turn away, he said, "Did I hear you running the Queen Mab speech?"

I nodded.

"Nice. Ironic. I like it."

"What do you mean, ironic?"

"A speech about the corrupting power of fantasy? For your Juilliard audition? Queen Mab hath been with all of us, bro. That's why we're here." He brought his thumb slowly underneath his chin as he said, "'Sometime she driveth o'er a soldier's neck, and then dreams he of cutting foreign throats.'"

"Are you doing it, too?" I said, my stomach teetering on the edge.

He shook his head. "*Henry V*, act three, scene one. Once more unto the breach, and all that."

As he followed the headset-and-clipboard lady through the stage door, I remembered where I'd seen him. Two years earlier, there'd been a fast food commercial— McDonald's or Wendy's, I think. It was on all the time— where a kid rode his bike in the drive-through lane, snatching a hamburger from an unsuspecting take-out customer. The burgers were so good, the commercial suggested, they were worth stealing.

No wonder Patrick Jade was so confident. His ad was national.

* * *

A woman's voice came at me from behind the lights. "Mr. David Ellison?"

I detected a challenge, as though they'd decided to admit David Ellison, but I had to prove I was actually him. I rolled back my shoulders to fight against a possible slouch. I stood center stage, with my hands at my side, remembering Big Pro's advice about auditions: eighty percent of the decision is made before you even open your mouth. "That's correct."

"When you're ready."

I took a deep breath. I closed my eyes. I'd been coming to plays in this very theater for the last six years, and now, for the first time, I wasn't in the audience. This was my time; this was my place. I'd put in the hours, and now all I had to do was relax and let it ride.

My eyes opened, slowly adjusting to the spotlight. The thick gold curtains had been pulled open completely, and I looked out over the three tiers of seating, reminding myself to project to the back row of the upper mezzanine, no matter where the judges were sitting. Own the space. I ran my toes across the scuffed black floorboards. A bead of sweat trickled from my temple. I began.

"'O, then, I see Queen Mab hath been with you . . .'"

It was as though there were two Davids on stage. One of them was performing, but the other was set apart, critiquing, commenting. "Too fast!" "Slow down!" "Don't forget to use your entire vocal register!" "Make your kneecaps stop bouncing!" The kiss of death for any audition is not being in the moment, and that second David, pulling me from myself like that, was a straight-up assassin.

I couldn't see the judges, but I could feel their energy, and it didn't feel good. It was slipping away from me, and I had to dig down. Who else was going to fight for it, if not me?

Forget about the second David and remember Patrick Jade. He was right. The dream was mine. I could do this! I was coming to the lines he'd quoted. "'Sometime she driveth o'er a soldier's neck, and then dreams he of cutting foreign throats—'"

A flash of panic brought me as far into the moment as I could have wanted.

There was a pause. A long pause. I opened my mouth, but nothing came out. I tried again, the second David cursing at me the entire time, but still nothing. I heard the sound of shuffling paper coming from the audience.

There was nothing. My mind was entirely, devastatingly, blank.

24

I refused to leave my bed, so terrified was I of reflective surfaces—a window, a doorknob, the back of a freshly washed spoon. I wanted nothing to do with myself, no reminders of who I was or what I had done. My official excuse was a stomachache. Then a headache. Then a general malaise. I don't know if I was more embarrassed by my "audition" or by the fact that I had dissolved into a cliché.

"This always happens to me when I push myself to a deadline," my mom said, poking her head into my room before she left to take Lisa to school. "Our bodies will tell us when they need to rest."

What I needed, in the absence of a time machine, was something to tear my mind away from the train wreck I'd engineered on that stage. It played like a horror film against the insides of my eyelids. The awkward clearing of the throat. The sound of papers rustling. The almost reluctant offer for me to start again.

Not only that, but leaving aside the psychological effects of my abject failure, there was also the practical issue to think about. Literally *hours* of my day had just opened up. No more practicing monologues. No more mental energy wasted on worrying. How was I supposed to occupy my time now? How was I supposed to get through my days? I'd have to find something new to obsess about.

I gave serious thought to skipping school altogether, but opening night was only a week away, and Oak Fields' official policy states that students who miss school are prohibited from taking part in after-school activities. My hand was forced. I wasn't about to give Big Pro a reason to pile on about my dedication to the theatre, not after the audition, so I arrived on campus before the third-period deadline.

I kept my head down, did the work, and went from room to room without looking at anybody. I made small talk like a champ when I had to. Classes and passing periods I could handle. But lunch was a different story. I wasn't ready to see so many people, all at once, in an unstructured environment.

I was wandering around the back of the dining hall when I saw my sister sitting cross-legged on the ground, leaning against the brick building. She looked about how I felt.

"Hey," I said, taking a spot next to her.

She glanced at me and looked away. "You're feeling better."

"What's wrong?"

"You know. Dumb freshman stuff."

"You have a life, too?" I said, and this time she laughed. "Want me to beat him up?"

"I've heard about your fighting skills. You might hurt his fist with your face."

"Ooh, direct hit." We were sitting on a narrow strip of grass between the dining hall and the campus perimeter. Some sort of drainage creek was barely visible through the ivy-covered fence. "Do you come here a lot?"

"Ahhh," she said. "So, how did it go yesterday? I didn't even see you when you came home, and this morning you were in bed."

"It was great," I said.

She flinched as if I'd screamed at her. "Oh, my God—"

"I said it was great. I don't know anything yet, but callbacks are in a few weeks, so I have a chance to—"

"Is that what you're telling people? Is that what *I* should be telling people?"

My mind flashed back to the audition. I'd waited until the end of my session for the callback list to be posted, just in case, but I'd known it would have taken a miracle. Of the thirty people in my session, only three had made the cut. Pumpkin Face girl was one of them. As was my good friend Patrick Jade.

I was more than just envious; I was embarrassed. Embarrassed that I'd stunk up the joint so bad, embarrassed that I'd thought I'd be able to handle the pressure. More than anything, I was ashamed that my assessment of myself was so wildly different from the reality of my audition. There's nothing worse for a small pond's big fish than being forced to recognize that the world is 80 percent water.

"How obvious is it?" I said.

"Not very, but I'm your sister. . . . I'm sorry," Lisa said.

She paused as if processing the information. "How did Mom and Dad take the news?"

My dad was the one to greet me at the door the night before. He'd been waiting, he said. He wanted to know how it went. And there was a bounce in his step as he steered me to the couch and an eagerness in his eyes that made me realize that no matter how much I'd tried to deny it, his opinion of me actually did matter. It was a humbling realization, actually, and one that stunned me into a painful silence.

"I didn't tell them."

Lisa's eyes flashed wide for an instant. "You're kidding."

"I couldn't. I didn't know what to say."

"You had to say something, didn't you? I can't imagine the silent—"

"I told them I got a callback, and even Dad was happy. Once I saw his face, I couldn't tell him the truth."

"Well, I guess that's one way to handle it."

"It was easy, actually. Lying to him like that. Easier than I would have thought. I wanted that look to stay on his face for as long as possible."

"What did your girlfriend say about that?"

My girlfriend, whom I still needed to talk to. Whom I'd been too ashamed to call after the audition.

"You guys *are* still dating, right? I can't keep up."

"As far as I know."

Lisa pulled a pinch of grass from the ground and tossed it into the air as if checking the wind. "What's the next step in Operation Lie Your Ass Off?"

"I was thinking I might pretend to get a phone call notifying me of an error in the judges' initial tabulations and apologizing for the mistake."

"How many people do you think that will fool?"

"Two is all I need, as long as they're Mom and Dad," I said. The wind rustled through the branches above us, swirling trash and a few wayward leaves into the courtyard. "I was supposed to get a callback, at least. It makes you wonder, did I just have a bad day, or was I kidding myself all along?"

"Aren't we all kidding ourselves? When it comes down to it?"

"It's probably a preservation instinct," I said. "If we always believed the reality of the situation, we'd be smothered by it."

"Exactly. Like there's one spot available in Stanford and everyone in your class is convinced they're going to be the one."

I took a deep breath. "Including me."

"Really?"

"I am," I said. "I'm going to apply."

It was the first time I'd said it out loud, and it felt like I meant it. There were plenty of other schools, plenty with great theatre departments, but I'd been after Juilliard because it was the best, and that's what my parents expected of me.

"It's kind of the only way I can think of to make up for everything."

Lisa didn't laugh, bless her, but she did squinch her face at me as though considering the options. "You could try the truth."

"Getting into Stanford might be easier."

"You're not worried about The Artist?"

This caught me by surprise. There had been another "attack" in the week following Iggy's, but I'd been focused so much on the audition that I hadn't paid too much attention to it. A collage, a caption, and Zoë Franklin, three-time Northern California Mathlympics Champion, accused of cheating.

"Why would I be worried?"

"Isn't The Artist going after all the hot shots? As long as people think you got into Juilliard, you're on the hit list. Now add wanting to go to Stanford, and you're pretty much asking for it."

Those were my options: tell the truth and let everyone know I'm a failure, or keep the lie going and risk the wrath of The Artist. "You're pretty insightful for a freshman."

"I'm like a cuter, thinner Buddha."

My phone rang. I looked at the caller ID but didn't answer. "That was Ellen. Maybe I should have answered, huh?"

Lisa snorted. "Yeah, maybe you should have."

"Don't tell anyone, okay? About Juilliard."

"You, my friend, are a piece of work." She stood up and wiped the grass from her backside. "No offense, but where you go to school isn't exactly an area of interest for me. Not quite gossip-worthy."

"So you say."

I watched her go. The certainty that Stanford was my only way out of this had just begun to squeeze my chest, and in a strange way, the pressure was almost a relief. Even now, I could feel it filling the void left by my Juilliard debacle. Don't think, don't dwell on it. Sometimes the most difficult thing is to make a decision, and a decision had been made.

I was an Oak Fields student, after all. The world was nothing if not my oyster. Now I just had to figure out how to make it happen.

My phone rang again, and this time I answered it.

"Where *are* you?" Ellen said. "I'm sitting here at lunch—are you avoiding me?"

"No, of course not. I just have some things on my mind."

"I figured you'd call last night. I don't even know how your audition went."

I cleared my throat, opened my mouth, and then it was done. Somehow I managed to lie to my girlfriend about something I'd been driving her crazy with for two years. It was one thing to lie to my parents, but this was an entirely different league of dick. I don't even know why I did it, either. Did I want to impress her? Did I not want her to think I was a failure?

"That's great news," she said, though her voice was almost completely devoid of emotion. "I kind of thought that would be something you'd want to tell me."

"Yeah," I said.

The noise she made was as unpleasant as it was

familiar—like something between a sigh and a scoff, with a healthy dose of weariness thrown in for good measure. I'd been on the receiving end of that sound plenty of times over the past two years, and not once had it been a good thing.

"This isn't working."

"Like, *not working* not working?"

"You know what I mean."

I knew the other shoe had been about to drop. I just didn't know it would be steel-toed. "Over the phone?"

"You want to meet up now so I can say it to your face? Or come over later. I have an AP Spanish presentation, and that History group project that I have to do by myself now that Iggy's gone, so I'll be up all night."

I stood up and pressed my forearm against the brick wall, resting my head against it. "Is this about the other night, at Geoff's house? With Francine?"

"What?"

"Because I didn't ask you to stay? You could have if you'd wanted to."

Her voice knifed through the receiver. "Are you insane? You and Vanessa get drunk together on Boone's, and you expect me to stick around and watch—"

"I'm just—"

"Do you think this is an easy conversation for me? After two years? Two years! I picked up the phone practically every hour for the last three days, but I never went through with it because—I don't know. I didn't want to ruin your focus before Juilliard, and then I thought that you'd call, that we'd work everything out . . . I'm not blind. I know you and Vanessa have your magical theatre connection; fine, I get it. I can't compete with that—"

"Nothing's going on," I said. Which was close to the truth. Only that kiss at Geoff's house, but that wasn't technically anything we hadn't done onstage dozens of times before.

"Don't embarrass yourself—"

"Ellen, I swear, we're not—"

"Don't talk, for one second, please. Let me talk."

There was a silence as I bit my tongue.

"David?"

"You asked me to let you talk," I said as calmly as possible.

"This isn't the first time we've had this conversation. Taking Vanessa out of it, I'm the one who goes over to your house and eats with your family. I'm the one who plans things for us to do on the weekends. I'm the one who spends time I could be using to study trying to convince you to take your college essay seriously—"

"Vanessa didn't even look at it for more than a second, remember? And my dad hired—"

"Still talking," she said.

I pinched my temples. "Go ahead."

"I just need some distance from you and your shit right now."

"Shouldn't we at least—"

"There's nothing more to talk about, David. It's a waste of time."

Two years. Two years of movies and study sessions, of bubble tea, opening night roses, afternoons at the mall, parties, music mixes, road trips, greeting cards, text messages, Milk Duds, phone bills, hookups. My mind was filled with thousands of images at once, still frames from our relationship, as though I'd just been shot and my life was flashing before my eyes.

"I didn't think this would ever happen over the phone," I said.

"Well."

The silence evolved from awkward to uncomfortable to excruciating. It felt as though she was expecting me to fight for her. She was giving me the chance to salvage something. I'd always thought that if it ever came to this, that's exactly what I would do. I believed in the future, after all.

"I packed a box with all your stuff," she said. "Your shirts and stuff. You can pick it up whenever you want."

"So we're really breaking up? At school? Over the phone?"

"David—"

"Are we?"

"Please tell me you're joking."

"I just want to know where we stand, for sure?"

"I packed a box! Just . . ." I pictured her gripping the phone with white knuckles until she got her breathing under control. "Good-bye, David."

I sat, numbed by her voice, staring at the perimeter fence, the ivy wrapped around each of the iron posts. I knew I'd have to get up soon, and I would. I'd try to push this all out of my mind, and after school I'd focus on the stage, and I'd remember my lines, and we'd rehearse the play. I would meet with my narrative coach after rehearsal as planned, and then I would go home and eat and go to sleep. I wouldn't tell anyone about Ellen because on some level I'd want to keep living in a world where we were still together. Besides, I didn't need to tell anyone; it would be all over school by the next morning.

The worst part about everything Ellen had said wasn't that she'd said it or even the way she'd said it. I couldn't feel slighted and self-righteous about being dumped, no matter how badly I wanted to. Because the worst part was that I knew everything she said was true.

25

Stephanie Blair took her coffee with four sugar packets and a two-second pour of half-and-half. She stirred it for at least thirty seconds. The weather was, once again, annoyingly perfect, even this late in the evening. Mid seventies with a slight breeze. Stephanie placed the wooden stirrer across a brown paper napkin on the table.

"I want to focus on getting me into Stanford," I said, dispensing with the small talk. "I want to go. That's my first choice. And I have to apply early."

She gave me the "stop" motion with both hands. "Whoa, there. Baby steps first."

"Forget baby steps."

"First of all, the early application is due less than three weeks from now. More important, there is only one spot available for your entire class, unless there's an injunction."

"No injunction," I said. "They dropped the suit."

"So you know what you're up against."

"If you want, we can think of it as rehearsal for the regular admissions. If we put me through the Stanford process, think about how much better my material will be for all the other schools. What's the harm in that?"

"No offense, but the harm is to my statistics. If *I* don't think you really want to go to a particular school, there's no way an admissions committee is going to let you in. I don't care how much I'm getting paid, if you're going to mess up my numbers, we're going to have a problem."

How could I explain to her that I felt like I'd let everybody down, everyone who believed in me, who supported me. Big Pro, Ellen, myself. I knew it was ridiculous to feel that way, given the raw percentage of applicants Juilliard accepted even under the best of circumstances, but what I felt and what I knew had nothing to do with each other. The only way to redeem myself was to make the biggest splash I could.

"My dad hired you, right? And there's nothing he wants more than for me to get into Stanford. So let's just say that you're doing what he hired you to do."

"The last time we talked you couldn't care less about that place. So why the change?" Stephanie said.

When I didn't respond right away, she grunted and chewed on the inside of her cheek, nodding as she sized me up.

"My essay is coming along and my scores are good. My grades have gotten better every year of high school. We could frame me as a late bloomer."

Stephanie choked on her mouthful of coffee. It seemed like an act until I had to sit back and wait for her to stop coughing. Tears leaked from the corners of her eyes, and her face was beet red. The man at the table next to us raised his eyebrows in alarm.

"Wrong pipe," I explained.

Stephanie blotted her eyes with a small paper napkin. "We don't say 'late bloomer.'"

"I can get in, I know I can. I just need your help."

She moved to take another sip, but froze when the cup touched her lips. She replaced it on the table. "Something happened."

"Nothing happ—"

"It's either a girl, or—"

"It's not a girl."

Now she took that sip. When she put the cup down, she crossed her arms on the table and leaned forward. "Do not—not—let relationships get anywhere near a decision this big."

"That's not what it is."

"So, why?" She pointed her index fingers at me while still keeping her arms crossed. "What made you change your mind?"

"Ms. Blair?" a male voice interrupted us. Felix Gutierrez stood three feet from our table. He wore a long-sleeved workout shirt, spotless white basketball shoes, and a pair of khaki shorts. Designer sunglasses sat atop his expertly tousled hair like a bird in a nest.

"Hi, Felix," she said.

"David," he said suspiciously. I nodded.

"How goes basketball?"

"Great," he said. Then to me: "Iggy's coming back next week."

"Of course he is," I said. Sending a message was one

thing, but the administration couldn't very well put the season in jeopardy.

Stephanie smiled at him. "With any luck, you'll win state this year."

"Luck is for the unprepared. See you in a couple days, right?" He eyed me warily and nodded good-bye to her and walked away.

"Sorry," Stephanie said. She must have mistaken whatever look was on my face for concern, because she said, "Don't worry. He's the only other client of mine from your school, and he's got his heart set on the northeast, although why anyone would choose to go to Vermont when he could live here is beyond me."

She sipped from her coffee, taking in the beautiful fall evening. "Okay, then. Where were we? Oh! You were about to explain to me why you've turned your back on what I was led to believe was a lifelong dream."

If I said it was about redeeming myself, about making amends and proving to my family that I wasn't a complete screwup, she would probably have told me I had my priorities all out of whack. She would've said that the college search is about finding the right fit and that vengeance applications were rarely successful. And she might have been right, but that didn't mean I was wrong.

"It's hard to explain. I haven't turned my back on it. Stanford has a theatre department—"

"Every college and university in the country has a theatre department—"

"I need to get in," I said. "It's important."

"Juilliard was a bomb, wasn't it?" Stephanie reached across the table as if to pat me on the arm, but when her hand was only inches away, she thought better of it, tapping the table with an open palm instead. "I'm sorry. I should have asked how that went."

"Please don't tell my dad. He doesn't even have to find out."

She took a mechanical pencil from her purse and opened up a small notepad. She scribbled something down, then pressed the lead into the pillow of her bottom lip. Then another scribble. A "hmmmm." Another scribble. The pencil back to her lip.

After a minute or two, I couldn't take it anymore. "What are you writing?"

"Anyone can get in anywhere," she said. "It's just a matter of framing it right. And just to be clear: *I* can't get you in; you're going to have to do the heavy lifting. So let me think about some options, and in the meantime, you still need to focus on what you're good at."

I could only assume she didn't mean lying to my parents.

26

walked on campus Friday morning feeling like I was the CIA and Ellen had hacked into my system. She knew everything, all my insecurities, my worries, my feelings of inferiority, and it was only a matter of time before she sold them on the black market.

I realized right away that Ellen had been both my rudder and my sail. Until I met Vanessa and Colter, I hadn't put any energy into maintaining other friendships because I neither had the time nor felt the need to do so. I was in the theater, or I was with Ellen. But now I wandered through the halls like a cracked dinghy, searching in vain for a friendly port. Pretending not to let it get to me was one of the hardest acting jobs I'd ever done.

At one point I stood in front of my locker the way you might stand in front of an open fridge. I held the door with one hand, kind of leaning on it, kind of not, staring into the inside at the stacks of books, the spines far too shiny and not nearly cracked enough for this late in the year.

Something hit me in the small of the back, and I lurched forward, only barely catching my balance in time to avoid hitting my head on the exposed metal edge of my locker. What the hell? Now I'm going to get bullied? Actually bullied?

I took a deep breath and gritted my teeth and turned to find Colter rocking back and forth on his crutches.

He wore a brand new Yale University hat—white dome, flat blue brim—with a hint of a gauze bandage underneath. His mane of hair jutted out from below the hat, a thick curtain of it covering his entire left eye. "Oops. A little too hard."

"Nice hat."

"Aim high, is what I always say." He smiled. "Dad's an alum. It's a sign of respect for me to wear it in public."

"Go Bulldogs. It's the Bulldogs, right?"

"Whatever." He shrugged and winced. "I heard about Ellen. You okay?"

"Fine," I said. "Never better. Peachy keen, in fact."

"You're lying, but that's fine. I get it."

"Iggy's back Monday," I said. "Keep your head on a swivel."

"He already did what he did; I can't imagine he'd want to come back for seconds."

"A week and a half hardly seems long enough."

"No witnesses, my word against his, maybe a couple teammates swear he was somewhere else. You expected anything different?"

"I'm surprised your parents didn't want to press charges."

Colter shrugged. "My dad wanted to. I didn't. We got into it after I threatened to misremember to the police."

"Look at you," I said, impressed. "Standing up to your dad."

"The crutches helped. Sorry, bad joke." He stood firmly on both feet and held the crutches out to me by the handles. "I don't even need them, by the way. But it's a great excuse to be late to class."

"This was all part of your master plan?"

He pulled something from his shirt pocket—a small piece of origami. The paper's golden foil glittered as he handed it to me. A little bird with a tail about three times the size of the body. "Here. As a gesture. It's a *houou*."

"A what?"

"Japanese phoenix," he said. "So you may rise again and all that."

I accepted his gift. Smug glances reached me from over his shoulder, but I didn't care. My friend had made me a little bird. "It's good to have you back."

"Agreed." Colter whacked me on the side of the leg with his crutch. "Now, about V. She's looking forward to rehearsal today. She told me."

"Jesus, man, the funeral meat's not even cold." I made a move to kick his crutch away, but he was too quick for me.

The truth was, I was looking forward to rehearsal more than anything, and although Vanessa was a part of it, she wasn't the only reason. Even with Ellen, I'd been a theatre guy, first and foremost. And now this play was all I had left.

As if to prove that point, I ran into Ellen just after school let out. I'd avoided her in History, managing to be the last one in and the first one out, never giving myself a chance to get caught in an awkward silence with her. I was completely aware of what a coward that made me, but at that point, coward didn't seem so bad compared to actually talking to her.

"You've been pretty busy," she said. "Hustling, running through the halls."

I swallowed. "Show's next week. You know how it is."

Each of us waited for the other to say something. It was like a game of emotional chicken—who was going to swerve first? It was almost excruciating enough to make me never want to date anybody ever again. Ever.

"You okay?" I said finally, the coward that I am.

"I heard you're applying to Stanford." The thin smile acquired a downward tilt at the corners. There was some judgment going on.

"News travels fast," I said.

Not all news. I still hadn't told her the truth about Juilliard; I hadn't told anyone but Lisa and Stephanie. But this wasn't exactly the time or place to describe what happened with the audition or try to explain why I'd lied about it. Honesty was going to have to take a number.

"It's a contingency plan," I said. "Just covering my bases, like we talked about."

"Stanford University is a contingency plan?"

"My narrative may still need a little work," I said.

"Among other things."

With that, she took a few steps backward and then spun away, leaving me in a puddle of my own deceit. That went just about as well as I thought it would.

"So sad." Iggy came up next to me, shaking his head. "Love lost. Never does get easier."

"Go beej yourself, Iggy." I turned away, but Iggy followed me. "You going to hit me again?"

"Come on, actor boy, you've got a better imagination than that." He sucked air in through his teeth. "I still owe you twenty bucks, right?"

I'd made it all the way down the hall. I was about to open the door and escape outside when Iggy stopped me. He put his arm around my neck and pulled me close as though offering up a juicy secret.

"Double or nothing says I fuck your ex-girlfriend by Christmas," he said. "See ya!"

Vanessa and I stood in the little courtyard behind the Performing Arts Center, a small, walled-in area with short bushes surrounding an industrial-size Dumpster we filled with theater trash during set construction. We were on a five-minute break while Big Pro and Jake confirmed a series of light cues, and it was a good thing; I needed to get outside. After so many years of the stage being the only place I felt comfortable, now I couldn't set foot inside the theater without feeling uneasy.

The news of my application to Stanford had spread throughout the school, no doubt with Lisa as the flash point. Not that my classmates took me as seriously as someone like Vanessa or Ellen, I'm sure. But the fact was that I'd increased the applicant pool. The odds for everyone else had just gotten slimmer, if only marginally so.

"So we're competitors now." Vanessa cracked her knuckles and wiggled her fingers. "Enemies."

"Frenemies?" I said.

"Stop it."

"Is that okay with you?"

"Why wouldn't it be okay?"

"I don't know. I thought maybe—"

"One thing you need to know about me, David, is that I'm a big girl. You want to apply to the same college as me? I'm not going to cry about it. I'm just going to crush you."

"Noted."

"Do you really think you can get in?" she said. "Or is this just something you're doing for your parents?"

I gave her my best look of feigned offense. "Of course I can get in. I'm well-rounded," I said. And then, quoting one of my lines from the show, "'The most limited of all specialists!'"

"When you put it like that, I'm going to have to take you seriously. So, tell me about the audition. We've been running around so much we haven't had the chance to talk about it. Which monologue did they like the best?"

I hesitated. "All of them, I think. They liked all of them equally." At least that was close to the truth. She smiled, and I knew I had to tell her what really happened. She was my friend. She would understand. She would be supportive.

"So . . ." she said. "About Ellen."

"She asked for distance, so I've decided to give it to her."

Vanessa smiled. "That sounds generous."

Corky poked her head outside. "There you guys are. Let's get back at it. Big Pro's off his meds."

Vanessa hopped to the door before I could say anything else. I followed her and Corky into the theater, and the anxiety hit me full in the chest when I saw the stage. There had to be a way to deal with that, a way to make that space seem familiar to me again. Operation Take Back the Theater was going to happen, and it had to happen fast.

27

Unlike at least half my class, I'd never bothered to get a fake ID, so my options were limited. Ultimately, I'd gone home after rehearsal, just long enough to have some leftover pizza and snag a bottle of Jack Daniel's from the liquor cabinet and stuff it in my backpack. I'd figure out how to replace it later.

I told them I was going to Ellen's for a bit, and they were fine with it. It was late, but not too bad for a Friday night. Besides, I'd gotten a callback to Juilliard. I'd proven to them that I could accomplish anything I set my mind to. I was their shining star.

By the time I returned to campus, it was almost ten o'clock and the theater doors were locked, so I had to use my key. I had expected the place to be empty by then, but I was only three steps inside when I noticed Big Pro looking up from an aisle seat. A coffee cup was balanced precariously on the armrest to his left, and he hunched to the right as he squinted down at the yellow legal pad he was scribbling on.

He glanced up at me. "You doing okay?"

My backpack felt surprisingly heavy. Would he wonder what was in it? Would he want to take a look? Could he even do that? "I didn't think you'd still be here."

"We don't talk as much as we used to, Sparkles," he said. "I miss that."

"Yeah." I was unprepared; aside from the backpack-inspired nervousness, I hadn't been expecting to have to talk to anyone.

"Sorry to hear about the audition."

I shrugged. "What are you gonna—wait, how did you know?"

"I may be a damn schoolteacher, but give me some credit. I still have a connection or two lying around." Big Pro capped the pen and clutched his coffee. "What happened?"

I said nothing. He grunted and pushed against the armrests to stand. He descended the aisle stairs and moved toward the door upstage left, but the closer he got, the more slowly he walked, like he wanted me to stop him.

"Big Pro?"

He turned around and leaned against the open door, coffee mug in one hand, legal pad tucked under the other arm.

"I choked."

I wanted him to meet me downstage, put his hand on my shoulder, and tell me to keep my chin up. He said, "Why?"

"I don't know. It just happened."

He nodded. "It's too bad about you and Ellen, by the way. I always liked her. But I guess when you have someone like Vanessa waiting in the wings, you have to do what you have to do."

"Excuse me?"

"What do you think we talk about in the faculty room? Lesson plans?" He took a step but stopped in the middle of the doorway. "Don't worry about the audition, okay, Sparkles? What's past is past. The show's next week. Clean slate. You're going to crush it."

The door latched behind him, sending the echo of its click off the empty walls.

I went up to the light board and killed the house lights, choosing a light cue that would feature a combination of blues and purples. I brought the cue up to 50 percent so the stage was only dimly lit. Then I took the backpack up to the catwalk and walked to a spot above center stage. I took a long swig from the bottle.

The air conditioner came to life occasionally with a series of whirrs and clicks. Cold air would hum down from the rafters and then shut down, and the silence would return.

Tension had accumulated in the center of my chest like the nucleus of an atom. I lay on my back, perfectly still, breathing in, picturing my body as though I stood above it, separate from it. I imagined pushing the stress from the fingertips of this body with a rolling pin, starting at the chest and then working out, to the shoulders, the arms, the hands. Down the abdomen, the thighs and shins, the feet, the toes. Again and again, but to no avail. The nucleus held form.

I heard the unmistakable sound of a key sliding into a lock. The side door opened slowly. "Hello?"

239

I scrambled to stuff the bottle into my backpack as quietly as possible, and I waited.

Heavy boots clomped on the carpeted stairs. Jake emerged from the shadows of the darkened houselights and stepped onstage. He wore his normal getup—black jeans and T-shirt. "Hello?" he said again, scanning the stage, the audience.

I waited for another beat or two, and then I finally said, "Up here."

"Sparkles?"

"Yeah, it's me."

Jake looked up at the catwalk, then he climbed up to meet me, much more confident on the mesh than I'd been. "Is this the cue for the Wilsons' garage?"

I nodded. "You're good."

"So," he said.

"So," I said. "You have a key, too?"

"What are you doing here, Sparkles?"

"Nothing," I said. I saw his eyes settle on the backpack, so I opened it and pulled out the bottle.

"Pretty high stakes. On campus."

"Yeah. Well."

"I'll leave you to it, then. I just came by to grab some stuff." He moved to the ladder and stopped. He turned around. "There's a crew getting together at Corky's tonight. If you're interested."

"No," I said. "I'm good."

"You want some company?"

My phone rang. I looked at it. Home. It rang again.

"Did you mean what you said the other day?" I said. "About me being a pussy?"

"You finish that," he said with a wink, "and all bets are off."

I watched him leave. My phone rang again. I turned it off.

Big Pro once told me that it's better to have loved and lost than never to have *lost* at all. It's how we deal with the heartbreak that defines us, not how we experience the pleasure of love.

I sat on the wire mesh, leaning back against one of the support posts, and looked at the bottle. I wasn't about to finish it—Jake could call me a pussy all he wanted—but a few sips wouldn't kill me. The chances of getting caught were slim, but the consequences were severe enough to send a thrill through me every time I put the bottle to my lips.

But with the thrill came the depressing realization that I hadn't ever done anything like this before. There were so many things I hadn't done, so many things I missed while cooped up in the theater: clubs and activities and relationships with real people. Maybe it was a good thing that I choked at Juilliard. Maybe now I'd get to experience life instead of thinking of ways to suggest the imagined life of a character.

28

I woke up with my face against the mesh and a grinding sensation behind my eyes. My lips and mouth were sandpaper. The bottle, mercifully capped and a third empty, lay at my side. The stage glowed blue.

I slowly eased myself to a sitting position and angled my watch toward the stagelights—2:47 a.m. Shit.

There were eleven voice mails waiting for me when I turned my phone back on. Two from Vanessa. One from Ellen. Two from my dad. Six from my mom. Oh, boy.

I stood up, wobbly both from the unstable mesh and my unsettled stomach, and tottered carefully to the ladder. There was no real need to turn the houselights back on, so I ditched the JD in a trash can outside the building and jogged to the parking lot as fast as my head would let me.

I was pretty sure I was still drunk, and that meant two things: I couldn't drive, and I couldn't call my parents to come get me. There was breath spray and gum in the White Horse, though, and the spray burned. I spat on the ground and sprayed again, repeating the cycle until actual saliva started to flow. Then I unwrapped two sticks of gum and pocketed the rest, and I started walking.

Even though they made me shiver, the gusts of cool

night air helped to sober me up. The closer I got to my house, the more comfort I took in the deserted streets. The mountains loomed creepy at night, but there was something oddly exciting about how the stoplights changed from green to yellow to red without so much as a car to prompt them.

Mercutio says in the Queen Mab speech that dreams are "children of an idle brain, Begot of nothing but vain fantasy, Which is as thin of substance as the air." He knows what he's talking about, too, considering that both he and Romeo are dead by the end of the play, thanks to Romeo's dream.

Where did that leave me? Was thinking that I could get into Stanford a vain fantasy? Was a relationship with Vanessa? Was wanting to impress my dad? Was my whole life a vain fantasy? Was it better never to have lost at all, or was losing the whole point?

I ducked behind my neighbor's tree as soon as I turned onto my street. The lights in my house were on. All of them. I saw silhouettes through the thin curtains in the living room; one was completely motionless while the other walked in and out of view, then sat. Then walked out of view again.

The nucleus of tension in my chest exploded, and I emptied my stomach right there in the neighbor's front yard. My eyes watered as the heaves became dry, then I chewed two new sticks of gum until the bile left my teeth. I dried my eyes on my sleeve and breathed in the cool air, and then it was time.

My mom met me at the door and enveloped me before I could say a word. I buried my face in her neck as I gathered myself. She smelled, for the first time in almost ten years, of cigarettes.

"It's okay, Mom," I whispered, "I'm okay. It's all fine."

But she didn't let go. She rocked from side to side. Empty mugs were scattered on the coffee table, and I heard the puffing and belching of a newly percolating batch of coffee in the kitchen. My dad stood by the couch, looking to all the world like a disappointed parent, but I could see relief in his eyes, too.

"I'm okay," I said again.

My mom held me at arm's length, and that's when the anger came from both of them. What was I doing? Why didn't I call? I had made them sick, didn't I know that? I was prepared for it, knew I deserved it, but that didn't make it any easier to take.

She grabbed my wrist and pulled me to the couch, where she instructed me to sit next to her.

"Where's your car?" Dad said.

"You're always home on time," my mom said, her hands still shaking. She touched my wrist, my shoulder, my hair as if probing to make sure that her son was really there, that the person on the couch wasn't some sort of impostor. "Even during your plays, you've never missed curfew, not even once."

My dad leaned forward. "We called Ellen, when you didn't come home. Your mother was frantic."

"You called Ellen?"

"I have her number." My mom nodded, then shook her head. "What happened between the two of you, sweetheart?"

My dad sat on the edge of the coffee table and rested his elbows on his knees. "She said you were probably with Vanessa, and she found someone who had the number, so we called—"

"Are you and Vanessa . . . ?" my mom said.

"Vanessa told us she didn't know where you were."

"We called the police. We called the hospitals." My mom squeezed my hand in both of hers. "What happened?"

"Where's your car?" Dad said again.

There had to have been some lie I could tell them. They would give me the benefit of the doubt because the alternative was worse. But whether it was my frazzled state of mind or the startling reappearance of my conscience, I couldn't bring myself to say anything other than, "I was drinking."

This was quite the admission. So I had to be contrite. I had to let them see that I knew it was wrong, and that I was sorry. It felt like I was teetering on the edge of a cliff as I waited for their response.

"At least you didn't drive," Lisa said from the hallway, rubbing her eyes. She yawned.

I could tell this irritated my dad. "I beg your pardon?"

"It could have been worse, right? If he'd—"

"I don't remember asking for your input," Dad said, pointing back down the hall.

"Hey, David," she said as though we were the only

two people in the room. "You okay?"

I nodded. "Thank—"

"Go!"

Lisa stormed off. A door slam rattled the walls. Her interference had given me time enough to muster the courage I needed to jump off the edge.

"I didn't get a callback to Juilliard. I didn't get in."

They said nothing; my dad grunted and stared at me while my mom seemed to look to him for help. I'd given them too much to process, but wait! There was more!

"Ellen and I broke up."

"Honey," Mom said, like a reflex.

"So I got drunk. I didn't think it was a good idea to drive."

"You didn't get into Juilliard?" my mom said, shaking her head as though she hadn't heard correctly.

My dad jumped in. "You had to know the charade wouldn't last."

"The callbacks?" Mom said. "The trip to New York?"

"I didn't want you to be disappointed in me." It was the most truthful thing I'd ever said.

Mom shook her head, mystified. "Why did you and Ellen—? I don't understand."

"I read a study," my dad said, his voice oddly robotic. Mechanical. "Over seventeen percent of teenagers are binge drinkers, did you know that?"

"I'm not a binge drinker, Dad—"

"Motor vehicle crashes remain the number one cause of death among people aged fifteen to twenty."

"That's why I didn't drive! I—"

"One good decision doesn't erase the bad one you made before it; you know that."

"It's late," Mom said. "We're just glad you're okay."

She gave me a reluctant kiss, and the look on my dad's face was worse that I could have imagined it would be, but they didn't say anything else. Their reactions would be different after they'd had the chance to sleep on it, to compare notes, but I'd have to cross that bridge when I got to it. If I hadn't burned it already.

Sure enough, Dad hustled me out of bed the next morning and led me to his car. My stomach hurt, and I didn't want to go anywhere, but as he said, not going wasn't one of my available options. We needed to talk.

We said nothing to each other as he drove toward the foothills and then up. He chose Page Mill Road, no doubt enjoying the effect all the hairpin turns had on my stomach. We passed the occasional cyclist, shrink-wrapped in spandex and gritting beneath a mask of pain and sweat, and after fifteen minutes of driving the speed limit, we turned into the parking lot of the Monte Bello Open Space Preserve. My dad parked facing the exit but left the engine running.

"I'm sorry about Ellen," he said. "That must be hard for you."

I stared out the passenger window at the tail end of the Bay in the distance. "Thanks."

"I spoke with Mr. Prokov two days ago."

"He told you?" This time I couldn't stop myself from looking at him. "You already knew? And you didn't say anything?"

"I was hoping I wouldn't have to . . . David, I'm sure you're disappointed, but I think we know it's all for the best."

"We do?"

"You weren't ready. You're not good enough, is what it comes down to. Someday, maybe, you will be. But for now, it would probably be—"

"You can stop trying to make me feel better any time," I said. He flinched, genuinely shocked at my anger.

"It's important that you don't take this the wrong way." It was clear by the rising panic in his voice that this was not how he'd expected our talk to go at all. I'm sure in his mind he'd planned to present the information and have me download it without complications. I would process it, understand it, and accept it.

"What other way is there?"

"David, please. I'm doing my best to understand you—"

My phone rang, and I took full advantage of the opportunity. "Hello?" I said, so quickly that I didn't even look to see who was calling.

"This play you're in, you're the lead, right?"

The voice was almost recognizable enough to be familiar. "Who is—"

"It's Stephanie."

I held a finger up to my dad and mouthed *narrative coach*. "Yes, I'm the lead."

"Okay, that's good. There's going to be someone from the Stanford drama department at the show on Saturday night. The department head. She won't have as much pull as the coach of a sports team, but it's the best I can do. It might even be good enough. But, David?"

"Yeah?"

"This is your shot, okay? The way I want to package it, you can't just be good. You have to bring the house down."

We hung up, and I sat with the phone in my lap and watched the breeze blow through the eucalyptus. How ironic that acting—the one thing my dad didn't want me to do—could very well be the thing that gave me a chance at Stanford. I smiled.

"David." His knuckles whitened slightly around the wheel. "David—"

"I get it, okay? I'm not going to Juilliard, you think it's what's best for me, and you want me to agree with you. Good. Done. I agree. Can we go home now?"

This time it was his turn to stare out the window. One of the cyclists we'd passed earlier chugged into view and strained toward us, standing on the pedals to make them turn over. It was kind of a pathetic sight, really, because even though he was working his ass off, he could probably have gotten off his bike and walked faster.

29

I t was all the orange that caught my eye the next Monday, standing out as it did on the muted beige walls outside the college counseling office.

Another collage had been glued to the bulletin board, a series of pictures of Mr. Edwards in Princeton University gear. They must have been from old yearbooks: him in an orange sweatshirt on College Decision Day, when seniors wore the clothing of their intended college and teachers represented their alma maters; pictures of him in a Princeton baseball cap; sporting a black and orange tie; waving a Princeton Tigers flag at a college rally; standing beneath the Princeton pennant in his office. And right in the middle was his résumé, printed out from the Oak Fields Web site, with the following information circled:

Undergraduate Education
Princeton University—1974–1976
New Mexico State University—1976–1978 (BA)

Graduate Education
University of Wisconsin, Madison—1978–1980
(MA English)*

Beneath the handwritten asterisk was scrawled, in red marker, NO RECORDS EXIST. Of course there was also a caption: OAK FIELDS PREP, WHERE EVEN THE TEACHERS ARE FRAUDS!

It was still so early that the halls were only just now starting to come to life. Mr. Edwards appeared at my side, his face a twisted mask of disbelief. We surveyed the scene together, and when he finally spoke, it was through clenched teeth. "What is this?"

He reached up to take it down, but this one had been glued to the board, not stapled, so he was only able to peel off one narrow sliver at a time. His arms went rigid at his side and he turned to me. His face took on the wrinkled and splotchy quality of an overripe tomato, the features distorted grotesquely by the effort of keeping his anger in check.

Mr. Edwards abruptly spun around and hustled down the hallway, the strips of poster drooping over his fists like strands of white hair. As he turned the corner, he nearly bumped into Ellen, who was focused on the open book in her hand. I heard him mumble an apology, and then he was gone.

I waved to her, and she gave me an irritated look, as if she'd just found mold on a piece of bread. Nevertheless, she had no real option other than to walk toward me.

"What're you reading?" I said.

"*How to Avoid Small Talk*," she said icily.

After two years together, I should have been able to come up with something. Anything, even a joke. But I was empty. How ridiculous that I would suddenly be unable to think of anything to say to her.

"It's *Heart of Darkness*," she said, softening just a little. "For the Humanities short-answer quiz today. What happened here?"

"Turns out Mr. Edwards didn't graduate from Princeton, or even go to grad school at all." I stepped aside and let her experience what was left of the message for herself. Other students wandered over, and soon we were surrounded.

"We need to talk," I whispered.

"Not now."

I leaned in. "Seriously, I have something to tell you, and I need to get it off my chest because I can't stand the thought of you walking aro—"

She held up her hand and motioned for me to follow her into Mr. Nadlee's empty History classroom. When the door closed behind us, she said, "You know the great thing about my life now? I don't have to be responsible for your drama anymore."

"It's not drama."

She crossed her arms and scraped her top lip between her teeth. Then she swayed a little bit back and forth, and it took all my self-control not to touch her. How bizarre to be confronted with her body now that I didn't have any claim over it. I knew it so well, after two years, and now it was supposed to go right back to belonging to a stranger? How was that possible?

"Okay," I said. "So it's a little drama, but it's still the

truth. Things have been happening so fast that I—"

"I'll save you the trouble," she said. "You and Vanessa are together now, and you'd rather I hear it from you than from someone else—"

"No—"

"Thanks to your parents for calling me the other night, by the way. That was really fun for me. Getting them Vanessa's number."

"Will you stop? Please? I have to tell you something, and it's not about Vanessa."

"Do you actually listen to the words when they come out of your mouth?" Her phone buzzed, and she didn't even show me the courtesy of waiting a few seconds before checking the screen. "It's Amber," she said. "We're meeting to go over the calc quiz."

"Ellen, wait—"

She brushed by me, and by the time we made it back down the hall, a large crowd had gathered. And Mr. Edwards had returned.

"This is defacement of Oak Fields property, people! Defacement!" he shouted to nobody in particular.

Watching the counselor come unglued like that was unexpectedly entertaining. He paced back and forth, his hands thrashing around, oblivious to the rest of us except to shout from time to time.

Amber stood among the cluster of students near the back. She turned to us and gave Ellen a double take when she noticed me, and I saw Ellen's shoulders rise as if to say, What can you do?

"Sorry," Ellen said. "You ready?"

Tell her about Juilliard, I screamed to myself. Just tell her you want to make things right with her, even if there's no future for the two of you. Tell her you never meant to hurt her and you appreciate everything that she's tried to do for you. Tell her all of that, you stupid, self-centered idiot.

Ellen took one last look at the door and turned to follow Amber down the hall. "We need to study."

"Can we meet at lunch?"

"I have Spanish club."

It didn't look good for me to be following her around like a stray dog, but I wanted to talk to her in person, and the longer she ignored me, the more likely it was that I'd lose my nerve.

"What about after school, just for a few minutes?"

"Go on, Am," she said. Amber shrugged whatever, and Ellen turned to me.

"Don't go out with Iggy," I said, surprising us both.

"You don't get to tell me who to go out with," she said.

"He's not your type."

"I don't know what my type is." I could tell that she hadn't even entertained the thought, but the way her eyes widened and her teeth bared into the hint of a smile meant she wasn't about to give me peace of mind. "I'm kind of excited to find out, though."

"Ellen—"

"There's really nothing to talk about, David. That's

what space from you means. It means lack of matter."

"Can you at least—"

"You people!" Mr. Edwards's voice barreled through the hallway. When I turned back to Ellen, she was gone.

30

The entire cast waited in the theater for Big Pro to return from a hastily organized faculty meeting. The assault on Mr. Edwards's honor had sent the administration into orbit. Naturally, The Artist was the topic du jour for us until Big Pro returned.

"He could be anybody," I said.

"Do you think it's just a prankster? A social provocateur? That would be kind of lame." Vanessa closed the book she was reading, some optional material about World War I. "A psychotic, college-obsessed serial-killer type would be more interesting. Taking out the competition one by one."

"That's what Lisa thinks, and he's got plenty of ammo if that's the case. There's a skeleton or two in every one of our closets." I shook my head. "Except mine, of course."

"I'm sure."

I didn't know how to act around her. If I was unaffected by my split with Ellen, would Vanessa wonder if I'd ever cared for Ellen at all? Would she think I was turning the page too quickly, and would that make her less likely to want to be with me? And the opposite reaction was just as risky. If Vanessa thought I cared too much about Ellen, she wouldn't want anything to do with me until I'd gotten over it, at which point it might be too late.

"Say that word again: provocateur."

She slapped me on the chest with the back of her hand. There was an intimacy in her pretend violence that I found thrilling.

"All I know is that I'm in trouble if he's a serial killer, what with Juilliard and all," I said, smiling, embracing the lie because it felt good to pretend.

"Oh, please."

"Look at the facts! Last year's Citizen? Boom. The best soccer player? Boom. The best basketball player? Three-time Mathlympics champion? Boom, boom. I've had the lead in every play for the last two years. I'm pretty much walking around with a target on my back."

She laughed. "You're more than a little full of yourself. I'm assuming you already know that."

"I wouldn't be so dismissive, new girl. He may not know all your gossip yet, but you'd better not become too big a star, or you're next."

"Chauvinist," she said.

"Huh?"

"You keep saying The Artist is a he, like a girl can't stir the pot now and then. I'm a little offended."

"Would you rather I say 'he or she'? Do the slash thing with my hand in between?"

She giggled and opened her book for a moment before closing it again. She really was the most beautiful person I'd ever had an extended conversation with. That kiss at Geoff's house was still the only nonperformance kiss we'd shared, but maybe once the play was over—starting of course with the cast party—we would make up for lost time.

The double doors slammed against the walls as Big Pro stormed into the theater.

"All right, everybody listen up," he bellowed, pacing back and forth downstage. "Just to get a few things off my chest: I hate my job. I hate administrators. I hate students, and their parents, and all their little problems. I hate myself for hating you people, and I hate you people for making me hate myself."

I leaned in to Vanessa. "That's how you command a room."

"I feel much better," Big Pro said, this time with a smile. "Now, then. Let's get started."

With only three days left, the energy at rehearsal was creeping up toward manic. The costumes were nowhere near ready, the lights still needed tweaking, and one of the underclassmen still wasn't off book yet. Plus, the *Palo Alto Daily News* was coming to Wednesday's final dress rehearsal so a review could come out in time for opening night.

The original Doctor T. J. Eckleburg had quit earlier that day because he wanted to streamline his schedule, and Big Pro volunteered Jake to step in until a permanent replacement could be found. The situation was ripe for an eruption of Mount Pro, and he didn't disappoint.

"Damn it, Jake, you're the personification of a billboard," Big Pro yelled suddenly. "That means no moving.

No crossing your arms, no taking off your spectacles—"

"They pinch my temples—"

"They pinch—Corky!" he yelled.

Corky sprang onstage seconds later, a vertically striped purple and yellow skirt billowing with each step.

"His spectacles hurt," Big Pro said.

She bounced to Jake, who handed her the glasses. "They pinch."

Corky opened them and slid them gently onto his face, then leaned back. "Where exactly does it—"

Big Pro threw up his arms. "Take your time, please. The show is seventy-two hours away."

"Don't be a baby," Corky said, getting away with it only because she was looking at Jake when she said it.

When Corky left with the spectacles, Big Pro went up to Jake and grabbed his wrists and pulled them down so that Jake's arms were at his side. "We're not supposed to notice you, understand? You're the background, watching over us. You're supposed to burrow into our subconscious, but if you move, the game is up. Get it?"

"Got it." Jake suppressed a smile.

Big Pro spun away and collapsed into a front row seat, his legs splayed out to either side. "From the top."

When we finally took five, Vanessa and I sat upstage on the wicker settee. Someone put her hands on my shoulders and began to massage them. Poorly. "I'll go out with you." The voice belonged to Corky. "I have a soft spot for charity cases."

"I'm honored." I tried to wiggle away, but Corky

tightened her grip on my neck. Jake clomped toward me holding a plastic grocery bag and smiling. "Something tells me I should run away right now."

Jake tossed the bag at my feet. "We've been worried about you."

I winced with each squeeze Corky delivered. "I think . . . I'm going . . . to be . . . okay."

"I know it hurts now," Corky said. "When Julius dumped me, at first I was actually afraid, can you believe it? I was petrified."

"Afraid?" I said, gritting my teeth against her grip. "I can't picture that."

"I know. I can't tell you how many nights I spent thinking how he did me wrong."

Vanessa picked up the grocery bag and poked her head inside. "Where did you get these?"

"But you grew strong," Jake said. There was a sparkle in his eyes that was neither familiar nor particularly welcome. "Didn't you?"

Corky mercifully released her death grip. "I did. I learned how to carry on."

Oh no, I thought. Vanessa looked up from the bag, a smile creeping across her face.

"One, two, three," Jake said, clapping. "Hit it!"

All of a sudden Corky started singing. Horribly. And at the top of her lungs. "'Go on now, go. Walk out the door. Don't turn around now, 'cause you're not welcome anymore.'"

Jake was behind her, stomping his badass boots side

to side and clapping to the beat. Big Pro watched with his arms crossed and a smile on his face, leaning against a scenery flat painted to look like the shores of East Egg.

"'You think I'd crumble? You think I'd lay down and die?'" Corky sang. And of course she attracted an audience. "'Oh no, not I. I will survive! As long as I know how to love, I know I'll stay alive.'"

Vanessa seemed to be getting a kick out of it. I looked back at Jake, swaying and clapping and singing like a big karaoke gangbanger, and that's what did it. I burst out laughing. I couldn't help myself.

"'I've got all my life to live, I've got all my love to give, and I'll survive. I will survive!'"

Corky and Jake bowed. There was applause. Jake walked over to me and gave me a friendly punch on the shoulder.

I tensed just in time. "I assume you were behind that?"

"Figured you could use a laugh."

"Don't get me wrong—it's not that I don't like her." Corky motioned to the theater. "But Ellen never really did get this."

Vanessa pulled a stack of books from inside the bag. "*Broken Hearts: A Love Story? Six Steps to a Better You? How to be a Player?*"

"There was a sale at Half Price Books," Jake said.

"It's so nice to have people who care," I said.

"We take care of our own," Corky said. She gave an awkward little curtsy and followed Jake backstage. There was a pause as Vanessa and I watched her go. When she didn't return right away, the pause became, as they say in the theatre, pregnant.

Vanessa leafed through one of the books. "Are they going to send scouts to the show, do you think?"

"Who?"

"Juilliard? Now that you made it through the first cuts?"

I noticed Big Pro still in front of the scenery flat, but I quickly looked back to Vanessa. "That's not how they do it," I forced myself to say. Big Pro grunted and left.

"I'm just going to put something out there," she said after what seemed like an hour of painful silence. "I like you."

My throat went dry. Now that the subject had been broached, it was like the space between us was electrified. She shifted on the settee, and the stage lights reflected off the golden skin of her knee. "Okay."

"Life is too short to wait around and let things happen to you. Trust me, I know all about that."

"Break's over." Big Pro yelled up to the catwalk, "Jake, cue forty-seven please!"

"You bet," came the disembodied voice.

"Everyone, that means places for act one, scene seven."

I forced a smile. Act one, scene seven meant the kiss. And even though we'd run it plenty since that first time— that unbelievably intense first time—now was going to be different. All those other times, I was still with Ellen.

"And Sparkles?"

"Present," I said.

"Thank God for that," Big Pro said with more than a hint of sarcasm. "It's dragging, by the way, so enough with the meaningful pauses. That okay with you?"

"Of course," I said. I whispered—jokingly, I hoped—to Vanessa, "Did that come off as too eager?"

"Not that I blame you," she said. "I'm pretty freaking hot."

She slapped me on the knee as she stood—a little farther up the thigh than the actual knee—and my insides lurched. "You're more than a little full of yourself," I said as I pushed myself to my feet. "I'm assuming you already know that."

I thought I'd handled it well, but the smile she gave me nearly obliterated every ounce of the self-control I'd managed to summon.

31

The morning of opening night, my mom rapped at my door with a blueberry muffin on a plate and a copy of the *Palo Alto Daily News*. A tradition was a tradition, after all, and she'd come through.

"Big day!" she said, handing me the paper as I sat up in bed.

I peeled off the top of the muffin and took a bite. "Did you read it yet?"

She hesitated for just an instant, but that instant was enough.

"It's that bad?" I said. My mouth went dry, and the bite of muffin turned to concrete. I forced it down as I searched for the right page.

"Oh, honey."

The picture accompanying the review was nearly half a page: Vanessa in the foreground, in perfect focus, shot from slightly below; me over her right shoulder, out of focus, half of my face cut off by her outstretched hand. The headline blared: *Birth of a Star*.

I scanned the review in disbelief and read the last line aloud: "Bottom Line—Even though this stage adaptation of *The Great Gatsby* was an ill-conceived mistake, there is no denying the star power of the young woman playing Daisy Buchanan."

Mom patted my feet beneath the covers as she stood. "You know it was just a dress rehearsal. I'm sure it will all come together. You say it always does."

I made it to the afternoon without anybody mentioning the review. I didn't know whether it was because people hadn't read it yet, or because they didn't know what to say, or because my focus was on psyching myself up for the performance and nothing else. I didn't care. The curtain was just over four hours away; Stephanie said I had to bring the house down.

And then the final bell rang, and the halls were packed, and I felt the scouring of passing eyes on my skin like light sandpaper. There were whispers. I tried to ignore them. And suddenly there I was, on the bulletin board.

A collage, with pictures from every performance I'd been in at Oak Fields. There was the photo of me and Vanessa from the *Palo Alto Daily News*, along with the headline from the accompanying review: *Birth of a Star*. In the center of the collage was the familiar blue and white Juilliard logo with REJECTED scrawled over it in red capital letters. There was a caption—there was always a caption: AND WE BELIEVE OUR FUTURE WILL SPARKLE.

Ellen appeared at my side like a ghost. We watched the board together. "Look at that, you're famous."

I couldn't have spoken even if I'd wanted to. I stepped back, but there were people behind me. Ten had become fifteen, and now there was nowhere to go. I was a part of this whether I wanted to be or not.

"Come tonight," I finally managed, my eyes still on the poster. "Or whenever. One of the shows."

"I don't think I need to see you and Vanessa lick each other's tonsils."

The people around us were no doubt talking, too, but aside from Ellen all I heard was a drone, like a chain saw in the distance. My heart started beating faster, and my breath came more rapidly with every passing second, but I couldn't move. I couldn't make myself tear the poster down or run away.

This one didn't have the sensationalism of the others—no marijuana or scantily clad underclassmen, no Internet résumés—but it had the knowledge of its victim that the other collages lacked. Maybe that was the danger of being what the headmaster had called "visible." There was no mystery as to what my dreams were, and now that very public knowledge had been used against me.

" 'Daisy and Nick's obvious chemistry is as unsettling as it is intriguing,' " Ellen said, quoting the *Daily News* review.

"Your photographic memory."

"Comes in handy from time to time, yes."

It had the odd quality of being both a private conversation and an extremely public performance. It was as though we were alone, so focused were we on each other, and yet—of course—we were not alone.

"Didn't you once tell me that chemistry is something people can't fake?" she said.

It was time to end this. I walked slowly through the gathered witnesses. They wanted a show, like Mr. Edwards had given us, but I wasn't about to provide one. Instead I kept my eyes on the collage and tried to block out the whispers. When I couldn't take the whole thing down I carefully removed each of the pictures one by one: *Godspell*, *The Sound of Music*, *Rumors*, *The American Plan*. *The Widow's Blind Date*. *The Crucible*. *A Midsummer Night's Dream*. Each moment of triumph turned into a taunt by its proximity to the Juilliard logo, which I removed last.

The theater was out of the question, so I walked across the senior parking lot to a small patch of grass at the base of the wrought-iron fence that surrounded the campus. I didn't know if anyone was following me. I still couldn't hear anything; it was as though I wore earplugs.

I arranged the pictures in chronological order on the ground in front of me: the young Rolf with a Nazi armband from *The Sound of Music*; a hipster Oberon in *Midsummer*; a Boy Scout leader in Big Pro's adaptation of *The Crucible*; a face-painted John the Baptist in *Godspell*; the tuxedo-wearing, whiplash-suffering accountant Lenny Ganz in *Rumors*. I was good in those roles. One of my lines from *The American Plan* popped into my head: "I cause happiness; that's what I do."

My face had changed as I'd gotten older, had become less round, more oval. The cheekbones were more visible, the jaw slightly more defined. But when I looked closer, I realized that there was one constant, no matter my age, no matter the character, no matter the costume. Big Pro had warned me about it, but this was the first time I'd seen the vacant, doe-eyed expression with my own eyes.

"Vanessa is wrong for you." Ellen stood above me, her fingers tucked under the straps of her backpack. "You know that, right?"

I returned my attention to the pictures, trying to remember the feelings I had when each of them was taken. "Says the objective observer."

"Even when you were at your most spacey, you still brought it to the theater every time."

"And now?" I whispered.

"You read the review. A star was born, and it wasn't you." I looked at her but didn't respond. Ellen sighed. "And Juilliard? You didn't even get a callback."

And then she looked at the pictures, and I understood. Her expression registered neither compassion nor anger. Not even humor, although something straightened her posture, a grin that didn't quite make it to her face. It was pride. Satisfaction.

"Oh," I said under my breath.

She hadn't sold my secrets on the black market—she'd done me one worse. She'd given them away for free. My insecurities about how people saw me, wanting to be recognized, wanting to be an actor, wanting to be famous. She knew what would hurt the most, and she went right for it.

I should have leaped to my feet and screamed something about respect and privacy and betrayal, but I was too numb to be outraged.

"I wondered why this one was different," I said. "This . . . It's too personal."

"Too personal for what?"

"There's no statement."

"Oh, there's a statement," she said.

"The Artist is a provocateur." I rolled the word around in my mouth and smiled in spite of myself. "This is just simple, uninspired retribution."

"Maybe. Maybe you deserved it. Maybe it was karma."

"I thought life coaches believed in self-reliance. Not karma."

"Life coaches." A cloud of disgust blew across her face. "I can quote you their program in my sleep," she said. "'Your response to life's challenges determines the person you choose to be. . . . You control how you prepare yourself for success. . . .' It's all bullshit if a bunch of hypocrites get to play by different rules."

"Everyone's a hypocrite, Ellen. This is high school."

"I thought you were different."

She hated me. People weren't supposed to hate me, but she did. Clearly, and with every fiber of her being. Was this feeling there in her all along? Buried and festering until she finally let it free?

She seemed to be expecting something more. Some sort of action. She still stood above me, still holding onto the straps of her backpack, as though she were waiting for me to remember my lines. She shifted her weight from one foot to the other, ready to prompt me if I asked.

Finally: "Aren't you even a little upset?"

That's what it was. That's why she was still here. She wanted me to be furious. She wanted to see me hurt. She wanted me to threaten to expose her. It was in my best interests, and not only out of revenge. We were both applying to Stanford, after all. With the bounty placed on The Artist, I could have turned her in—at least for this— taken her out of the running, improved my chances.

But I was more confused than angry. More worried about the fact that I hadn't seen this side of her in two years; I didn't even know she was capable of such a thing, and that called into question our entire relationship. If I hadn't seen this, what else had I not seen?

Slowly, deliberately, I stacked the pictures on top of one another. Then I stood. She wanted to know that she'd affected me, and no matter how I was feeling, I couldn't let her.

"I have to get ready for the show." I took a step toward her; now she was looking up at me. "I'm leaving a ticket for you at the box office. Every night. Front row and center, just in case."

It was only when I started walking away that I lost it.

32

Dozens of four-inch square sheets of paper covered the living room coffee table. Colter sat on the edge of the couch and leaned forward, his hands expertly folding and pressing, running the back of his thumbnail across the paper to sharpen the crease. In front of him was a collection of marine animals: blowfish, turtle, clam, shark, each one as crisp and confident as something out of a manual.

In front of me was a collection of crumpled disasters, a dozen frustrated attempts at a peace crane, the classic-est origami pattern there was, according to my self-appointed paper sensei. "When you said you had just the thing to calm me down, I thought you meant weed."

"This is nature's weed," he said.

"Weed is already from nature."

I seemed to have stumped him. "So is paper?"

"Colter," I said, "this is way out there, even for you."

"Did you know a lot of the newer patterns have over a hundred folds? That's five times as many as back in the day. There's wicked math involved now. Huzita axioms, angle quintisections. I don't know what any of it means, but doesn't it sound cool? There are even computer programs that design the patterns for you."

"Kind of takes the Zen out of it."

"You can laugh if you want—"

"Oh, I want—"

"But without origami we probably wouldn't have airbags, or solar panels on satellites—"

"Or paper airplanes. Or napkins."

He ignored me, instead concentrating on the paper in front of him. "I'm going to make you a little pouch to store all that cynicism."

"I'm not becoming more mellow, in case you were wondering."

My sister came through the door and stopped when she saw us. "You didn't tell me it was crafts day. Can I make Mom a potholder?"

"I'm learning how to relax," I said, motioning to all the crumpled-up sheets. "Can't you tell?"

"At least you're not humping the air."

Colter chuckled. I tried to fold a damn piece of paper.

Lisa said, "I'm sorry about what happened today. I heard."

Colter held up a half-folded creation and peeked at it with one eye closed. "Is The Artist a topic of discussion among the yapping freshmen?"

"Are you kidding? He's a hero."

"A what?"

"He's fighting The Man. Which I guess makes him more of a folk hero." Lisa put her hands out in a half-hearted surrender. "Until today, of course, at least for me."

"How do you know it's a he?" I said.

"Do you know who it is?" She cocked her eyes at me. "You do know, don't you?"

Colter said, "You do?'

"It could be anybody, couldn't it?" I said. Ellen's copycatting was my secret to do with whatever I wanted. It made me feel powerful to keep it to myself, and right then I needed all the power I could muster. "That's what makes it so exciting."

"Who, exactly, is The Man in this case?" Colter said.

"Seniors are The Man." Lisa sighed. "No offense, David, but everyone's all perfect and annoying. It's kind of hard to live up to."

I stood up. Curtain was two hours away. "I should just go back to the theater."

Colter pointed. "Sit. Focus. Paper."

"Grasshopper wants to kick your ass. I think my blood pressure is triple what it was when you came over."

Lisa went to the kitchen and rummaged around in the fridge. Colter sat next to me and slid over another piece of paper. "You're too worried about what you want it to look like. All you should care about is the next fold."

I crumpled the paper into a little ball with both hands and threw it at him. "I made a marble."

"Look, there are only two rules. You use one square sheet, and you can't tear or cut it. Everything else is up to you. Trial and error. Fold and fold."

"How do I make a middle finger?"

"You know something?" He selected a new white

square and began folding. "I never liked any of Vanessa's boyfriends before. Let's not keep the streak alive."

I tried to force saliva into a mouth that had become surprisingly dry. "We're not—"

"Not yet, at least. Maybe that all changes at the cast party? Wink, wink, if you know what I mean?"

"What do you think she would say if she heard you talking like that?"

"I love it. Defending her honor and everything. We'd be like brothers-in-law. . . ." He trailed off, becoming lost in the little white paper in front of him. He flattened it back out into a square, with sharp creases crisscrossing the sheet like little scars.

My phone rang. Stephanie Blair.

"I'm kind of busy right now," I said. "Opening night."

"I read the review in the paper this morning. It sounds like a fascinating play, and I'm very excited to see it on Saturday. But there's one thing I don't understand. You said you were the star."

"I am the star."

"Not to put too fine a point on it, David, but I have a reputation to think about. I called in favors."

"I'm the star," I said again, but it came out sounding petulant.

She exhaled into the mouthpiece. "If it takes tonight and tomorrow to work yourself into shape, that's fine. But I'll be there Saturday night, and Sue Douglas will, too. She's the head of the drama department. Remember, I can only do so much. This is your shot."

I thanked her, though my voice was so tight that I must have sounded like I was in a tunnel. I closed the phone and felt its heft in my hand.

"Who was that?" Lisa said. She stood by the kitchen table eating sherbet out of the container.

"Stephanie."

"Stephanie?" Colter raised an eyebrow, as if to say, There's more?

"His narrative coach," Lisa said. "She's writing his essay for him."

"That's not what she's doing," I said. "She's assisting in the development of a specific angle through which to position the applicant as an attractive prospective member of the institution of higher education of his choice."

"Man," Colter said. "I thought Boston was crazy. JJ wouldn't even have made it to junior year out here—" He stopped talking and froze as if I'd caught him shoplifting red-handed.

"That's okay," I said. "Your sister told me."

He exhaled.

I said, "Do you think it was V's fault?"

"What are you talking about? How could it have been her fault?"

"The car accident."

Colter shook his head. "If by 'car accident' you mean 'carbon monoxide from her car's exhaust in her family's garage while her parents and younger brother were inside sleeping,' then yes, I guess it was a car accident." He must have noticed the surprise on my face, because the caught-shoplifting look was back on his face. "I take it you didn't get the whole story?"

"She committed suicide?"

"My parents thought it would be best for us to get away from all the distractions, what with the college application process being so important," he said, gathering all the unfolded sheets into a tidy little pile. "You know, because you'll forget all about your best friend killing herself as long as you move three thousand miles away."

It felt wrong to be talking about this, like I was gathering dirt behind Vanessa's back.

"Vanessa said it was her fault," I said. "That's what she told me. If it hadn't been for her—"

"My sister has been known to put herself in the center of the story from time to time. A common thread among actors, I've been told." He stood, looking a little agitated. "See you after the show?"

"You're not leaving, are you?" Lisa said from the kitchen. "I still haven't made my lanyard."

He extended his arm. Pinched between his thumb and index finger was a miniature hammer. "Break a leg tonight."

33

The thick scent of nerves and foundation filled the makeup room on Saturday night. Curtain for the final performance was just an hour away.

"I thought it would fade after the first couple of times," Vanessa said. "This feeling? This expectation in the pit of your stomach? Dread and euphoria mixed together?"

"You have nothing to dread," I told her. "You of all people."

She winked into the mirror. "Say it again and I might believe you."

On the heels of the *Palo Alto Daily News* review, our school paper, the *Oak Fields Observer*, had called Vanessa a "revelation" and had lamented that it was too bad she'd only graced us with her senior year. My Nick Carraway, on the other hand, was called "serviceable" and "appropriately distant."

I was happy for her, but of course I was envious as well, and with the head of the Stanford drama department in the audience tonight, I couldn't afford to choke again. The problem with constantly telling yourself not to choke is that you're reminding yourself that the possibility of choking exists. You've already lost.

I'd been worried about how my fellow theatre freaks

would react to the truth about my audition, but to my great surprise—and even greater relief—they'd rallied around me. The Artist had attacked one of their own, after all. As for lying about Juilliard, everyone said they would have done the same thing.

Vanessa brushed rouge over cheekbones that hardly needed highlighting. The cast party—the *real* cast party— would take place after the show. That's when we'd have the time to continue what we'd started at Geoff's house.

"We have obvious chemistry," she said as though reading my mind; her reflection winked at me. "You don't find it unsettling?"

What was unsettling was that every time she looked at me that way—so innocent as to be suggestive—I still thought of Ellen. I couldn't explain it. I should have wanted to erase her from my memory, but I didn't know how.

"Very unsettling," I said. "Very much so."

"Can you believe tonight is the last time we'll make out?" She leaned in, so close that I felt the heat of her breath against my ear and neck. "In public?"

Geoff nodded at me from across the room, giving the kind of frown-smile that guys give each other when they don't think girls are looking. That's my boy, is what the look says. You better hit that. I'd been out of the game for so long that I couldn't remember the last time I'd gotten that look.

But I wasn't playing the role of the popular guy who does what he pleases with the ladies. I was the doofus who never manages to say anything right, who always seems to shake his head ruefully at the camera later. I was mentally and emotionally weak, and the worst part was that I knew it.

With five minutes to places, I stood in the wings, stealing a glance through the side curtain. The theater was filling up quickly, but Ellen's seat was still empty, as it had been last night and the night before.

She'd come to every show of every play I'd been in since we'd started dating. I'd grown addicted to peeking at her through the curtain, to letting my peripheral vision wander to her seat after my laugh lines, to her being my first hug backstage afterward. I knew that her absence on the first two nights of *Gatsby* had affected my performance, and that's one of the reasons why, for the first time in two years, I didn't get the reviews I was supposed to get.

Vanessa's hand rested on my shoulder. "Break a leg, Nick," she said.

"Daisy." I reached up to cover her hand with my own.

Stephanie Blair sidestepped to her seat near the back, followed by a woman wearing a flowing sage-colored shirt belted at the waist over black tights. Her hair was platinum blond and close-cropped, like my dad's, and she wore horn-rimmed glasses.

A flash of unease struck me. It was more than knowing the head of the Stanford drama department was in the house. It was more than just the melancholy of the last performance, when people who've spent the last three months together realize that there's only two hours of the experience left.

It was this: Vanessa had become the star of the show. With all my help, all the extra rehearsals, the heart-to-hearts about how to prepare, I may as well have wrapped Stanford up in a box with a little red bow and given it to her myself.

"You okay?" Vanessa said.

"Of course." Stepping away from the curtain, I realized that half of me wanted her to be fantastic tonight, and the other half wanted her to fail spectacularly. What kind of person thought like that? "Final show jitters."

Two minutes before curtain, the stage manager shouted, "Places." Vanessa squeezed my hand and rushed silently to the wings stage left. I hid behind the curtains stage right and closed my eyes. Breathed in. Breathed out.

The houselights throbbed. Less than a minute left.

Colter was in the audience, in an aisle seat near the back, his legs stretched sideways in a clear violation of the fire code. My parents were there, and Lisa. Big Pro would be standing by the wall near the back exit. Ellen's seat was still empty.

The houselights faded to black. A beat later, a dim yellow wash illuminated Tom Buchanan's drawing room and the enormous divan in the center, with a freshman as Jordan Baker perched across one end and Vanessa's Daisy Buchanan bent slightly forward, looking like the most beautiful person I had ever known.

I scanned the audience from one side to the other,

smiled gently, adjusted the lapels of my sport coat. This moment was my favorite, just before the first word was spoken, when the audience's expectation became tangible, charged like the air before a lightning strike. It was in this moment—and only this moment—that the performance was perfect. Everything that came afterward, no matter how well-executed, was just a cruel bastardization of what had been possible.

Showtime.

34

Halfway through the second scene, Vanessa as Daisy leaned forward with her elbow on the table and her chin resting on her fingertips, and with her fork poised daintily in the other hand.

"I'll tell you a family secret," she stage-whispered. "It's about the butler's nose. Do you want to hear about the butler's nose?"

I was supposed to play my response as a laugh line. Nick had come to Daisy and Tom's house for dinner for the first time, and it was an essential moment for the audience. They had to experience Nick's cleverness and understand that, though he wasn't at all like the Buchanans, he could still play their game. But whether it was the timing or the words I chose to stress, I'd always had trouble with the line. I'd never quite gotten it right.

Until now.

"That's why I came over tonight," I said. The deadpan was perfect. The delivery was perfect. The little glance to Jordan Baker halfway through the line was perfect. I nailed it.

The audience responded with a surprised but appreciative laugh. Gosh, it seemed to say, that Nick Carraway is actually quite witty. We think we'd like to spend our evening with him!

Whatever had been wrong with me during the previous performances was no longer an issue. I had it tonight. I was on. Every line, every cue. I could feel it. You hear about athletes who get in the zone, like a quarterback who completes every pass or a basketball player who can't seem to miss a shot. That rarely happened to me onstage; I was often focused on the mechanics of my performance. But tonight I was finally there, firmly inside the creative zone where I knew—*knew*—that every word, every gesture, every look was flawlessly executed.

Vanessa pointed her fork at me and laughed her flighty Daisy laugh. "I love to see you at my table, Nick. You remind me of a—of a rose, an absolute rose."

"This is untrue," I said. "I am not even faintly like a rose."

I'd gotten good at the surreptitious glance at Ellen over the years, and now I could feel my peripheral attention turning to the horn-rimmed face of the drama department, gauging her reaction. Was she laughing? Had I sold the double take well enough? She was. I had. It was working.

During an early scene change, in the instant before the lights went back up, Ellen took her seat in the front row. I watched from the wings as she glanced at the people on either side of her and made apologetic gestures regarding her lateness. My reaction to seeing her there surprised me. No heartbreak, no regret at having invited her; I was happy. I *wanted* her to see me like this.

"We're killing it tonight," Corky whispered backstage. "Killing it!"

Daisy's white linen dress was sleeveless, with an inch of lace trim around the neck and arm holes. The neck was scooped, offering a glimpse of her collarbones and a hint of something more, and the dress came down just past her knees. She wore a necklace of tiny white pearls. Her hair was covered by a white cloche hat with a brilliant blue ribbon just above an almost nonexistent brim.

My heart was pounding the inside of my rib cage. The lights were warm on my face. It was the best we'd ever run the scene. I knew it; Vanessa knew it. With Ellen twenty feet away, there was an unease that couldn't be faked, and with the events of the impending cast party in the back of my mind, a passion that was undeniable.

"Are you sure we should be doing this?" I said.

There was knowledge in her eyes, perhaps even a twinkle, when she said, "Absolutely."

She eased back against the small table and pulled me in with her left hand. She reached behind my neck, and I felt every one of her fingertips on my skin with such clarity that she may as well have scanned them onto me. We held the kiss an extra beat longer, not out of any malice for Ellen, but because we were there, in the moment. Both of us.

I wanted her. I wanted this.

One of the party scenes came to a close with a little slapstick routine involving a ditch, some partygoers, and a missing car wheel. Geoff emerged from the driver's seat of the pantomimed wreckage and staggered around drunkenly. He stuck his hands on his hips, looking as if he'd just woken up.

"Whasa matter?" he said. "Did we run outa gas?"

The audience laughed—some even clapped—and Geoff responded by overacting the rest of his lines with an uproariously gleeful gusto.

Then the party was over and the stage cleared, and I stepped downstage to address the audience, the last lines of the first act.

"I am slow thinking and full of interior rules that act as brakes on my desires," I said, looking at Ellen for this one. I delivered the line with feeling, and with a hint of apology.

I took two confident steps stage left, brought the flap of my linen suit back with the outside of my wrist as I put one hand in my pants pocket. There was a long beat as I took in the audience I knew was mine. The department head leaned forward, her hands resting on the knee of her crossed legs, expectation in her eyes.

"Everyone suspects himself of at least one of the cardinal virtues," I said, "and this is mine: I am one of the few honest people that I have ever known."

I was deeper into the moment than I had ever been in my life, and the feeling I had as I spoke was proof. There was an emotional connection to the words I'd never felt before. David was Nick and Nick was David. I was in the zone.

And it was exactly *because* I was in the zone that I was ripped from it.

The department head smiled, and it should have filled me with pleasure, or with gratitude, or with hope, but it didn't. Her smile brought disgust. Anger. It was instant and inexplicable. Something was happening to me. Not as a character. Not as an observer. But to *me*. A feeling of shame.

I looked at my parents. Stephanie. Big Pro. Everyone important to me was either in the audience tonight or onstage with me. And I was lying to all of them.

There was supposed to be a long beat as I scanned the audience, followed by a light cue to darkness and then the intermission. The lights were slowly fading.

"I am one of the few honest people I have ever known," I said again.

I heard a surprised grumble up at the light board, and then the lights came back up to full. For the first few moments at least, the audience went along with me. We were bound together by an energy that felt eerily similar to Francine's slow-motion fall.

"My name is David Ellison."

And . . . impact. The fall was over. I knew from the look on the department head's face that I was throwing Stanford away. I'd pinned my hopes on her recommendation, and up to this moment I'd done everything possible to ensure it would be mine. But you simply did not break character in the middle of a play, and I had done so deliberately, maliciously. The disgust behind her horn-rimmed lenses told me I had lost her. I glanced back at Vanessa, who stood upstage behind me, her confusion morphing into fury before my eyes.

Iggy Rockwell hated basketball but played it anyway. Vanessa felt responsible for JJ's death but couldn't help achieving for her parents' sake. Even poor Mr. Edwards thought the only way we would respect him was to lie about having graduated from a community college. We all had our roles to play.

I was in a regional commercial when I was eleven years old because I thought it would be fun to audition and some casting director liked the way I said, "Mmmboy." That was it. But what if that's all it took?

Did everything that came after happen because I liked acting? Or was it because I liked that I'd become known as an actor? Had I let everyone else's expectations define me, or—in the case of my dad—had I defined myself against those expectations? Either way, I was a liar.

Self-disgust quickened my pulse. I'd thought I was different, but I wasn't some grand rebel, choosing a different life path, going my own way. Stanford and Juilliard were the same. I was playing my role; I wanted to be *known* as the guy who was going to Juilliard. *Known* as the guy who'd gotten into Stanford.

But the machine no longer had any hold on me, not anymore. And I knew just how to prove it. Here. Now. A stand taken in private is meaningless, is nothing more than an idle thought.

"Gatsby dies in the end," I said. "You all know that.

But at least he believes in his vision of the future."

People checked their programs. Ellen sat up straight. Colter chewed on his thumbnail, a tiny curl lifting the corners of his mouth. I noticed Jake up at the light board, waving frantically as the lights began to dim again.

"They may have been vain fantasies," I said, raising my voice so Jake had no choice but to bring the lights up to full again, "but at least Gatsby's dreams were his own. You try to fight for someone else's dream, and you lose sight of who you are in the first place."

We'd invested so much energy into who we proclaimed to be that we never had a chance to be who we were. He was careless, The Artist, careless with other people's lives, but at least he'd gotten that much right.

I panned across the audience, where each expression became more horrified than the next. A low buzz started to build, but I kept talking. Big Pro had stepped into the glow of the stage lights at the back of the audience, his arms crossed and his head shaking, his bottom jaw protruding out like a ledge.

The department head looked on in shock. She grimaced at her program. Stephanie pressed her lips into an odd flat smile and sat forward, as if eager to witness the carnage.

"The only future we can believe in," I said, "is the one we create for ourselves."

I held the moment for a beat longer. My fingertips were trembling. I couldn't believe I'd done what I'd just done— Big Pro would hate me, Stephanie would be furious with me, and the department head would think I was a joke. I'd lost Ellen already, and I was about to lose Vanessa as well, I knew—yet in the face of it all, I felt an enormous weight disappear from my shoulders.

I turned my back to the audience and the lights faded to black, and as I walked directly upstage past Vanessa, I didn't even feel my feet hit the floor.

35

t is now mid-December. A bowl of punch sits half-empty, watery from the melted ice. My parents' friends eat tiny sandwiches on plastic plates and offer heartfelt congratulations my mom and dad are only too happy to accept. White and Cardinal Red streamers decorate the trees in my backyard. Colter is here. Ellen is not. Vanessa will be leaving soon.

"It's the happiest day of your life," Lisa says.

"It's just a school."

Colter pats me on the back. "Spoken like someone who just got in."

It turns out that an act of defiance such as the one I perpetrated makes for the subject of a spectacular college essay, so long as one's narrative coach is able to frame it the right way. I had finally asserted myself, Stephanie helped me say, and while I now understood the time and place were not entirely appropriate, epiphanies should never be denied. Etcetera.

Francine walks through the sliding glass door holding a bouquet of balloons and a medium Frosty with the spoon sticking out. "I ate half of it," she says. "I couldn't resist."

"Who doesn't love a Frosty?" I say.

"This is what I try to tell people. Congratulations, though. It's pretty awesome. Stanford. Even if everyone hates your guts."

My act of rebellion did not go over as well with my classmates as it did with the admissions committee, it's true. My name would not grace the plaque in Big Pro's office for a second year in a row. I'd let everybody down, had put my own interests before those of the group. It had earned me near universal scorn, and that was just the theatre people. The general population resented me on principle.

We never heard from The Artist again. It may have been Ellen after all, and she'd stopped with me, though I wonder. More likely, whoever it was gave up once Ellen imitated him. Regardless, I was the last person to see himself on the bulletin board. As for Ellen, well, we don't really talk much anymore. I miss her.

Vanessa wanders over to me, a tiny dab of ranch dressing at the corner of her mouth. "Sorry I have to go," she says, licking the dressing away. "It's a nice party. And congratulations again."

"Which is this one?" I say.

"There's a production of *An Irish Play* up in Redwood City."

"Break a leg," I tell her. "They'd be idiots not to cast you."

She gives me a quick hug, no kiss. And I watch her walk away.

I wasn't welcome at the cast party the night of the

final show, so the connection promised between us never happened. *We* never happened. She's just my best friend's friendly sister, life being too short to hold grudges, as she says. And now, with her new passion having liberated her from the shadow of JJ's death, she auditions for every role she can find. She's even made progress finding an agent. She has the bug, as they say.

"My parents hate you," Colter said. "You know that, right? You may as well have sold her heroin."

"She seems happy, though."

Colter laughs. "Like I said."

"David," my mom says, waving. "Come over here!"

I wander over near the punch bowl to my father, who wears a "Stanford Dad" baseball cap and holds a half-finished light beer. He puts his free hand on my shoulder and toasts Stephanie's camera. Then we take a couple pictures with my mom.

"Come on, Lisa," Mom says. "The whole family!"

My sister groans and shuffles toward us as if being dragged with a rope. "I liked it better when you were a screwup," she says under her breath.

"Give me a few minutes," I whisper back.

With my dad's hand still resting proudly on my shoulder, I glance over at Francine and Colter arguing playfully over the last of my Frosty. Francine jams the spoon in Colter's mouth with her fully recovered left hand. They make a good couple.

Stephanie snaps her fingers above the camera. "Okay now, say 'Cardinal!'"

The thing is, I meant what I said onstage. I did. I took a stand, and I'm proud of it, and I still believe every word. It's just that, looking at the situation objectively, when you're offered your school's only spot at one of the top three universities in the whole country, you'd have to be an idiot to turn it down.

Acknowledgments

For a critical eye right from the get-go, I want to thank Alexander Parsons and the Forms class at the University of Houston: Ian Schimmel, Eddie Gonzalez, David Lombardi, Irene Keliher, Laurie Cedilnik, Maranatha Bivens, Erin Namekawa, and Garret Johnson. I also feel fortunate to have benefited from the wonderful readers of the Antidote Workshop. Rice University and the Parks Fellowship provided invaluable time and space. I'm grateful to Arianne Lewin for her super-keen insight, to Catherine Onder for helping bring out what I'd hoped was there all along, and to Sara Crowe for always having my back. Special thanks to my parents for always telling me I could do whatever I put my mind to, even if they didn't believe it, and to my sister for going along with them. And of course the most special thanks of all go to Molly, Dayton, and Annie for their ongoing patience, understanding, and support.